HAPPY FAMILIES ARE ALL ALIKE

BOOKS BY PETER TAYLOR

A Long Fourth and Other Stories
A Woman of Means
The Widows of Thornton
Tennessee Day in St. Louis
Happy Families Are All Alike

Happy Families

A COLLECTION OF STORIES BY

NEW YORK

Are All Alike

PETER TAYLOR

McDOWELL, OBOLENSKY

Acknowledgment is here made to the following publications in which the
stories in this volume first appeared (a number of them under different
titles): *The Kenyon Review* for "Venus, Cupid, Folly and Time," and "A
Friend and Protector" (formerly "Who was Jesse's Friend and Protector?");
The New Republic for "A Walled Garden" (formerly "Like the Sad Heart
of Ruth"); *The New Yorker* for "1939" (formerly "A Sentimental Journey"),
"The Other Times," "Promise of Rain" (formerly "The Unforgivable"),
"*Je Suis Perdu*" (formerly "A Pair of Bright-Blue Eyes"), "The Little Cous-
ins" (formerly "Cousins, Family Love, Family Life, All That"), "Heads of
Houses," and "Guests."

for
my son
Peter Ross Taylor

Contents

———◆———

I

CHATHAM

II

OTHER PLACES

"Happy families are all alike; every unhappy family is unhappy in its own way."

TOLSTOY, *Anna Karenina*

I
CHATHAM

I

MARRIAGE

The Other Times

———◆◆———

Can anybody honestly like having a high-school civics teacher for an uncle? I doubt it. Especially not a young girl who is popular and good-looking and who is going to make her début someday at the Chatham Golf and Country Club. Nevertheless, that's who the civics teacher was at Westside High School when we were growing up in Chatham. He was the brother of Letitia Ramsey's father, and he had all the failings you would expect of a high-school civics teacher and baseball coach. In the classroom he was a laughingstock for the way he butchered the King's English, and out of school he was known to be a hard drinker and general hell-raiser. But the worst part of it was that he was a bachelor and that the Ramseys had to have him for dinner practically every Sunday.

If you had a Sunday afternoon date with Letitia, there the civics teacher would be, out on the front lawn, playing catch with one of Letitia's narrow-eyed little brothers. Somehow, what disturbed *me* about this particular spectacle when I was having Sunday dates with Letitia was the Uncle's and the little brother's concentration on the ball and the kind of real fondness they seemed to feel for the thing. When either of them held it in his hand for a minute, he seemed to be wanting to make a pet of it. When it went back and forth between them, smacking their gloves, they seemed to hear it saying, yours, mine, yours, mine, as though nobody else had ever thrown or caught a baseball. But of course that's not the point. The point is that it was hard to think of Letitia's having this Lou Ramsey for an uncle. And I used to watch her face when we were leaving her house on a Sunday afternoon to see if she would show anything. But not Letitia!

It may not seem fair to dwell on this unfortunate uncle of a girl like Letitia Ramsey, but it was through him that I got a clearer idea of what she was like, and the whole Ramsey family, as well. They were very well-bred people, and just as well-to-do, even in the depression. Mr. Ramsey, like my own father, was from the country, but, also like my father, he was from one of the finest country families in the state. And Mrs. Ramsey and my mother had gone through Farleigh Institute together, which was an old-fashioned school where they studied Latin so long that it made a difference in the way they spoke English all the rest of their lives.

Anyway, though I didn't take Latin, fortunately I didn't take civics, either (since I was hoping to go to college if the depression eased up), and fortunately I didn't go out for the baseball team. This made it not too hard for me to pretend not to notice who Letitia's uncle was. Also, since Letitia didn't go to the high school but went to Miss Jordan's, a school that has more or less replaced Farleigh Institute in Chatham, it could have been as easy for her to pretend not to notice as it was for me.

It could have been, except that Letitia didn't want it that way. When she and I went across the lawn to my father's car on those Sunday afternoons and her uncle and one of her little brothers were carrying on with that baseball, she would call out something like "Have fun, you two!" or "Come see us this week, Uncle Louis!" And her voice never sounded sweeter than it did then. After we were in the car, if I hadn't thought of something else to talk about she would sometimes begin a long spiel like "I always forget you don't really know my uncle. I wish you did. You probably know how mad he is about sports. That's why my little brothers adore him. And he's just as shy as they are. Look at him and Charlie there. When I'm dressed up like this to go out on a date, he and the boys won't even look at me."

The truth is I felt that Letitia Ramsey was just as smart as she could be—not in school, necessarily, but in the way she handled subjects like undesirable relatives. I think she was very unusual in this. There was one of her friends, named Nancy O'Connor, who had a grandmother that had once run a fruit stand at the old curb market, up on the North Side. The grandmother lived with the O'Connors and was a right funny sort of person, if you know what I mean, and Nancy was forever apologizing for her. Naturally, her apologizing did nothing but make you uncomfortable. Also, there was Trudie Hauser, whose brother Horst was a good friend of mine. The Hausers lived out in the German section of town, where my mother hadn't usually gone to parties in her day, and they still lived in the kind of castlelike house that the first one of the Hausers to get rich had built. Poor Trudie and poor Horst! They had not one but three or four peculiar relatives living with them. And they had German servants, to whom their parents were apt to speak in German, right before you, and make Trudie and Horst, who were both very blond, blush to the roots of their hair the way blonds are apt to do. Then there was also a girl named Maria Thomas. She had a much older brother who was a moron —a real one—and if he passed through the room, or even came in and sat down, she would simply pretend that he wasn't there, that he didn't even exist.

This isn't to say, of course, that all the girls in Chatham had something like that in their families. Lots of girls— and lots of the boys, too—had families like mine, with nobody in particular to be ashamed of. Nor is it to say that the girls who did have something of this kind weren't just as popular as the others and didn't have you to their houses to parties just as often. Nancy O'Connor's family, for instance, lived in a most beautiful Spanish-style house, with beamed ceilings and orange-colored tile floors downstairs, and with a huge walled-in sort of lawn out in the back, where Nancy gave a big party every June. But, I will say, at those parties you always felt that everybody was having more fun than Nancy, all because of the old grandmother. The peculiar old woman never came out into the light of the Japanese lanterns at the party, or anywhere near the tennis court, where the dancing was.

She kept always in the shadows, close to the walls that enclosed the lawn. And someone said that Nancy said this was because her grandmother was afraid we would steal the green fruit off the trees she had trained to grow like vines up the walls.

Whether or not Nancy had a good time, her June party was always one of the loveliest events of the year in Chatham. Even though it was the depression, we had many fine and really lovely parties, and Nancy O'Connor's usually surpassed all others. It was there, at one of them, two nights after we had graduated from high school, that Horst Hauser and Bob Southard and I made up our minds to do a thing that we had been considering for some time and that a lot of boys like us must have done at one time or another. We had been seniors that year, you understand, and in Chatham boys are apt to go pretty wild during their senior year in high school. That is the time when you get to know a city as you will never have a chance to again if you come from the kind of people that I do. I have lived away from Chatham quite a long while now, mostly in places which are not too different from it but about which I never kid myself into thinking I know very much. Yet, like a lot of other men, I carry in my head, even today, a sort of detailed map of the city where I first learned to drive a car and first learned to make dates with girls who were not strictly of the kind I was brought up to date. And I don't mean nice girls like Nancy and Trudie, whose parents were different from mine but who were themselves very nice girls indeed. Chatham being only a middle-sized city—that is, without a big-league baseball team, yet with almost a quarter of a million big-league fans—and being not thoroughly Middle Western and yet not thoroughly Southern either, the most definitely complimentary thing I usually find to say about it is that it was a good place to grow up in. By which I don't mean that it is a good place to come *from,* or anything hateful like that.

For I like Chatham. And I remember everything I ever knew about it. Sometimes, when I go back there for a visit, I can direct people who didn't grow up there to a street or a section of town or even to some place out in the country nearby that they wouldn't have guessed I had any knowledge of. And whenever I am there nowadays, the only change I notice and the only thing that gives me a sad feeling is that the whole city is so much more painted up and prosperous-looking than it used to be during the depression. And in connection with this there is something I cannot help feeling is true and cannot help saying. My father, who came from a country town thirty-five miles east of Chatham, used to tell us how sad it made him to see the run-down condition of the house where he was born, out there in the country. But my feeling is that there is something even more depressing about going back to Chatham today and finding the house where I lived till I was grown—and the whole city, too—looking in much better shape than it did when I called it home. There are moments when I almost wish I could buy up the whole town and let it run down just a little.

Of course, that's an entirely selfish feeling, and I realize it. But it shows what wonderful times we had—decent good times, and others not so decent. And it shows that while we were having those fine times we knew exactly what everything around us was like. We didn't like money's being so tight and didn't like it that everything from the schoolhouse to the country club was a little shabby and run-down. We boys certainly *minded* wearing our fathers' cut-down dinner jackets, and the girls certainly *minded* wearing their older sisters' hand-me-down evening dresses; although we knew that our party clothes looked all right, we knew, too, that our older brothers and sisters, five years before, wouldn't have put up with them for five minutes. We didn't like any of this a bit, and yet it was *ours* and the worriers among us worried even then about how it was all bound to change.

Of course, when the change came, it wasn't at all what anyone had expected. For it never occurred to us then that a war would come along and solve all the problems of the future for us, in one way or another. Instead, we heard so much talk of the depression that we thought that times were bound to get even worse than they had been, and that all the fun would go out of life as soon as we finished high school, or, at the latest, after college. If you were a worrier, as I was, it didn't seem possible that you would ever be able to make a living of the kind your father had always made. And I sat around some nights, when I ought to have been studying, wondering how people would treat me when I showed that I couldn't make the grade and began to go to pieces. It was on those nights that I used to think about Letitia Ramsey's uncle, whom I considered the most dismal failure of my acquaintance, and then think about how he was treated by Letitia. This became a thing of such interest to me that I was never afterward sure of my own innocence in the way matters developed the night of Nancy O'Connor's party.

I don't need to describe the kind of mischief the boys in

my crowd were up to that year—that is, on nights when we weren't having movie dates or going to parties with the usual "nice girls" we had always known. Our mischief doesn't need going into here, and besides it is very old hat to anyone who grew up with the freedom boys have in places like Chatham (especially at a time like the depression, when all the boys' private schools were closed down). Also, I suppose it goes without saying that we were pretty careful not to mix the one kind of wonderful time we were having with the other. To the girls we had known longest, we did make certain jokes and references they couldn't understand, or pretended they couldn't. We would kid each other, in front of them, about jams we had been in when they weren't along, without ever making any of it very clear. But that was as far as we went until, toward the end of the year, some of the girls got so they would beg us, or dare us, to take them with us some night to one of our "points of interest," which was how we referred to the juke joints and roadhouses we went to. We talked about the possibility of this off and on for several weeks. (Five years before, it wouldn't have taken our older brothers five minutes to decide to do such a thing.) And finally, on the night of Nancy O'Connor's party, Horst Hauser and Bob Southard and I decided that the time had come.

The three of us, with our dates, slipped away from the party just after midnight, telling Nancy that we would be back in about an hour, which we knew we wouldn't. And we didn't tell her mother we were going at all. We crossed the lawn and went out through a gate in the back wall at one of the corners, just behind a sort of tool house that Nancy called "the dovecote." She had told us how to find the gate, and she told us also to watch for her grand-mother. And, sure enough, just as we were unlocking the gate, there came the old grandmother running along the side wall opposite us, and sticking close to it even when she made the turn at the other corner. She was wearing a long black dress, and at the distance from which we saw her I thought she might easily have been mistaken for a Catholic nun.

But we got the gate open and started through it and into the big vacant lot we had to cross to get to Horst Hauser's car. I held the gate for the other couples, and then for my own date. While I was doing this, I kept one eye on the old woman. But I also peered around the dove-cote and saw Nancy O'Connor leave the bright lights of the tennis court and head across the grass under the Japa-nese lanterns, walking fast in order to catch her grand-mother before she reached us. And when I shut the gate after me, I could just imagine the hell the old woman was going to catch.

It wasn't very polite, leaving Nancy's party that way and making trouble in the family—for Nancy was sure to blame the old woman for our going, somehow—but the whole point is that the girl who happened to be my date that night and for whom I had stood there holding the gate was none other than Letitia Ramsey.

Now, there is no use in my not saying right here that all through that spring Letitia's uncle, whom the high-school students generally spoke of as "the Ram," had been having the usual things said about him. And there is no use in my denying that by this time I knew those things were so. For we hadn't had our *other* wonderful times all winter long without running into the Ram at a number of our points of interest—him, along with a couple of his star athletes and his and their girl friends. In fact, I knew by this time that the rumors all of us had heard about him every year since we entered high school were true, and I knew, too, that it was the very athletes he coached and trained and disciplined from the day they first reported for practice, after junior high, that he ended by making his running mates when they were seniors.

But all that sort of thing, in my opinion, is pretty much old hat to most people everywhere. The important thing to me is that when we decided to leave Nancy's wonderful party that night and take our dates with us out to a dine-and-dance joint called Aunt Martha's Tavern, something crossed my mind. And I am not sure that it wasn't something I hoped for instead of something I dreaded, as it should have been. It was that this Aunt Martha's Tavern was exactly where we were most likely to run into the Ram on a Saturday night, which this happened to be, with, of course, one of his girl friends and a couple of his athletes with their girl friends, too.

Well, it couldn't have been worse. We all climbed into Horst Hauser's car and drove out west of town to Aunt Martha's. It was the kind of place where you had to ring several times before they would come and let you in. And when we had rung the bell the second time and were standing outside under the light, with its private flock of bugs whirling around it, waiting there for Aunt Martha to have a look at us through some crack somewhere and decide if she would let us in, a rather upsetting thing happened to me. We were all standing on the stoop together, facing the big, barnlike batten door to the place.

Letitia was standing right next to me, and I just thought to myself I would steal a quick glance at her while she wasn't noticing. I turned my head only the slightest bit, but I saw at once that *she* was already looking at *me*. When our eyes met, I felt for the first second or two that she didn't realize they *had* met, because she kept right on looking without changing her expression. I couldn't at once tell what the expression meant. Then it came over me that there was something this girl was expecting me to say—or, at least, hoping I would say. I said the first thing that popped into my mind: "They always make you wait like this." And Letitia Ramsey looked grateful, even for that.

At last, the door was pulled open, though only just about six inches, and inside we saw the face of Aunt Martha's old husband. The old fellow gaped at the girls for a couple of seconds with a stupid grin on his face—he was a deaf-mute and a retired taxidermist—and then he threw the door wide open. We went inside—and, of course, there the Ram was, out on the floor dancing.

There weren't any lights on to speak of, except around the sides, in the booths, and the curtains to some of the booths were drawn. But even so, dark as it was, and with six or eight other couples swinging around on the dance floor, right off the bat I spotted the Ram. Maybe I only recognized him because he was doing the old-time snake-hips dancing that he liked to do when he was high. I can't be sure. But I have the feeling that when we walked into that place that night, I would have seen the Ram just as plainly even if he had not been there—seen the freckled hand he pumped with when he danced, seen the white sharkskin suit, seen the head of sandy hair, a little thin on top but with the sweaty curls still thick along his temples and on the back of his neck.

Once we were inside, I glanced at Letitia again. And for some reason I noticed now that either before she left the party or in the car coming out here she had moved the gardenia corsage that I had sent her from the shoulder strap of her dress to the center of its low-cut neckline. When I saw this, I suddenly turned to Bob and Horst and said, "Let's not stay here."

Letitia and the other two girls smiled at each other. "I think he thinks we'll disgrace him," Letitia said after a moment.

I don't know when she first saw her uncle. It may have been when I did, right off the bat. It being Letitia, you couldn't tell. Or *I* couldn't. The one clue I had was that when the old deaf-mute made signs for us to follow him across the floor to an empty booth, I saw her throw her little powder blue evening jacket, which was the same color as her dress, around her shoulders. It was a hot night, and before that she had only been carrying it over her arm.

Yet it wasn't necessarily her uncle's presence that caused Letitia to put the jacket around her bare shoulders. It could have been just the kind of place we were in. It could have been Martha's crazy-looking old husband, with his tufts of white hair sticking out in all directions. It seemed to me at the time that it might be only the sight of the old man's stuffed animal heads, which were hung all around the place. You didn't notice most of these with it so dark, but above the beer counter were the heads of three collie dogs, and as we went across the floor, the bubbly lights of the jukebox would now and again catch a gleam from the glass eyes of those collie dogs. Any other time in the world, I think the effect would have seemed irresistibly funny to me. I would have pointed it out to Horst and Bob, and afterward there would have been cryptic references made to it before girls like Letitia who normally wouldn't ever have been inside such a place.

We went into our booth, which was a big one in a corner, and almost as soon as we sat down, I saw two of the Ram's athletes come out on the dance floor with their girls. The Ram had disappeared, and I didn't see him dancing again. But every so often the two athletes would come out and dance for the length of about half a record and then go back to their booth, pushing the curtains apart just enough to let themselves slip through. None of us said a word about seeing them out there. And, of course, nobody mentioned the Ram. I guess we were all pretty uncomfortable about it, because we made a lot of uncomfortable and silly conversation. All of us except Letitia. We joked and carried on in a very foolish way, trying to cover up. But everything we said or did seemed to make my toes curl under.

For instance: Bob pretended he was going to close the curtains to our booth, and there was a great scramble between him and his date over keeping them open. And all the while, across the way, the curtains to the Ram's booth were never opened wider than it took for one person to slip in or out.

Also: "Where in the world *are* we?" one of the girls asked. That we were way out in the country, of course, they knew, but *where?* And it had to be explained that Aunt Martha's Tavern was across the line in Clark

County, about twelve miles due west of Chatham, which is in Pitt County, and this meant we were only about three miles from Thompsonville. Thompsonville, I knew, if some of the others didn't, was where Letitia's uncle and her father grew up. We were in an area that Letitia's Uncle Louis must have known pretty well for a long time.

And finally: There was the business about Aunt Martha. She came herself to take our orders. None of us was hungry, and the girls wouldn't even order Cokes. But she took us boys' orders for mixers, and while she was there, Horst Hauser tried to get her to sing "Temptation" for us. Martha wasn't so very old—you could tell it by her clear, smooth skin and her bright green eyes—and nobody really called her Aunt Martha. But she must have weighed about three hundred pounds and she hadn't a tooth in her head. She wore her hair in what was almost a crew cut. And she was apt to be barefoot about half the time; she was barefoot that night. She wouldn't sing "Temptation" for us, but she talked to the girls and told them how pretty their dresses were and asked them their names—"Just your first names, I'm no good at last names," she said—so she would be sure to remember them next time they came. "You know," she said. "In case you come with some other fellows, and not these jelly beans." And she gave them a big wink.

We three boys pretended to look very hurt, and she said, "They know I'm a tease. These here boys are my honey babes." Then she looked at us awfully close to make sure that we did know. She hung around telling the girls how her old husband had built the tavern single-handed, as a wedding present for her, and how, after practicing taxidermy "in many parts of the world and for over forty years," he had given it up and settled down in the country with her, and how generally sweet he was. "It mayn't seem likely to you girls," she said, her green eyes getting a damp look, "but they can be just as fine and just as noble without a tongue in their head as with one." Then, from fear of being misunderstood, maybe, or not wanting to depress the customers, she added, "And just as much fun, honey babes!" She gave us boys a wink and went off in a fit of laughter.

When she had gone, we all agreed that Martha was a good soul and that the old deaf-mute was a lucky man. But we couldn't help trying to take her off. And I laughed with the others till, suddenly, it occurred to me that her accent and her little turns of speech sounded, on our lips, just like things the Ram was quoted as saying in his civics class. He said "territory" and "A-rab" and "how come" and "I'm done." I knew that Letitia's own father didn't say things like that; it only showed the kind of low company Lou Ramsey had always kept, even as a boy in Clark County.

Well, when Martha went for the mixers, it was time for Bob and Horst and me to flip a coin to see who was going outside and buy us a pint of whiskey at the back door, which was where you always had to buy it. Unfortunately, I was odd man, and so I began collecting the money from the other two. Letitia didn't understand about the whiskey, and we had to explain to her about local option and Clark County's being a dry county, and about bootleg's being cheaper than the legal whiskey in Chatham. But while we explained, she didn't seem to listen. She only kept looking at me questioningly, and finally she squinted her eyes and said, "Are you sure you know how to buy it, and where?"

I went out the front door and around to the kitchen door, and bought the whiskey from Martha's husband, who had gone back there to meet me. I was glad for a breath of fresh air and to be away from the others for a few minutes. And yet I was eager to get back to them, too. I hurried toward the front, along the footpath between the parking lot and the side wall of the tavern—a dark wall of unpainted vertical planking. The night seemed even hotter and muggier now than it had earlier. The sky, all overcast, with no stars shining through anywhere, was like an old, washed-out gray sweater. On the far side of the parking lot, a few faint streaks of light caught my eye. I knew they came from Aunt Martha's tourist cabins, which were ranged along the edge of the woods over there. The night was so dark it was hard to tell much about the cars in the parking lot, but I could tell that they were mostly broken down jalopies and that the lot looked more like a junkyard than any real parking lot. Everything I saw looked ugly and raw and unreal to me, and when I came round to the front, where the one big light bulb above the entrance still flickered brightly in its swarm of bugs, I could see a field of waist-high corn directly across the road, and somehow it looked rawer and more unreal to me than anything else.

When I rang at the front door to be let in again, the old man had already come through the place. He opened up for me, grinning as though it were a big joke between us —his having got there as soon as I did. But I didn't want any of his dumb-show joking just then. He was making all kinds of silly signs with his hands, but I passed by him and went on back to our booth. And I was struck right away by how happy Letitia looked when she saw me. She didn't seem to be concerned about her uncle at all, which, of course, was what I was watching to see. I was glad, and yet it didn't ease my mind a bit. What were you to make of such a girl? Ever since we got there, I had been watching her in a way that I felt guilty about, because I knew it was more curiosity than sympathy. And I was certain now that she had been watching me, for some kind of sign. I couldn't have been more uncomfortable. It was strange. She was such a marvellously pretty girl, really!—with her pale yellow hair and her almond eyes, with her firm little mouth that you couldn't help looking at when she opened it a little and smiled, no matter how much respect you had for her, and no matter what else you had on your mind. I kept looking at her, and I tried not to seem too self-conscious when I drew the pint of whiskey out of the pocket of my linen jacket and put it on the table.

But I did feel self-conscious about it, and even more so because she continued to sit there just as casually as though we were having a milkshake somewhere after the show and were settling down to enjoy ourselves for the rest of the evening. When I first came back, she had looked at me as though I were a hero because I had gone around to the back door to buy a pint of bootleg whiskey and had got back alive, and now she commenced puttering around with the glasses and the mixers with a happy, helpful attitude. Bob and Horst and their two dates were still jabbering away as much as before, but Letitia made me feel now that they weren't there at all. She had set the three tumblers in front of me, and so I worked away at opening the pint bottle and then began pouring drinks for us three boys. I wasn't sure how much we ought to have right at first, and I decided I had got too much in two of the glasses. I tried to pour some back into the bottle, and made such a mess of it that I cursed under my breath. During this time, the jukebox was playing away, of course, but I do think I was half aware of some other noise somewhere, though it didn't really sink in. It didn't even sink in when Letitia put her hand on my sleeve, or when I looked up at her and saw her looking at me very much as she had outside the door a while before. The others still went on talking, and after a second Letitia drew away her hand. She began fidgeting with her gardenias, and she wasn't looking at me any more. For a moment, I wondered if she hadn't really expected us to have the drinks. But it wasn't that, and now I saw that she had tilted her head to one side to get a better view of something across the floor. I cut my eyes around and saw that the curtains to the Ram's booth had been pulled apart and that there he was, in plain view, with his girl and his star pitcher and outfielder and their two girls. I thought to myself, She's just now realized that they're all here together. Then I took another look over there, wondering why in hell they hadn't kept those curtains drawn, and I saw that something very unusual was up.

This all happened in an instant, of course—much quicker than I can tell it. The Ram was getting up very slowly from his seat and seemed to be giving some kind of orders to his pitcher and his outfielder. His own girl was still sitting at the table, and she stayed there, but the two other girls were climbing on top of the table. Pretty soon, they had opened the little high window above their booth —there was one above each of the booths—and you could see that the next thing they were going to do was to try to climb out that window. I guess they did climb out, and it wasn't long before people in some of the other booths were doing the same thing.

After a minute or so, there was nobody left on the dance floor, and all of a sudden someone unplugged the jukebox. Without the music, we could hear the knocking on the doors of the tourist cabins, and I began to notice lights flashing outside the little window above our booth. I knew now there was a raid on the cabins, but I didn't want to be the first to mention the existence of those cabins to the girls. And though I was sure enough of it, I just couldn't make myself admit that the raid would be happening to the tavern, too, in about three minutes.

I saw the Ram leave his booth, and he seemed to be starting in the direction of ours. Letitia looked relieved now, and actually leaned forward across the table as though she were trying to catch his eye. Both Bob Southard and I got up and started out to meet him, but he held out a stiff arm, motioning us back, and he went off toward the beer counter without ever looking at Letitia.

When Bob and I turned back toward our booth, Horst and the girls were standing up, saying nothing. But Letitia gave me a comforting smile and she opened her mouth to say something that she never did say. I can almost believe she had been about to tell me how shy her uncle was, and to ask if I noticed how he wouldn't look at her when she was dressed up this way.

But now the Ram was headed back toward us with Martha, and Martha had slipped on some brown loafers. There was loud banging now on the front and back doors of the tavern, but apparently she and her husband weren't set to open up yet; I guessed the old man hadn't finished hiding the whiskey. By now, anybody who was going to get away had to chance it through the windows. We could hear people dropping on the ground outside those little high windows, and hear some of them grunting when they landed.

As soon as the Ram and Martha got near us, he said, "We're going to put you out of sight somewhere. They won't want to take too many in. They just want their quota."

Martha wasn't ruffled a bit. I suppose she could see we were, though. She looked at the girls and said, "Chicka-biddies, I wouldn't have had this happen for nothing in this world."

The Ram glanced back at his own booth, to make sure that his athletes were still there—and maybe his girl friend. They hadn't moved a muscle. They just sat there very tense, watching the Ram. You would have thought they were in the bullpen waiting for a signal from him to come in and pitch. But they never got one. The Ram said to Martha, "Just anywhere you stick her and the rest of them is all right, but upstairs in your parlor would be mighty nice." From the way he said it, you would have thought he was speaking to one of the old lady teachers at Westside.

"You know I ain't about to hide nobody upstairs," she said firmly but politely. "Not even for you, honey baby."

"Then put them in the powder room yonder," he said.

"If they'll fit, that's fine," she said. She led the way and we followed.

It was over at the end of the counter—just a little closet, with "SHE" painted on the door and a toilet in-

side, and not even one of the little high windows. Martha
made sure the key was in the lock, inside, and told us to
turn off the light and lock ourselves in. We had to squeeze
to get in, and one of us would have stood on the toilet
except there wasn't a lid. While we were crowding in, the
banging on the doors kept getting louder and began to
sound more in earnest, and Martha's husband ambled up
and stood watching us with his mouth hanging open.
Martha looked around at him and burst out laughing.
"He can't hear it thunder, bless his heart," she said. And
the old fellow laughed, too.

The Ram said, "Get them inside, please, Ma'am.
They'll *have* to fit."

But Martha merely laughed at him. "You better git
yourself *out*side if you expect to git," she said.

"I don't expect to git," he said.

"What'sa matter?"

He looked back over his shoulder at the room, where
there were only eight or ten people left, most of them
staggering around in the shadows, looking for a window
that wasn't so high. "They'll have to have their quota of
customers," he said, "or they might make a search."

"Well, it's your funeral you're planning, not mine,"
Martha said, and she winked at nobody in particular.
Then her little green eyes suddenly darted another look
at her husband. "OK," she said, "and I better take a quick
gander to see he left out their quota of whiskey-take."
With that, she slipped her feet out of her shoes again and
padded along behind the counter and into the kitchen,
with the old man following her. The banging on the
doors couldn't get any louder, but they could have
knocked the doors down by this time if they had really

been as earnest about it as they made it sound. And we would long since have been locked inside the toilet except that while the Ram and Martha were having their final words, Letitia had put one foot over the sill again and was waiting to say something to her uncle.

"Uncle Louis," she began very solemnly. The Ram's faced turned as red as a beet. Not just his face but the top of his head, too, where his sandy hair had got so thin. And, from the quick way he jerked his head around and fixed his eyes on the front door, it seemed as if he hadn't heard the banging over there till now. The truth was he *didn't* want to look at Letitia. But of course he had to, and it couldn't wait. So he sticks out that square chin, narrows his eyes under those blond eyebrows of his, and gives Letitia the hardest, impatientest look in the world. But it was nothing. The thing that was something was not the expression on *his* face but the one on hers. I won't ever forget it, though I certainly can't describe it. It made me think she was going to thank him from the bottom of her heart or else say how sorry she was about everything, or even ask him if something couldn't be done about hiding those poor athletes of his. I thought most likely it would be something about the athletes, since their being there with him was bound to make a scandal if it got into the newspapers. But in a way what she said was better than any of that. She said, "I don't have any money with me, Uncle Louis. Do you think I ought to have some money?"

"*Good* girl!" he practically shouted. And the guy actually smiled—the very best, most unselfish kind of smile. He reached down in his pocket and pulled out a couple of crumpled-up bills. I saw that one of them was a five. Letitia took the two bills and stuffed them in the pocket of her jacket. "Good girl," he said again, not quite so loud. He was smiling, and seemed nearly bursting with pride because Letitia had thought of something important that he had overlooked.

"It's going to be all right, isn't it?" she said then.

"Why, sure it is," he said. It was as though the whole raid was something that was happening just to them and concerned nobody else. And now she gave him that look again, and what it showed, and what it had shown before, was nothing on earth but the beautiful confidence she had in him—all because he was an uncle of hers, I suppose.

"Good night, darling," she said. She stepped back into the toilet with the rest of us, and it was every bit as exciting to see as if she had been stepping into a lifeboat and leaving him on a sinking ship. My guess, too, is that when the Ram watched her pulling the door to, he wished he *was* about to go down on a real ship, instead of about to be arrested and taken off with his girl friend and his two athletes to the jail in Thompsonville, the town where he grew up, and then to have it all in the Chatham papers and finally lose his job as civics teacher and baseball coach at Westside High. For that, of course, is the way it turned out.

Somebody locked the door and we stood in there in the dark, and then we heard Martha come back and put on her shoes and go to open the front door. But we couldn't hear everything, because at the first sound of the deputies' voices the two other girls began to shake all over and whimper like little sick animals. Bob and Horst managed to hush them up pretty much, however, and before long I heard a man's voice say, "Well, Lou, haven't *you* played hell?" The man sounded surprised and pleased. "This is too bad, Lou," he said. It was a mean, little-town voice, and you could hear the grudge in it against anybody who had got away even as far as Chatham and amounted to even as little as the Ram did. Or that was how I felt it sounded. "That wouldn't be some of your champs over there, would it, Lou?"

Letitia didn't make a sound. She just shivered once, as though a rabbit had run over her grave, or as though, in the awful stink and heat of that airless toilet, she was really cold. It was black as pitch in there, but I was pressed up against Letitia and I felt that shiver go over her. And then, right afterward, I could tell how easily she breathed, how relaxed she was. I wanted to put my arms around her, but I didn't dare—not in a place like that. I didn't dare even think about it twice.

Once our door was shut, we never heard the Ram's voice again.

In a very few minutes, the sheriff's men seemed to have got everybody out of the tavern except Martha and her husband. The two girls had stopped all their whimpering and teeth-chattering now, and we heard one of the men —the sheriff himself, I took it—talking to Martha while the others were carrying away whatever whiskey had been left out for them to find.

"Kind of sad about Lou Ramsey," he said, with a little snicker.

"I don't know him," Martha said, cutting things short. "I don't know any of them by their last names. That's your business, not mine."

The man didn't answer for a minute, but when he did, he sounded as though she had hurt his feelings. "You ought to be fair, Mrs. Mayberry," he said, "and not go blaming me for taking in them that just stands around waiting for it." I thought I could tell now that they were both sitting on stools at the counter.

"I don't mind, if he don't mind," she said. "It's his funeral, not mine." And now it sounded as though it was the Ram she was mad at, even more than the man she was talking to.

After a minute, he said, "I never been so hot as to-night."

"It's growing weather, honey baby," she said, and slapped her hand down on the counter.

"There's not nobody else around?" he asked her suddenly.

"What are you asking me that for, honey baby?" she said. "You got as many as your little jail will 'most hold."

We heard him laugh, and then neither of them said anything more for a minute. The other men seemed to have made their last trips to the kitchen and back now, and I heard the man with Martha get down off his stool at the counter.

"Well'm," he said, "which one of you cares to make the ride this time?"

"Whichever one you favors," she said.

"You know me," he said. "How's them kids?" For a second I was absolutely sure he meant us. But then he said, "How you manage to keep 'em quiet enough up there? You put cotton in their ears?" Martha didn't answer him, and finally he said, "What'sa matter with you tonight, Mrs. Mayberry?"

"You wouldn't kid me about something like my kids, would you, Sheriff?" she asked, in a hard voice.

"Like what?"

"Like saying nobody's never told you they was born just as deaf as their daddy, yonder."

"You don't say, Mrs. Mayberry," he said, sounding out of breath. "Nobody ever told me that, I swear to God. Why, I've seen them two tow-heads playing around out there in the lot, but nobody said to me they was deaf."

"Can't hear it thunder," she said, and all at once she laughed. Then she let out a long moan, and next thing she was crying.

"Mrs. Mayberry," the sheriff said, "I am sure sorry."

"No," she said, and she stopped crying just as quick as she had begun. "When somebody says they're sorry about it, I say no, it's a blessing. My kids ain't never going to hear the jukebox play all night, and no banging on doors, neither. It's a blessing, I say, all they won't hear, though it's a responsibility to me. But I won't be sitting up wondering where they are, the way you'll likely be doing with your young'uns, Sheriff. It's a blessing the good Lord sends to some people. It's wrong, but it's *something*. It's *something* I got which most people ain't. Till the day they die, they'll be just as true to me as the old man there."

Just then, one of the sheriff's men called him from outside to say they'd better get going, and I couldn't help being glad for the sheriff's sake. "Hell," he said to Martha, "it's too bad, but one of you has to come with me."

I was glad for us, too, because we were about to smother in there and be sick at our stomachs besides. The sheriff went on out then, taking one of the Mayberrys along.

Everything was quiet after that, except for the motor of the sheriff's truck starting up. At first, we couldn't even tell for certain whether it was Martha or the old man who had gone with the sheriff. We waited a couple of minutes, and then, from the way the floor was creaking overhead, we knew it was Martha who had stayed. In the excitement, and after her outburst, she had forgotten all about us and had gone tiptoeing upstairs to see about her little deaf children.

All at once, Bob Southard said, "Let's get out of here," and he turned the key. We burst out onto the dance floor, and the first thing my eyes hit on was Martha's two brown loafers on the pine floor at the end of the counter. They were the first thing I saw, and about the only thing for a minute or so, for we stood there nearly blinded by the bright lights, which the sheriff's men had turned on everywhere and which Martha hadn't bothered to turn out.

It was awful seeing everything lit up that way—not just the mess the place was in, which wasn't so bad considering that there had been a raid, but just seeing the place at all in that light. Those stuffed animal heads of the old man's stared at you from everywhere you could turn—dogs, horses, foxes, bulls, even bobcats and some bears, and one lone zebra—leaning out from the walls, so that their glass eyes were shining right down at you. We got out of there just as quick as we could.

The front door was standing wide open. We didn't stop to pull it to after us. We went outside and around the corner toward the parking lot, and when we showed ourselves there, it was the signal for about twenty or thirty people to begin coming out of the woods, where they had been hiding. Some of them came running out, and others kind of wandered out, and at least one came crawling on his hands and knees. With the sky still that nasty gray, we couldn't have seen them at first except for the broad shafts of light that came from the open doorways of the cabins. It was a creepy sight, and the sounds these people made were creepy, too. As they came out of the woods, some of them were arguing, some of them laughing and kidding in a hateful way, and here and there a woman was crying and complaining, as though maybe she had got hurt jumping down from one of those high little windows.

We knew that as soon as they climbed into their old jalopies, there would be a terrific hassle to get out of that parking lot, and so we made a dash for Horst's sedan and all piled into it without caring who sat where or who was whose date. And we were out of that lot and tearing down the road before we even heard a single other motor get started.

All the way to Chatham, and then driving around to take everybody home, we just kept quiet except to talk every now and then about Martha and her old husband's children, about how unfair and terrible it seemed for them to be born deaf, and how unfair and terrible it was to bring up children in a place like that. Even then, it seemed to me unnatural for us not to be mentioning what had happened earlier. But I suppose we were thankful at least to have the other thing to talk about. I was sitting in the back seat, and Letitia was sitting up in the front. I watched her shaking her head or nodding now and then when someone else was talking. There was certainly nothing special I could say to her from the back seat. But when we finally got to her house and I took her up to her door, I did make myself say, "We certainly owe your uncle a lot, Letitia."

"Yes, poor darling," she said. "But it's a good thing he was there, isn't it?" That's all she said. The marvelous thing, I thought, was that she didn't seem to hold anything against me.

I was away from Chatham most of that summer. The first of July, I went down to New Orleans with a friend of mine named Bickford Harris, and he and I got jobs on a freight boat and worked our way over to England and back. We got back on the fourteenth of September, which was only about a week before I had to leave for college. I had seen Letitia at several other parties before we went off to New Orleans, and had called her on the telephone to say goodbye. I sent her a postcard from New Orleans and I sent her three postcards from England. I didn't write her a letter for the same reason that I only telephoned her, instead of asking her for a date or going by to see her, before we left. I didn't want her to think I was trying to make something out of our happening to be put together that night, and didn't want her to think it meant anything special to me. But when we got back in September, I did ask her for a date, and she gave it to me.

And, of course, Letitia hadn't changed a bit—or only a very little bit. I could tell she hadn't, even when I talked with her on the telephone to make the date. She said she loved my postcards, but that's all she said about them, and it was plain they hadn't made any real impression on her. She told me that she was going to be leaving within a couple of weeks, to go to a finishing school in Washington, D.C., and the next summer she was going to Europe herself, before making her début in the fall. She talked to me about all these plans on the telephone, and I knew that when a girl in Chatham begins talking about her plans to make her début, she already has her mind on meeting older guys. That's the "very little bit" I mean she had changed. But she did give me the date—on a Monday night, it was. I was awfully glad about it, yet the minute I walked into her house, I began wishing I had left well enough alone.

For right off the bat I heard her uncle's voice. He was back in the dining room, where they were all still sitting around the table. And I had to go in there and tell them how I'd liked working on a freight boat and how I'd liked England. I also had to shake hands all around, even with the Ram, who was already standing up when I came in, speaking rather crossly to Letitia's three little brothers and hurrying them to get through with their dinner. When I shook his hand, I could tell from the indifferent way he looked at me that he didn't know he had ever seen me before. And suddenly I said to myself, "Why, all he knows about me is that I'm not a Ramsey and I'm not a baseball player."

Most of the time I was in the room, he was still hurrying Letitia's little brothers, under his breath, to finish their dinner. Everyone else had finished, and he was waiting to take her brothers somewhere afterward. I knew what he had been doing since June, when he found out he wouldn't be teaching at the high school in the fall. He had landed a soft daytime job with one of the lumber companies in Chatham, which had hired him so it would have him to manage the company's baseball team. As we were going out through the living room, I heard his voice getting louder and very cross again with the boys, the way it had sounded when I came in. Letitia heard it, too, and only laughed to herself. Outside, when we were walking across the lawn toward my car, she explained that her uncle was taking her little brothers to a night baseball game, in the commercial league, and that there was nothing in the world they loved better.

Letitia and I had a nice time that night, I suppose. It was just like other dates we'd had. We ran into some people at the movie, and we all went for a snack somewhere afterward. The thing is I don't pretend that I ever did get to know Letitia Ramsey awfully well. As I have said, it was only by chance that she and I were put together for Nancy O'Connor's dance that year. We simply ran with the same crowd, and in our crowd the boys all knew that they would be going to college (or hoped so), and the girls that they would be going off to finishing school, up East or in Virginia, for a year or two and then be making their débuts, and so we tended not to get too serious about each other. It wasn't a good idea, that's all, because it could break up your plans and your family's. The most that usually happened was some terrific crushes and, naturally, some pretty heavy necking that went along with the crushes. But there was never even anything like that between Letitia and me. I never felt that I knew her half as well as I did several of her friends that I had even fewer dates with.

Still, I do know certain things from that evening at Aunt Martha's Tavern. I know how Letitia looked at an uncle who never had—and never has yet—amounted to anything. And I know now that while I watched her looking at him, I was really wishing that I knew how to make a girl like her look at me that trusting way, instead of the way she had been looking at me earlier. It almost made me wish that I was one of the big, common fellows at Westside High who slipped off and got married to one of the public-school girls in their class and then told the teachers and the principal about it, like a big joke, after they'd got their diplomas on graduation night. But the point is I *didn't* know how to make a girl like her look at me that way. And the question is why *didn't* I know how?

Usually, I tell myself that I didn't because I was such a worrier and that I wouldn't have been such a worrier if there hadn't been a depression, or if I had known a war was going to come along and solve everything. But I'm not sure. Once, during the war, I told this to a guy who didn't come from the kind of people that I do. He only laughed at me and said he wanted to hear more about those other times we were having that year. I pointed out that those other good times weren't the point and that a girl like Letitia Ramsey was something else again. "Yea," he said, looking rather unfriendly. "That's how all you guys like to talk."

But the worst part, really, is what it's like when you see someone like Letitia nowadays. She may be married to a guy whose family money is in downtown real estate and who has never had a doubt in his life, or maybe to some guy working on commission and drinking himself to death. It doesn't matter which. If it is a girl like Letitia who's married to him, he's part of her family now, and all men outside her family are jokes to her. And she and this fellow will have three or four half-grown children, whom nobody can believe she is really the mother of, since she looks so young. Well, the worst part is when you are back home visiting and meet her at a dinner party, and she tells you before the whole table how she was once on the verge of being head over heels in love with you and you wouldn't give her a tumble. It's always said as a big joke, of course, and everyone laughs. But she goes on and on about it, as though it was really something that had been worrying her. And the more everybody laughs, the more she makes of it and strings it out. And what it shows, more than any number of half-grown children could ever do, is how old she is getting to be. She says that you always seemed to have your mind on other things and that she doesn't know yet whether it was higher things or lower things. Everyone keeps on laughing until, finally, she pretends to look very serious and says that it is all right for them to laugh but that it wasn't funny at the time. Her kidding, of course is a big success, and nobody really minds it. But all I ever want to say—and don't ever say—is that as far as I am concerned, it isn't one bit funnier now than it was then.

Promise of Rain

———◆◆———

Understand, there was never anything *really* wrong with Hugh Robert. He was a well-built boy, strong and quick and bursting with vitality. That, at least, was the impression of himself he managed to give people. I guess he did it just by carrying himself well and never letting down in front of anyone. Actually, he was no better built than my other boys. And how is one really to know about a person's vitality? He had a bright look in his blue eyes, a fresh complexion, and a shock of black curly hair on a head so handsomely shaped that everybody noticed it. It was the shape of his head, I imagine, that made people feel Hugh was so much better looking than his older brothers. All the girls were crazy about him. And even if

I am his father, I have to say that he was a boy who seemed fairly crazy about himself.

When Hugh was sixteen, I kept a pretty close watch on him—closer than I ever had time to keep on the others. I observed how he seldom left for school in the mornings without stopping a moment before the long gilt-framed mirror in the front hall. Sometimes he would seem to be looking at himself with painful curiosity and sometimes with pure admiration. Either way it was unbecoming of him. But still I wasn't too critical of the morning looks he gave himself. I did mind, however, his doing the same thing again when he got home from school in the afternoons. Many a winter's afternoon I would already be home when he came in, and from where I sat in the living room, or in the library across the hall, I could tell by his footsteps that he was stopping to see himself in that great expanse of looking-glass.

For Hugh's own good I used, some afternoons, to let him catch me watching him at the mirror. I thought it might break him of the habit. But his eyes would meet mine without the least shame and he would say something he didn't mean, like "I'm not much to look at, am I, Mr. Perkins?" And he continued to stop there and ogle himself in the mirror whenever it suited him to. He would often call me Mr. Perkins like that, and call his mother Mrs. Perkins. We could never be quite sure how it was meant, and I don't think he intended us to be. When he was being outright playful, he was apt to call us Will and Mary.

Hugh kept his schoolbooks in a compartment of the cupboard in the downstairs hall. The cupboard I speak of was a big oak, antique thing, a very expensive piece of furniture, which Hugh's mother had bought in Europe during our 1924 trip—ten years before. Hugh's school-books seldom got farther into the house than the hall cupboard. If I complained about this to Mary, she would refer me to his report card, with its wall of straight A's. If I carried my attack further and mentioned the silly kind of subjects he was taking, she would sigh and blame it on his having to go to the public school. As though I *wanted* Hugh to go to the public school! And as though I wanted to be home those afternoons when he came in from school! It was just that Hugh Robert grew up during bad times for us, which, as I see it, was no more my fault than it was his. Those were years when it seemed that my business firm might have to close its doors almost any time. I couldn't *afford* to keep a boy in private school. And as for myself, I just couldn't bear to hang around the office all of those long, dead winter afternoons at the bottom of the depression.

I can see Hugh now in his corduroy jacket and sheep-skin collar stooping down to slip his books always in the same corner of the same compartment of the hall cup-board. He was orderly and systematic about everything like that. His older brothers had never measured up to him in this respect. In an instant he could tell you the whereabouts of any of his possessions. He had things stashed away—ice skates, baseball gloves, and other ath-letic equipment, as well as sets of carpentry tools, car tools, and radio parts—had them pushed neatly away in nooks and shelves and drawers all over the house. They were all things he had been very much excited about at one time or another. Hugh would plague us to buy him something, and then when we did and he didn't get the satisfaction out of it he had expected, he would brood about it for weeks. Finally, he would put it away somewhere. If it was something expensive and we asked him what became of it, he would say it was just one of his "mistakes" and that we needn't think he had forgotten it. Sometimes when I was looking for something I had misplaced, I would come on one of those nests of "mistakes" and know at once it was Hugh's. I remember its occurring to me once that it wouldn't take Hugh Robert thirty seconds to lay his hands on anything he owned, and that he would be able in ten minutes' time to assemble *everything* he owned and be on his way, if ever that notion struck him. It wasn't a thought that would ever have occurred to me in connection with the other children.

Our daughter and the two older boys were married and gone from the house by this time, but when they were home with their spouses on a Sunday they'd say we were still babying Hugh, and say that they knew what would have happened to *them* if they had ever tried calling us by our first names. I suppose you really can't help babying the youngest, in one way or another, and favoring him a little over the others, especially when he comes along as a sort of trailer after the others are already up in school. But to Hugh's mother it was very annoying to have the older children point this out, and she would deny it hotly. If on a Monday morning, after the others had been there on Sunday, Hugh came down to breakfast and began that first-name or Mr.-and-Mrs. business, Mary was likely to try to talk to him as she used to talk to the other children, and tell him that it was not very respectful of him. It never did any good, though, and she would say afterward that I never supported her in these efforts. I don't know. I do know, though, that disrespectful is hardly the word for my son Hugh Robert Perkins—not when he was sixteen, not when he was younger than that, not even nowadays, when he favors us with one of his rare visits and sits around the house for three days talking mostly about himself and about how broke I was when he was growing up. Mary says he's the only person who can remind me, nowadays, of how hard up we were then without making me mad. If that is so, it is because he seems to take such innocent pleasure in remembering it. He talks about it in a way that makes you feel he is saying, "I owe *every*thing to that!"

It got to be the fashion in those days for high-school boys to wear the knee bands of their golf knickers unfastened, letting the baggy pants legs hang loose down to their ankles. They went to school that way, and it looked far worse to me than even the shirttail-out fashion that came along after the war. I had never seen Hugh wearing his own plus-fours that way, but I remarked to him one day that I regarded it as the ugliest, sloppiest, most ungentlemanly habit of dress I had ever encountered. And I asked him what in the world possessed those boys to make them do it. I think he took this as a nasty slam against his classmates. "I don't know why they do it," he said, with something of a sneer, "but I could find out for you, Mr. Perkins." I told him never mind, that I didn't want to know.

Next day Hugh appeared at breakfast with his knickers hanging down about his ankles. He lunged into the room with the buckles on his knee bands jangling like spurs.

Naturally, I was supposed to blow up and tell him to fasten them. But I pretended not even to notice, and I wouldn't let Mary mention it to him. He wore them that way for a couple of days, and then, seeing he wasn't going to get a rise out of me, he stopped. He seemed dispirited and rather gloomy for a day or so. Then, finding me at home after school one afternoon, he said out of the clear: "I made a discovery for you, Dad."

"What's that?" I said. I really didn't know what he meant.

"I found out why those fellows wear their plus-fours drooping down. I tried wearing my own that way for a couple of days, though you didn't even notice it." And he had the cheek to wink at me in the hall mirror.

"Well?" I said noncommittally. I remembered I had said I didn't want to know why. But I didn't remind him, because I knew he remembered, too.

He had already put his books away, and he was about to take his jacket to the closet behind the stair. He stood running one finger along the ribbing of the corduroy jacket, which he had thrown over his arm, and he had a dejected look on his face. "It makes them feel kind of reckless and devil-may-care and as if they don't give a darn for what anybody thinks of how they look." This he volunteered, mind you. I had only said, "Well?"

I thought he would continue, but when he didn't, I asked, "You don't recommend it? You didn't like the feeling?"

"It didn't make *me* feel that way. It only made me understand how it makes *them* feel. I didn't get any kick out of it. I don't blame them too much, though. Those guys don't have much to make them feel important."

I had to bite my tongue to keep from asking the boy what he had to make him feel important. But I let it go at that, because I saw what he was getting at. I realized I was supposed to feel pretty cheap for having criticized the people he went to school with.

Hugh didn't have any duties at home. We weren't people who lived in any do-it-yourself world in those days, no matter how bad business was. I still kept me a yard man in summer and a furnace man in winter. I can't help saying that in that respect I did as well by Hugh as by his older brothers. When he came home in the afternoon and had stuck his books in the cupboard he was *free*—free as a bird. He might have looked at himself in the mirror all afternoon if he had wanted to. Or he might have been out on the town with a bunch of the high-school roughnecks. But Hugh wasn't a ruffian, and he wasn't an idler, either; not in the worst sense. He was vain and self-centered, but you knew that while he stood before that looking-glass unbuckling his corduroy jacket he was trying to make judgments and decisions about himself; he was checking something he had thought about himself during the day.

In the mirror Hugh's blue eyes would seem to study their own blueness for a time, and then, not satisfied, they would begin to explore the hall—the hall, that is, as reflected in the glass, and with himself, of course, always in the foreground. If I had purposely planted myself in the library doorway, that's when his eyes would light on me. He would look at me curiously for a split second—before he let his eyes meet mine—look at me as he did at everything else in view. The first time it happened, I thought the look meant he was curious and resentful about my being home from the office so early. Next time, I saw that this wasn't so and that he was merely fitting me into his picture of himself. I remember very well what he said to me on one of these occasions: "Mr. Perkins, even among mirrors there's a difference! Especially the big ones. They all give you different ideas of how you look." He rambled on, seemingly without any embarrassment. "I saw myself in a big one downtown one day and there was a second when I couldn't place where I'd seen that uncouth, unkempt, uncanny individual before. And at school there's a huge one in the room where we take typing—don't ask me what it's there for. It makes me look like everybody else in the class, with all of us pecking away at typewriters. We all look so much alike I can hardly find myself in it." When Hugh finished that spiel, I found myself blushing —blushing for him. I hated so to think of the boy gaping at himself in mirrors all over town the way he did in that one in my front hall.

During the summer after Hugh turned seventeen I had the misfortune to learn, first-hand, something about his habits away from home—that is, when he did take a notion to use his freedom differently and go out on the town with his cronies from the high school. I am not speaking of night life, though there was beginning to be some of that, too, but of the hours that young people have to kill in the daytime. The city of Chatham, which is where we have always lived, is not the biggest city in the world, by a long shot. It isn't even the biggest city in our state. Since the Second World War it has grown substantially, and the newspapers claim that there are now half a million people in the "municipal area," by which they mean almost the whole county. But twenty-five years ago people didn't speak of it as being more than half that size. For me to encounter my son Hugh downtown or riding along Division Boulevard couldn't really be thought a great coincidence—especially not since, almost without knowing it, I had developed the habit of keeping an eye out for that head of his.

I would catch a glimpse of him on the street and, with my mind still on some problem we had at the office, wouldn't know right away what it was I had seen. Often I had to turn around and look to be sure. There Hugh would be, his dark head moving along in a group of other youthful heads—frequently a girl's head for every boy's—out under the boiling July sun, in a section of the city that they couldn't possibly have had any reason for being in. There was at least one occasion when I was certain that Hugh saw me, too. I was in the back seat of the car, and when I turned and looked out the rear window, Hugh was waving. But I was crowded in between two hefty fellows—two of my men from the office—and couldn't have returned his wave even if I had tried. On that occasion, we were riding through a section of town that used long ago to be called the Irish Flats. The men with me were both of them strictly Chatham Irish, and as we rode along I commenced teasing them about how tough that section used to be and how when I was a boy a "white man" didn't dare put foot in that end of town.

Perkins Finance Company, which was the name of our firm before we reorganized in 1946, used to make loans on small properties all over Chatham. Since the boys took over—my two older boys and my daughter's husband— they haven't wanted to deal much in that kind of thing. We have bigger irons in the fire now, and the boys have even put a cable address on the company stationery, along with the new name: Perkins, Hodgeson Investments. (The Hodgeson's for my daughter's husband.) But our small loans were what saved us in the depression. The boys weren't with me in the firm then, of course. When they came back from college up East, just at the time of the crash, I wouldn't let them come in with me. I got them jobs in two Chatham banks which I *knew* weren't going to fail. They were locked up down there in their cages all day and went home to their young wives at night without ever having any notion of the kind of hide-and-seek games Hugh and I were playing in our idleness. What I would often do—when I didn't go home in the afternoon—was to ride around town with some of my men and look at the property we had an interest in. Aside from any business reason, it did something for me— more than going home did, more than a round of golf, or going to the ball game even. It did something for me to get out and look at the town, to see how it had stopped building and growing. The feeling I got from it was that Time itself had stopped and was actually waiting for me instead of passing me by and leaving me behind just when I was in my prime. At the time, I already had a son-in-law and two daughters-in-law, but I wasn't an old man. I had just turned fifty. In the hot summertime of the depression I could sometimes look at Chatham and feel about it that it was a big, powerful, stubborn horse that wouldn't go. I was still in the saddle, it seemed—or I had just dismounted and had a tight grip on the reins near the bit and was meaning to remount. Perhaps I even had in mind beating the brute somehow, to make it go; for I was young enough then to be impatient and to feel that I just couldn't wait for the town to begin to move again. I know I had to have my second chance. Hugh could take whatever pleasure and instruction he would from exploring the city as it was in those days and getting to know different kinds of people. It corresponded to something in his make-up. Or it answered some need of his temperament. Anyway, he seemed to be born for it. But, as for me, I could hardly wait for things to begin to move again and to be the way they had been before.

Yet I was a man old enough to take a certain reasonable satisfaction in everything's suddenly stopping still the way it did in the depression and giving me the chance to look at the city the way I could then. It has a beauty, a town like Chatham does. Even with things getting mighty shabby, as they were by 1933, Division Boulevard was a magnificent street with handsome stone and tile-faced office buildings and store buildings downtown, with the automobile showrooms taking up beyond the overpass at the Union Station—a cathedral of a building!—and after that a half mile of old mansions from the last century, most of them long since turned into undertaking parlors, all of them so well built that no amount of abuse or remodeling seemed to alter them much; and then almost a mile of small apartment houses, and after that the clinics and the State Medical Center and the two big hospitals.

Beyond the hospitals, Division Boulevard runs right through Lawton Park. On one side you get a glimpse among the trees of the Art Gallery; farther along on that side, there is the bronze monument to the doughboy. On the other side is a mound with Lawton Park spelled out in sweet alyssum and pinks and ground myrtle; and away over on that side you can see among the tree tops the glass dome of the bird house at the zoo. It's a handsomely kept park—was all the way through the depression even—and when you come out at the other end there before your eyes is the beginning of Singleton Heights!

From Singleton Heights on out past the Country Club to the Hunt and Polo Grounds it's all like a fairyland. Great stucco and stone houses, and whitewashed brick, acres upon acres of them. All of them planted round with evergreens and flowering fruit trees, with wide green lawns—the sprinklers playing like fountains all summer long—lawns that are really meadows, stretching off to little low stone walls or rustic fences or even a sluggish little creek with willow trees growing along its banks in places. It's the sort of thing that when you've been off to New York, or maybe to Europe for the summer, and come back to it, the very prettiness of it nearly breaks your heart.

But I ought to say, before speaking of Hugh again, that Singleton Heights and the Country Club area beyond are not the only fine neighborhoods in Chatham and it is not of those sections of Chatham that I think when I'm up at the lake in the summer or away on a business trip. My own house, for instance, is in one of the gated-off streets that were laid out just north of Lawton Park at the turn of the century. The houses there are mostly big three-story houses. There's a green parkway down the center of the street, and we have so many forest trees you would think you were in the middle of Lawton Park itself. But, actually, it's not even the Lawton Park area that's most typical of Chatham, any more than Singleton Heights or the Country Club area. And, in my mind, it is certainly not the new do-it-yourself ranch-house district that means

Chatham to me. . . . It is the block after block of modest
two-story houses, built thirty to forty years ago now, that
seem most typical and give me a really comfortable feeling. It was the people in those houses who managed to
keep paying something on their loans in the depression.
Whenever I think of Chatham when Mary and I go away
in the summer and think of how pleasant it can be to be
there despite the awful heat I think first of those bunga-
lows built of good wirecut brick, with red and orange tile
roofs and big screened porches, of the little privet hedges
that divide their sixty-foot lots and of the maples and
oaks and sycamores whose summer shade their front
yards share.

The summer Hugh was seventeen I must have seen him
hoofing it along the sidewalk or standing at the curb of
every block of Division Boulevard. I could never be certain that the men with me recognized him, and once I
asked Joe McNary, "What were those kids doing back
there on the curb?"

"They're hitch-hiking, Will," he said.

"Hitch-hiking?" I had never heard the term before, but
I knew at once what it meant. "Where are they going?" I
said.

"Nowhere. They're just doing the town. There's no
harm in it, I guess."

I guess he was right. Hugh never got into any trouble
that I know of, except over a car that he and his buddies
made a down payment on, one time. They put down
seven dollars on an old Packard touring car and drove it
around town till it ran out of gas. They had bought the
car in Hugh's name, and so when the police found it

parked at the roadside out near the Polo Club, they gave me a ring. I told them just to take it back to the dealer and that I'd pay whatever fine there was. But they were pretty inquisitive, and I had to go down to the police station and answer a lot of questions. It was an embarrassing experience for me, because I had to confess that I hadn't known of Hugh's part in the adventure and didn't know the names of the other boys who went in on it with him. From the police station I had to get Hugh on the telephone at the high school and find out the names of the other boys. He didn't want to tell me. And we had to argue it out right then, which was the bad part, with him talking from the principal's office and with me at the sergeant's desk at the police station. Hugh ended by giving me the boys' names, and we never heard any more about it from the police, though I did have to pay the used-car dealer something to make him forget the whole business.

Hugh Robert was in the dumps for a couple of weeks afterward. Instead of excusing himself from the dinner table, as he had always done when his mother and I sat dawdling over our coffee, he would sit there pretending to listen to what we had to say, or he would just gaze despairingly up into the glass prisms of the chandelier above the table. One night when I felt I couldn't stand his black mood any longer, I gave his mother a sign to leave us alone. At first she frowned and refused to do it. Finally though, when I grew as silent as Hugh, she invented a reason to have to go to the kitchen. As soon as I heard hers and the cook's voices out there, I said, "What's the matter, Hugh. What are you thinking about?"

He said, "I was thinking about how sorry I am. I really am, Dad."

"What's this?" I said.

"I'm sorry you had to pay that money on the car."

"Is that all?"

"No. Worse than that was their having you down at the station. I know you hated that worse than paying the money." Right away, you see, he was making me out as some kind of pantywaist.

"I didn't give a hoot in hell about going to the police station," I said. "But it was a damn-fool idea you boys had."

"You don't have to tell me that," he said. "It was the stupidest idea I've ever had. It was an awful mistake."

What could you say to such a boy? I wanted to ask him where they would have gone if they had had more gas, but his mother came bustling back from the kitchen then, followed by Lucy May, the cook, who began pressing Hugh to have a second helping of chocolate pie, which, if I remember correctly, he did.

One other time, when I was out with another group of men, and in another part of town, I asked, "What do you suppose those kids are doing out here?"

"*Out* here?" One of them said, and I could tell from his lack of interest that he hadn't recognized Hugh. But I think the fellow who was driving the car that day must have known that what I meant was: What was a son of mine doing so far from home?

"Oh," he said, "I can guess pretty well what they're doing. They've heard there's a drugstore in this end of town that sells milk shakes for a nickel. It's something like that; you can just count on it." We were in a perfectly decent neighborhood out on the south side, where a lot of the rich Germans used to live. It's a nice section and didn't get too awfully run-down during the depression. I could hardly have told the difference between it and my own section if I hadn't known Chatham so well.

Still another time, we had parked the car and were crossing the street toward a little Italian grocery store and lunchroom, a place just west of Court Square and near the old Canal. It was a pretty rough and slummy part of town. (Not long afterward F.D.R. had the whole area demolished and put one of his housing projects there.) But the little joint, which was called Baccalupo's Quick Lunch & Grocery, was getting to be well known for its rye and prosciutto and its three-point-two draught beer. We were just stopping for some cold beer. As we headed across the street, I saw Hugh and two other boys running out of the place, with Tony Baccalupo, a swarthy little dwarf of a man, after them. I watched Tony overtake them and snatch some fruit away from them. Then the boys went off laughing together at Tony, who stood shouting something in Italian at the top of his voice. Tony was himself a sort of half-wit, I suppose. He was not the proprietor but the proprietor's younger brother—or older brother. When we got inside, I found the opportunity to ask him about the boys who had gone out just before we came in.

"They jellybeans," he said. "They just-a jellybeans. They think they plenty smart and I see 'em making the fun of me, winking in the mirror over the counter. But they got no money, got no jobs, not even know how to make-a the real trouble. They steal them grapefruit just-a to make-a me hafta run out in the street and get a sweat." He spat in the sawdust on the floor, and began taking our orders.

It got so, instead of watching for Hugh, I tried not to

see him. All summer, he was wandering about town, hitch-hiking from one point to another, never with any real destination, sometimes driving my old Pierce-Arrow, when his mother didn't need it. He didn't really like to take the car, however; it was an old limousine with a glass between the front and back seats, and used too much gas. He and his friends drifted about town, not ever knowing where they were, really, because to them the different parts of the city didn't mean anything. I would be riding in the back seat of a car or walking on the sidewalk, aware only of how all business and progress had bogged down, wondering if and when we could ever get it going again, searching for the first sign of a comeback. Hugh and his gang were searching for something, too, you might say. Searching for mirrors to admire themselves in. Or that's how it seemed. Every time I saw them, I would think of Tony's word: jellybeans.

One night when I got up from the dinner table, Hugh was just coming in from one of his days of wandering about town. We met in the dining room doorway. "I hope you're making the most of your freedom, son," I said.

He looked at me for a moment, almost squinting. Then he opened his eyes wide, and turned his blue gaze on the room in general, blinking his eyelids two or three times as though they were camera shutters, his eyes registering everything, including the black cook; Mary had buzzed for her when she heard Hugh shut the front door, and Lucy May was now holding the swinging door a little way open. Finally he squinted at me again—squinted so that you couldn't have told the color of his eyes. And I repeated, "I hope you're making the most of your freedom."

"I wonder if I *am*," he said, smiling, with a tinge of contempt in his smile and in his voice, I thought.

I looked over my shoulder at his mother, and she shook her head, meaning for me not to say anything more.

It was as though Hugh and I were drifting about through two different cities that were laid out on the very same tract of land. I used to feel we were even occupying two different houses built upon one piece of ground— houses of identical dimensions and filling one and the same area of cubic space. It was just a feeling I had. It first came to me one afternoon when I watched Hugh looking at himself in the mirror. I imagined that the interior that Hugh and I saw there wasn't the same as the one I stood in. That's all there was to it. But probably even to mention that feeling of mine is carrying things too far. I don't want to be misleading about this mirror business. I don't think the mirror-gazing itself was any real fetish with Hugh. In the first place, he didn't *always* make for the mirror as soon as he came in. Sometimes he would slip his books into the hall cupboard and go straight to the telephone; he was a great one for the telephone.

And what a lot of common talk we had to listen to on the telephone:

"Did she say that? . . . I saw her looking at me and I wondered what she thought. . . . What do you mean? I mean what she thought about *me*. . . ."

Always himself. Often as not, one of his girls would call him.

There was a girl named Ida, who nearly drove us all crazy. In the beginning, Hugh was mightily smitten by her. Of that I am quite certain. She was the belle of the class when Hugh entered the tenth grade at the high school, and throughout most of that year it seemed as though he looked for excuses to mention Ida Thomas's name at the dinner table. We didn't get much notion of her except that she was "a gorgeous redhead" and that she had so many admirers that Hugh "couldn't get near her with a ten-foot pole." Nevertheless, he clearly liked for us to tease him about her, though he would always insist that "she didn't know he existed." But at last—and after considerable effort, I gather—he managed to make Ida aware of his existence. From that day the girl gave him no peace.

She would telephone him two or three times in one evening. She was a brash little thing and would engage Hugh's mother in conversation if she answered the telephone, or even me, if I answered it: "How are *you*, Mr. Perkins? . . . How's Mrs. Perkins? . . . And how's that good-looking son of yours—your pride and joy, so they tell me?" Hugh had a time shaking her, I guess. He got so he wouldn't come to the telephone if Mary or I answered and recognized Ida's voice, and he would never answer it himself. She took to writing him letters at home and finally to sending postcards that were obviously intended to embarrass the boy with his family. One card said, "Roses are red, violets are blue. Sugar's sweet and so is Hugh." Another said, "Some day I'll ride in your Pierce-Arrow, Hugh Robert Perkins."

One Sunday, I got Hugh to go for a walk with me while his mother was at church, and I asked him outright why he put up with so much nonsense from the girl. "I feel sorry for her," he said. As though that were any kind of an excuse.

"She's not as popular as she used to be?" I asked.

"Certainly she is!" he said.

"Oh," I said. "Then you feel sorry for her because she has all the other fellows but *not* you?"

He laughed aloud. "I never thought of it that way, Mr. Perkins," he said, as if he thought I was only joking.

So I laughed, too, and took the opportunity to ask another question. "Tell me, son," I said, "what turned you against her? Was it the telephone calls?"

"No. Not exactly. You see, it wasn't even *me* she was interested in. She was impressed by your old Pierce-Arrow. And still more by our living in West Vesey Place."

"But you didn't exactly like those telephone calls. And what about those postcards, Hugh?"

"Why, she didn't know any better, Dad!" For a minute he stopped there on the street on Sunday morning and looked at me as though it was I who didn't have good sense about such things. "That's why I had to put up with it. That's why I felt sorry for her."

He was very cagey, and I didn't bother him any further about Ida, since it was all over with by then anyway. But judging from the gloom he dwelt in for several months, he must have considered Ida one of his worst mistakes.

Hugh wouldn't study, and he wasn't really too hot an athlete, although certainly for a while he thought he was going to be. He made several of his "mistakes" in the athletic line, and would, of course, fall into a black mood each time he was dropped from a team or was even kept on the sidelines. His mother said he couldn't excel in athletics because he had to compete with the big, tough fellows who went out for sports at Chatham West High. And she said that the schoolwork at the public school was too easy and didn't occupy him. Maybe she was right. I know that when his two brothers had finished at Chatham Academy they had had trigonometry and Latin and even some Greek. Both of them passed the College Board examinations with flying colors and had a summer in Europe before starting college. Hugh wouldn't even *talk* about going to college—not to any local college that I could afford to send him to. Since the war, of course, he has gotten himself some kind of degree at Columbia University on the G.I. Bill. But during high school, when we mentioned college to him, he only laughed at the idea. One Sunday in his senior year, when the other children were at the house and the subject came up, he said, "Why, I've already been to the best college in our part of the country, the College of William and Mary"—meaning his mother and me, of course. "I've been studying diplomacy, and next June I'll be ready for the foreign service."

The others took this as a joke, but it made me realize how soon he might be gone from us to wherever he had in mind going. I was only half through my meal, but involuntarily I began searching my pockets for my pipe and a match. It's hard having your youngest be the one who disappoints you. I sat there searching for my pipe, thinking that I could just imagine how the letter he would leave would look on the library table, or how he would come down to breakfast one morning and say he had written off and gotten himself a job somewhere away from us—away from Chatham! I suppose it was rather simple-minded and old-fashioned of me to think about it the way I did.

In his senior year, Hugh actually began to show an interest in his schoolwork—in a certain part of it, in a part I wouldn't have called work. You would just hardly believe the things they offered in the curriculum of that school. But anyway, the first indication I had of what was stirring was Hugh's coming to me one morning with a very odd sort of request. From some neat, dark, and no doubt carefully protected corner of the house, known only to himself, he had pulled out an old dictation machine—a Dictaphone—which I had given him as a little fellow. It was an old model that I had brought home from the office and let him use as a plaything. I had forgotten about it. It had been seven or eight years since he had asked me to take the wax cylinders downtown and have them scraped so he could use them again. But he came to me after breakfast one morning, when he was all ready to leave for school, carrying the case of cylinders that came with the Dictaphone. He looked a little shamefaced, I must say, like any big boy caught playing with one of his old toys. I was touched to see that he had hung on to something I had given him so long ago. He handed the case to me and as I examined it I remarked silently that it seemed to be in as good condition as on the day I gave it to him. "Where did you resurrect this from Hugh?" I asked.

"I've had it put by against a rainy day," he said.

"Do you still have the machine itself?" I asked.

"Oh, yes, of course," he said.

I held the case of cylinders and then I said, "You intend to sell it, I suppose—the whole outfit?"

"Why, no, Mr. Perkins. I want you to have these cylinders scraped for me."

"You know it costs something to have it done?" It occurred to me that as a child he mightn't have realized that.

"Oh, certainly. I'll pay for it. I have some *money* put by, too," he said, giving me one of his quick winks, "against the same rainy day." He was no spendthrift, to be sure. I doubt that there was ever a week when he spent the whole of the small allowance his mother gave him.

I set the case of cylinders on the floor beside me and picked up the paper I had been reading when he came in. "What are you going to use them for?" I said from behind the paper.

"In connection with one of my classes," he said. "A readings course."

I looked at him over my paper. He was still standing before me and was clearly willing for me to pursue the subject. "A reading course?"

"Oral readings," he explained. "A class in oral readings, for additional speech credit." He was in dead earnest. He said they were graded according to some kind of point system and that it had been wonderful help for him to be able to hear himself on the Dictaphone, that he had already made terrific progress.

"You've already been using the Dictaphone, then?" I inquired. "The cylinders were clean when you got them out?"

"Yes," he said. "Don't you remember, I got you to have them scraped before I ever put them away?"

"No, I didn't remember," I said. "It's been a pretty long time, Hugh."

Now I found myself wondering how many nights had he already been up there in his room listening to his own voice on the Dictaphone. I went back to my paper again, because I knew I didn't want to hear any more about this business. Sooner or later, I thought, he will see it as just as another of his mistakes.

But for some months to come, Hugh's concern with his voice was all we did hear about. My theory was that the boy had been trying a long while to decide what it was about himself that charmed him most. And at last he thought he knew. All that winter he was as busy as a beaver with his "speech lessons" and "exercises." I would bring home the set of cylinders freshly scraped, and they wouldn't last him much more than a week. Finally, I guess he wore them out, because well before spring he quit asking me to take them. But his interest didn't stop there. He continued to engage me now and then in discussions of his current "problems" in speech, as openly and seriously as though he were talking about math or history. And first thing his mother and I knew, he was on the debating team, was trying out for a part in the class play, was even getting special instructions from the teacher in "newscasting."

It occurred to me once during this time that maybe Hugh had fallen in love with his speech teacher, Miss Arrowood. In recent months his mother had complained of a tendency in him to resent any questions about the girls he was having dates with on the weekends. If, under pressure, he mentioned the name of a particular girl, it wasn't a name that his mother knew. I couldn't explain such a business to Mary—there was no use in it—but I think I understood pretty well what Hugh was going through in that respect. And I could remember that a boy, hating himself for his own fallen and degraded state, is apt at such times to begin idealizing some attractive, sympathetic woman who is enough older than himself to seem quite beyond his aspiration—particularly if she is even vaguely the intellectual type. I didn't ask Hugh how old Miss Arrowood was or what she looked like. I just dropped by the school one afternoon in March when I knew there was to be a rehearsal of the class play.

It wasn't even necessary for me to go inside the auditorium to see what I had come to see. Through a glass panel in one of the rear doors I could see the whole stage. The play they were practicing for was one of those moronic things that they give big grown-up boys and girls to act in. (They did it even in the private schools when my older children were coming along.) This one was called "Mr. Hairbrain's Confession: A Comedy." I read the title in a notice on the bulletin board beside the auditorium door.

After two seconds I spotted Miss Arrowood, who was giving directions from a position at the side of the stage, and I knew that my conjecture had been a false one. I say "after two seconds" because for about two seconds I mistook that lady to be one of the cast and already in costume and make-up. Her bosom was of a size and shape that one of the youngsters might have effected with a bed pillow. Her orange-colored hair may really have been a wig. On the far end of her unbelievable nose rode the inevitable pince-nez. The woman's every gesture had just the exaggeration that you could expect from any member of the cast on the night of the performance.

I realized who she was when she started giving some directions to Hugh, who was now posturing in the center of the stage. No, she wasn't directing him, after all; she was applauding something he had already done or said. Hugh, like his fellow-actors, was reading his lines from the book. Every time he opened his mouth or so much as turned his dark head or struck a new position, she either nodded approval or shook with laughter. She hardly took her eyes off him. Hugh no doubt had a comic role, but I knew that nothing in that play was so funny or so interesting as Miss Arrowood's conduct would have led me to believe. I can't say exactly how long I stood watching, lost in my own damned thoughts. When finally I did leave it was because someone in the cast—not Hugh—saw me and called Miss Arrowood's attention to my presence. At once she began motioning to me to go away, waving her book in the air and shooing me with her other hand. She didn't know who I was and didn't care. Miss Arrowood knew only that she wasn't going to have any interruption of the pleasure she took from watching Hugh.

There was no more to it than that. Miss Arrowood was just another old maid schoolteacher with a crush on one of her pupils. I doubt very much that Hugh's experience with her had any influence on his finally going into the theatre the way he has. Quite naturally she must nowadays imagine herself to have been his first great influence and inspiration, but if Miss Arrowood has ever gotten to New York and found her way over to the East Side, to that little cubbyhole of a theatre where my son Hugh Robert directs plays, I'll bet she doesn't understand the kind of plays he puts on any better than I do. At any rate, she didn't succeed in turning him into any radio announcer or even into an actor, thank God. I doubt that she hoped to, even; for in my opinion Hugh Robert didn't have any better voice than any of the rest of the family. Physically he is very much like the rest of us. But it is my opinion also that the lady tried to play upon Hugh's vanity that year, for the sake of keeping him near her. And it must cer-

tainly have been she who arranged for a certain phonograph record, which he made on a machine at the school,
to be put on the local radio. This happened one miserable
Sunday afternoon in May. It capped everything else that
had happened.

Hugh rose early that Sunday morning in order to plug
in the charger to the batteries of the radio. Our set was an
old battery-type table model, one that I had paid a lot of
money for when it was new. Hugh was fond of giving it a
big thump and saying in his best smart-aleck voice, "They
don't make 'em like that any more." But he would have
been the first to admit—especially on the Sunday I'm
speaking of—that there are times when the electricity
goes off just as you want to hear some program. I hung on
to my battery set all through the depression, just the way
I did my Pierce-Arrow. And it is true, of course, that we
did sometimes find, when a favorite program was due to
come on, that we had forgotten to charge the batteries.

But the batteries didn't need charging at all that Sunday in May, and Hugh knew they didn't. He simply
wasn't taking any chances. When I came down to breakfast, I saw the ugly little violet light burning in the
charger at the end of the living room. I observed Hugh
coming in there to check on them off and on all morning.
Apparently when the idea of charging the batteries first
struck him, he had jumped out of bed and thrown on some
clothes without bothering to comb his hair or put on his
shoes. He came down wearing his old run-over bedroom
slippers, his everyday corduroy pants, and a wrinkled shirt
that he must have pulled out of the clothes hamper. He
wandered around the house like that all morning. When

his mother was leaving for church at ten-thirty, I asked
her if she didn't think she ought to remind him to get
properly dressed before the other children came for dinner. But either she forgot to, or she decided against it, or
she just "hated to" and didn't.

During the two hours his mother was gone, I could hear
Hugh moving about all over the house. First he would be
in the basement, then at the closet in the back hall, then
upstairs somewhere, even on the third floor. Every so often
he would come back to the living room to have a look at
the batteries. He would sit down and try to get interested
in some section of the Sunday paper. But he couldn't stay
still except for short intervals. Every time he got up, the
first thing he did was to go and look out one of the living-
room windows. I suspect that during his wandering
through the house he must now and then have stopped
and looked out windows in most of the other rooms, too.
To him, that day, the weather outside was the most important matter in the world.

And in spite of its being May, the weather outside was
quite wintry and nasty. Rain fell during most of the morning, and there was occasional thunder, with streaks of
lightning away off across town. We had been having a
series of electrical storms, which generally come to us a
month earlier than they did that year. This bad weather
was what Hugh had pinned his hopes on. The understanding was that if the ball game—the third of the season
—was called that Sunday, then Station WCM was going to
fill in the first ten minutes or so of the time with a re-
corded reading Hugh had made of "A Message to Garcia."
Though I had been unaware of it before, it seems that the ··

station made a practice of devoting such free periods to activities of the public schools. Hugh managed that Sunday to make us all keenly aware of the fact.

I seldom missed listening to the Chatham Barons' home games. When it was a good season, I even used to go out to Runnymede Park and watch the games. The Barons, however, hadn't had such a season in almost a decade. The last time they had won their league's pennant was in 1925. But, even so, I have never been one to go running off to Cincinnati or St. Louis to see big-league games when we have a team right in Chatham to support and root for. It happened that this year the Barons had won their first two games, and I was hopeful. In particular, I hoped to be listening to the broadcast of a third game in what might turn into a winning streak. I knew why Hugh kept looking out the windows, and soon I was looking out windows, too. The rain came down pretty steady all morning and only began to let up about noon. I found I was pitting my hopes against his. I was, at least, until I saw how awfully worked up the boy was. Then I tried my best to hope with him. But I don't think I ever before had such mixed feelings about so small a thing as whether or not a ball game would be rained out.

Hugh's mother returned from church at twelve-thirty. The other children came for dinner just before one. Hugh was off upstairs somewhere when the others arrived, and had to be called to come to the table. I supposed that he had finally gone up to get himself dressed, but he came down in the same state of undress, with his hair still uncombed, and I saw at once that it offended his brothers and his sister. I saw Sister trying to signal her mother, indicating that Hugh ought at least to go and comb his hair. But her mother's eye was not to be caught that day.

Hugh was unusually silent during the meal, and his silence was contagious. From time to time I saw every member of the family taking a glance out the window to see how the weather was. After raining all morning, the skies seemed to be clearing. It was mostly bright while we sat there, with only an occasional dark interval. During those dark intervals, Hugh ate feverishly; otherwise he only picked at his food. I'm afraid that with the rest of us the reverse was true.

Once, while Lucy May was passing round a dish, I even saw her turn her black face toward a sunlit window at Hugh's back. Just as she did so, there came from outside the clear chirping of a redbird, which brought a beautiful smile to her face. The others were making a show of keeping up the conversation while a servant was in the room, and so when she offered Hugh the dish she was able to mumble to him without their taking notice, "You hear that redbird, don't you, Hugh! He say, 'To wet! To wet!' That's a promise of rain, honey!" Hugh may or may not have heard the redbird. But he paid no more attention to Lucy May's encouraging words than he had to the encouragement and applause of Miss Arrowood.

The very instant we rose from the table, there was a flash of lightning so close to us that it brightened the windows. And there followed a deafening crack of thunder. Hugh galloped across the hall into the living room and commenced disconnecting the batteries from the charger and hooking them up to the radio. The rest of us followed, just as if there were no other room in the house we could have gone to. By the time I got in there, Hugh was tuning in on WCM. There was a roar of static, and then, as the static receded, the announcer's voice came through, saying, "The next voice you hear will be that of Hugh Robert Perkins," and went on to tell who Hugh's parents were, to give his street address, and to say that he was a senior at West High and a member of Miss Arrowood's class in oral readings. Outside, a sheet of rain was falling, and there was more thunder and lightning than there had been all morning.

Through the loudspeaker the voice of Hugh Robert Perkins began with some introductory remarks, telling us how, why, when, and by whom "A Message to Garcia" had been written. It didn't sound especially like Hugh's voice, but even at the outset the static was so bad that I missed about every third word. After the first half minute of the "Message" itself, it seemed hopeless to try to listen. Yet we had to sit there, all of us—and without any assistance from Miss Arrowood or Lucy May—and suffer through the awful business with Hugh. At least, it seemed to us we had to; and we *thought* that's what we were doing.

Hugh never once looked around from the radio. His eyes were glued to the loudspeaker, which was placed on top of the set. He had pulled up a straight chair, and he sat with his legs crossed and his hands clasped over one knee. He held his neck as straight and stiff as a board and didn't move his head to left or right during the entire ten minutes. The storm and the static got worse every second, and he didn't even try to improve the reception. He didn't touch the dials. Toward the very end, I saw his mother raise her eyebrows and tighten her mouth the way she does when she's about to cry, and I shook my head vigorously at her, forbidding it. I knew what she was feeling well enough; we all were feeling it: Poor boy had endured his uncertainty, had for days been pinning his hopes on the chance of rain, and now had to hear himself drowned out by the static on our old radio. I thought it might be more than flesh and blood could bear. I thought that at any moment he might spring up and begin kicking that radio set to bits. But I knew, too, that his mother's tears wouldn't help matters.

What a fortunate thing for us all that I stopped her. Because not ten seconds after I did, the reading was finished and Hugh was on his feet and facing us with a broad grin of satisfaction. I saw at once that for him there had been no static. Or, rather, that he had heard the clear, sweet, reassuring tones of his own voice calling to him through and above the static, and that his last doubts about the kind of glory he yearned for had been swept away. He ran his hand through his tangled hair self-consciously. His blue eyes shone. "There!" he said. And after a moment he said it again: "There!" And I felt as strongly then as I feel it now that that was the real moment of Hugh's departure from our midst. He tried to fix his gaze on me for a second, but it was quite beyond his powers to concentrate on any one of us present. "It's a shame. . . ." he began rather vaguely, "it's a shame you had to listen to my sorry voice instead of hearing the game. But maybe the game will come on later. . . . Did you hear the place where my voice cracked? That was the worst part of all, wasn't it? I'm glad it's over with." He gave a deep sigh, and then he said, in a voice full of wonder and excitement and confidence, "Gosh!"

At once, he went upstairs and dressed himself in his

Sunday clothes and left the house, saying that he had a date, or maybe it was that he was going to meet some of his cronies somewhere. I didn't bother to listen. I knew that he would be back for supper that night and that he wasn't really going to leave us for some time yet. And I knew it wouldn't be a matter of a letter on the breakfast table when he did go, because it couldn't any longer be a matter of a boy running away from home. While the other children were laughing over what had happened and were talking about what a child Hugh still was, I was thinking to myself that Hugh Robert Perkins hadn't many more of his "mistakes" ahead of him. I felt certain that this afternoon he had seen his way ahead clear, and I imagined that I could see it with him.

The other children left the house soon after lunch that Sunday. Mary went upstairs to take a nap, as she often did when we had been through something that there was no use talking about. I wandered through the downstairs rooms, feeling not myself at all. Once, I looked out a window in the library and saw that the weather had cleared, but I didn't go and turn on the radio. And I had a strange experience that afternoon. I was fifty, but suddenly I felt very young again. As I wandered through the house I kept thinking of how everything must look to Hugh, of what his life was going to be like, and of just what he would be like when he got to be my age. It all seemed very clear to me, and I understood how right it was for him. And because it seemed so clear I realized that the time had come when I could forgive my son the difference there had always been between our two natures. I was fifty, but I had just discovered what it means to see the world through another man's eyes. It is a discovery you are lucky to make at any age, and one that is no less marvelous whether you make it at fifty or fifteen. Because it is only then that the world, as you have seen it through your own eyes, will begin to tell you things about yourself.

Venus, Cupid, Folly and Time

———•———

Their house alone would not have made you think there
was anything so awfully wrong with Mr. Dorset or his old
maid sister. But certain things about the way both of them
dressed had, for a long time, annoyed and disturbed everyone. We used to see them together at the grocery store,
for instance, or even in one of the big department stores
downtown, wearing their bedroom slippers. Looking more
closely we would sometimes see the cuff of a pajama top or
the hem of a hitched up nightgown showing from underneath their ordinary daytime clothes. Such slovenliness in
one's neighbors is so unpleasant that even husbands and
wives in West Vesey Place, which was the street where the
Dorsets lived, had got so they didn't like to joke about it
with each other. Were the Dorsets, poor old things, losing

their minds? If so, what was to be done about it? Some
neighbors got so they would not even admit to themselves
what they saw. And a child coming home with an ugly report on the Dorsets was apt to be told that it was time he
learned to curb his imagination.

Mr. Dorset wore tweed caps and sleeveless sweaters.
Usually he had his sweater stuffed down inside his trousers with his shirt tails. To the women and young girls in
West Vesey Place this was extremely distasteful. It made
them feel as though Mr. Dorset had just come from the
bathroom and had got his sweater inside his trousers by
mistake. There was, in fact, nothing about Mr. Dorset
that was not offensive to the women. Even the old touring
car he drove was regarded by most of them as a disgrace
to the neighborhood. Parked out in front of his house, as
it usually was, it seemed a worse violation of West Vesey's
zoning than the house itself. And worst of all was seeing
Mr. Dorset wash the car.

Mr. Dorset washed his own car! He washed it not back
in the alley or in his driveway but out there in the street
of West Vesey Place. This would usually be on the day
of one of the parties which he and his sister liked to give
for young people or on a day when they were going to
make deliveries of the paper flowers or the home-grown
figs which they sold to their friends. Mr. Dorset would appear in the street carrying two buckets of warm water and
wearing a pair of skin-tight coveralls. The skin-tight coveralls, of khaki material but faded almost to flesh color,
were still more offensive to the women and young girls
than his way of wearing his sweaters. With sponges and
chamois cloths and a large scrub brush (for use on the canvas top) the old fellow would fall to and scrub away, gen-

tly at first on the canvas top and more vigorously as he progressed to the hood and body, just as though the car were something alive. Neighbor children felt that he went after the headlights exactly as if he were scrubbing the poor car's ears. There was an element of brutality in the way he did it and yet an element of tenderness too. An old lady visiting in the neighborhood once said that it was like the cleansing of a sacrificial animal. I suppose it was some such feeling as this that made all women want to turn away their eyes whenever the spectacle of Mr. Dorset washing his car presented itself.

As for Mr. Dorset's sister, her behavior was in its way just as offensive as his. To the men and boys in the neighborhood it was she who seemed quite beyond the pale. She would come out on her front terrace at mid-day clad in a faded flannel bathrobe and with her dyed black hair all undone and hanging down her back like the hair of an Indian squaw. To us whose wives and mothers did not even come downstairs in their negligees, this was very unsettling. It was hard to excuse it even on the grounds that the Dorsets were too old and lonely and hard-pressed to care about appearances any more.

Moreover, there was a boy who had gone to Miss Dorset's house one morning in the early fall to collect for his paper route and saw this very Miss Louisa Dorset pushing a carpet sweeper about one of the downstairs rooms without a stitch of clothes on. He saw her through one of the little lancet windows that opened on the front loggia of the house, and he watched her for quite a long while. She was cleaning the house in preparation for a party they were giving for young people that night, and the boy said that when she finally got hot and tired she dropped down in an easy chair and crossed her spindly, blue veined, old legs and sat there completely naked, with her legs crossed and shaking one scrawny little foot, just as unconcerned as if she didn't care that somebody was likely to walk in on her at any moment. After a little bit the boy saw her get up again and go and lean across a table to arrange some paper flowers in a vase. Fortunately he was a nice boy, though he lived only on the edge of the West Vesey Place neighborhood, and he went away without ringing the doorbell or collecting for his paper that week. But he could not resist telling his friends about what he had seen. He said it was a sight he would never forget! And she an old lady more than sixty years old who, had she not been so foolish and self-willed, might have had a house full of servants to push that carpet sweeper for her!

This foolish pair of old people had given up almost everything in life for each other's sake. And it was not at all necessary. When they were young they could have come into a decent inheritance, or now that they were old they might have been provided for by a host of rich relatives. It was only a matter of their being a little tolerant —or even civil—toward their kinspeople. But this was something that old Mr. Dorset and his sister could never consent to do. Almost all their lives they had spoken of their father's kin as "Mama's in-laws" and of their mother's kin as "Papa's in-laws." Their family name was Dorset, not on one side but on both sides. Their parents had been distant cousins. As a matter of fact, the Dorset family in the city of Chatham had once been so large and was so long established there that it would have been hard to estimate how distant the kinship might be. But still it was something that the old couple never liked to have mentioned. Most of their mother's close kin had, by the time I am speaking of, moved off to California, and most of their father's people lived somewhere up east. But Miss Dorset and her old bachelor brother found any contact, correspondence, even an exchange of Christmas cards with these in-laws intolerable. It was a case, so they said, of the in-laws respecting the value of the dollar above all else, whereas they, Miss Louisa and Mr. Alfred Dorset, placed importance on other things. — ? youth, family history

They lived in a dilapidated and curiously mutilated house on a street which, except for their own house, was the most splendid street in the entire city. Their house was one that you or I would have been ashamed to live in —even in the lean years of the early thirties. In order to reduce taxes the Dorsets had had the third story of the house torn away, leaving an ugly, flat-topped effect without any trim or ornamentation. Also they had had the south wing pulled down and had sealed the scars not with matching brick but with a speckled stucco that looked raw and naked. All this the old couple did in violation of the strict zoning laws of West Vesey Place, and for doing so they would most certainly have been prosecuted except that they were the Dorsets and except that this was during the depression when zoning laws weren't easy to enforce in a city like Chatham.

To the young people whom she and her brother entertained at their house once each year Miss Louisa Dorset liked to say: "We have given up everything for each other. Our only income is from our paper flowers and our figs." The old lady, though without showing any great skill or talent for it, made paper flowers. During the winter months her brother took her in that fifteen-year-old tour-

ing car of theirs, with its steering wheel on the wrong side
and with isinglass side-curtains that were never taken
down, to deliver these flowers to her customers. The flowers looked more like sprays of tinted potato chips than like
any real flowers. Nobody could possibly have wanted to
buy them except that she charged next to nothing for
them and except that to people with children it seemed
important to be on the Dorsets' list of worthwhile people.
Nobody could really have wanted Mr. Dorset's figs either.
He cultivated a dozen little bushes along the back wall of
their house, covering them in the wintertime with some
odd looking boxes which he had had constructed for the
purpose. The bushes were very productive, but the figs
they produced were dried up little things without much
taste. During the summer months he and his sister went
about in their car, with the side-curtains still up, delivering the figs to the same customers who bought the paper
flowers. The money they made could hardly have paid for
the gas it took to run the car. It was a great waste and it
was very foolish of them.

And yet, despite everything, this foolish pair of old people, this same Miss Louisa and Mr. Alfred Dorset, had become social arbiters of a kind in our city. They had at-
tained this position entirely through their fondness for
giving an annual dancing party for young people. To
young people—to *very* young people—the Dorsets' hearts
went out. I don't mean to suggest that their hearts went
out to orphans or to the children of the poor, for they
were not foolish in that way. The guests at their little
dancing parties were the thirteen and fourteen year-olds
from families like the one they had long ago set them-

selves against, young people from the very houses to which, in season, they delivered their figs and their paper flowers. And when the night of one of their parties came round, it was in fact the custom for Mr. Alfred to go in the same old car and fetch all the invited guests to his house. His sister might explain to reluctant parents that this saved the children the embarrassment of being taken to their first dance by mommy or daddy. But the parents knew well enough that for twenty years the Dorsets had permitted no adult person, besides themselves, to put foot inside their house.

At those little dancing parties which the Dorsets gave, peculiar things went on—unsettling things to the boys and girls who had been fetched round in the old car. Sensible parents wished to keep their children away. Yet what could they do? For a Chatham girl to have to explain, a few years later, why she never went to a party at the Dorsets' was like having to explain why she had never been a debutante. For a boy it was like having to explain why he had not gone up east to school or even why his father hadn't belonged to the Chatham Racquet Club. If when you were thirteen or fourteen you got invited to the Dorsets' house, you went; it was the way of letting people know from the outset who you were. In a busy, modern city like Chatham you cannot afford to let people forget who you are—not for a moment, not at any age. Even the Dorsets knew that.

Many a little girl, after one of those evenings at the Dorsets', was heard to cry out in her sleep. When waked, or half waked, her only explanation might be: "It was just the fragrance from the paper flowers." Or: "I dreamed I could really smell the paper flowers." Many a boy was ob-

served by his parents to seem "different" afterward. He
became "secretive." The parents of the generation that
had to attend those parties never pretended to understand
what went on at the Dorsets' house. And even to those of
us who were in that unlucky generation it seemed we
were half a lifetime learning what really took place during
our one evening under the Dorsets' roof. Before our turn
to go ever came round we had for years been hearing
about what it was like from older boys and girls. Afterward, we continued to hear about it from those who followed us. And, looking back on it, nothing about the one
evening when you were actually there ever seemed quite —
so real as the glimpses and snatches which you got from
those people before and after you—the second-hand impressions of the Dorsets' behavior, of things they said, of
looks that passed between them.

Since Miss Dorset kept no servants she always opened
her own door. I suspect that for the guests at her parties
the sight of her opening her door, in her astonishing attire, came as the most violent shock of the whole evening.
On these occasions she and her brother got themselves
up as we had never seen them before and never would
again. The old lady invariably wore a modish white evening gown, a garment perfectly fitted to her spare and
scrawny figure and cut in such high fashion that it must
necessarily have been new that year. And never to be worn
but that one night! Her hair, long and thick and newly
dyed for the occasion, would be swept upward and forward in a billowy mass which was topped by a corsage of
yellow and coral paper flowers. Her cheeks and lips would
be darkly rouged. On her long bony arms and her bare
shoulders she would have applied some kind of suntan

powder. Whatever else you had been led to expect of the evening, no one had ever warned you sufficiently about the radical change to be noted in her appearance—or in that of her brother, either. By the end of the party Miss Louisa might look as dowdy as ever, and Mr. Alfred a little worse than usual. But at the outset, when the party was assembling in their drawing room, even Mr. Alfred appeared resplendent in a nattily tailored tuxedo, with exactly the shirt, the collar, and the tie which fashion prescribed that year. His gray hair was nicely trimmed, his puffy old face freshly shaven. He was powdered with the same dark powder that his sister used. One felt even that his cheeks had been lightly touched with rouge.

A strange perfume pervaded the atmosphere of the house. The moment you set foot inside, this awful fragrance engulfed you. It was like a mixture of spicy incense and sweet attar of roses. And always, too, there was the profusion of paper flowers. The flowers were everywhere —on every cabinet and console, every inlaid table and carved chest, on every high, marble mantel piece, on the book shelves. In the entrance hall special tiers must have been set up to hold the flowers, because they were there in overpowering masses. They were in such abundance that it seemed hardly possible that Miss Dorset could have made them all. She must have spent weeks and weeks preparing them, even months, perhaps even the whole year between parties. When she went about delivering them to her customers, in the months following, they were apt to be somewhat faded and dusty; but on the night of the party the colors of the flowers seemed even more impressive and more unlikely than their number. They were fuchsia, they were chartreuse, they were coral, aquamarine, brown, they were even black.

Everywhere in the Dorsets' house too were certain curious illuminations and lighting effects. The source of the light was usually hidden and its purpose was never obvious at once. The lighting was a subtler element than either the perfume or the paper flowers, and ultimately it was more disconcerting. A shaft of lavender light would catch a young visitor's eye and lead it, seemingly without purpose, in among the flowers. Then just beyond the point where the strength of the light would begin to diminish, the eye would discover something. In a small aperture in the mass of flowers, or sometimes in a larger grotto-like opening, there would be a piece of sculpture—in the hall a plaster replica of Rodin's *The Kiss,* in the library an antique plaque of Leda and the Swan. Or just above the flowers would be hung a picture, usually a black and white print but sometimes a reproduction in color. On the landing of the stairway leading down to the basement ballroom was the only picture that one was likely to learn the title of at the time. It was a tiny color print of Bronzino's *Venus, Cupid, Folly and Time.* This picture was not even framed. It was simply tacked on the wall, and it had obviously been torn—rather carelessly, perhaps hurriedly —from a book or magazine. The title and the name of the painter were printed in the white margin underneath.

About these works of art most of us had been warned by older boys and girls; and we stood in painful dread of that moment when Miss Dorset or her brother might catch us staring at any one of their pictures or sculptures. We had been warned, time and again, that during the course of the evening moments would come when she or he would reach out and touch the other's elbow and indicate, with a nod or just the trace of a smile, some guest whose glance had strayed among the flowers.

To some extent the dread which all of us felt that evening at the Dorsets' cast a shadow over the whole of our childhood. Yet for nearly twenty years the Dorsets continued to give their annual party. And even the most sensible of parents were not willing to keep their children away.

But a thing happened finally which could almost have been predicted. Young people, even in West Vesey Place, will not submit forever to the prudent counsel of their parents. Or some of them won't. There was a boy named Ned Meriwether and his sister Emily Meriwether, who lived with their parents in West Vesey Place just one block away from the Dorsets' house. In November Ned and Emily were invited to the Dorsets' party, and because they dreaded it they decided to play a trick on everyone concerned—even on themselves, as it turned out. . . . They got up a plan for smuggling an uninvited guest into the Dorsets' party.

The parents of this Emily and Ned sensed that their children were concealing something from them and suspected that the two were up to mischief of some kind. But they managed to deceive themselves with the thought that it was only natural for young people—"mere children"—to be nervous about going to the Dorsets' house. And so instead of questioning them during the last hour before they left for the party, these sensible parents tried to do everything in their power to calm their two children. The boy and the girl, seeing that this was the case, took advantage of it.

"You must not go down to the front door with us when we leave," the daughter insisted to her mother. And she persuaded both Mr. and Mrs. Meriwether that after she and her brother were dressed for the party they should all wait together in the upstairs sitting room until Mr. Dorset came to fetch the two young people in his car.

When, at eight o'clock, the lights of the automobile appeared in the street below, the brother and sister were still upstairs—watching from the bay window of the family sitting room. They kissed Mother and Daddy goodbye and then they flew down the stairs and across the wide, carpeted entrance hall to a certain dark recess where a boy named Tom Bascomb was hidden. This boy was the uninvited guest whom Ned and Emily were going to smuggle into the party. They had left the front door unlatched for Tom, and from the upstairs window just a few minutes ago they had watched him come across their front lawn. Now in the little recess of the hall there was a quick exchange of overcoats and hats between Ned Meriwether and Tom Bascomb; for it was a feature of the plan that Tom should attend the party as Ned and that Ned should go as the uninvited guest.

In the darkness of the recess Ned fidgeted and dropped Tom Bascomb's coat on the floor. But the boy, Tom Bascomb, did not fidget. He stepped out into the light of the hall and began methodically getting into the overcoat which he would wear tonight. He was not a boy who lived in the West Vesey Place neighborhood (he was in fact the very boy who had once watched Miss Dorset cleaning house without any clothes on), and he did not share

Emily's and Ned's nervous excitement about the evening. The sound of Mr. Dorset's footsteps outside did not disturb him. When both Ned and Emily stood frozen by that sound, he continued buttoning the unfamiliar coat and even amused himself by stretching forth one arm to observe how high the sleeve came on his wrist.

The doorbell rang, and from his dark corner Ned Meriwether whispered to his sister and to Tom: "Don't worry. I'll be at the Dorsets' in plenty of time."

Tom Bascomb only shrugged his shoulders at this reassurance. Presently when he looked at Emily's flushed face and saw her batting her eyes like a nervous monkey, a crooked smile played upon his lips. Then, at a sign from Emily, Tom followed her to the entrance door and permitted her to introduce him to old Mr. Dorset as her brother.

From the window of the upstairs sitting room the Meriwether parents watched Mr. Dorset and this boy and this girl walking across the lawn toward Mr. Dorset's peculiar-looking car. A light shone bravely and protectively from above the entrance of the house, and in its rays the parents were able to detect the strange angle at which Brother was carrying his head tonight and how his new fedora already seemed too small for him. They even noticed that he seemed a bit taller tonight.

"I hope it's all right," said the mother.

"What do you mean 'all right'?" the father asked petulantly.

"I mean—," the mother began, and then she hesitated. She did not want to mention that the boy out there did not look like their own Ned. It would have seemed to give away her feelings too much. "I mean that I wonder if I should have put Sister in that long dress at this age and let her wear my cape. I'm afraid the cape is really inappropriate. She's still young for that sort of thing."

"Oh," said the father, "I thought you meant something else."

"Whatever else did you think I meant, Edwin?" the mother said, suddenly breathless.

"I thought you meant the business we've discussed before," he said although this was of course not what he had thought she meant. He had thought she meant that the boy out there did not look like their Ned. To him it had seemed even that the boy's step was different from Ned's. "The Dorsets' parties," he said, "are not very nice affairs to be sending your children to, Muriel. That's all I thought you meant."

"But we *can't* keep them away," the mother said defensively.

"Oh, it's just that they are growing up faster than we realize," said the father, glancing at his wife out of the corner of his eye.

By this time Mr. Dorset's car had pulled out of sight, and from downstairs Muriel Meriwether thought she heard another door closing. "What was that?" she said, putting one hand on her husband's.

"Don't be so jumpy," her husband said irritably, snatching away his hand. "It's the servants closing up in the kitchen."

Both of them knew that the servants had closed up in the kitchen long before this. Both of them had heard quite distinctly the sound of the side door closing as Ned went out. But they went on talking and deceiving themselves in this fashion during most of the evening.

Even before she opened the door to Mr. Dorset, little Emily Meriwether had known that there would be no difficulty about passing Tom Bascomb off as her brother. In the first place, she knew that without his spectacles Mr. Dorset could hardly see his hand before his face and knew that due to some silly pride he had he never put on his spectacles except when he was behind the wheel of his automobile. This much was common knowledge. In the second place, Emily knew from experience that neither he nor his sister ever made any real pretense of knowing one child in their general acquaintance from another. And so, standing in the doorway and speaking almost in a whisper, Emily had merely to introduce first herself and then her pretended brother to Mr. Dorset. After that the three of them walked in silence from her father's house to the waiting car.

Emily was wearing her mother's second best evening wrap, a white lapin cape which, on Emily, swept the ground. As she walked between the boy and the man, the touch of the cape's soft silk lining on her bare arms and on her shoulders spoke to her silently of a strange girl she had seen in her looking-glass upstairs tonight. And with her every step toward the car the skirt of her long taffeta gown whispered her own name to her: *Emily . . . Emily*. She heard it distinctly, and yet the name sounded unfamiliar. Once during this unreal walk from house to car she glanced at the mysterious boy, Tom Bascomb, longing to ask him—if only with her eyes—for some reassurance that she was really she. But Tom Bascomb was absorbed in his own irrelevant observations. With his head tilted back he was gazing upward at the nondescript winter sky where, among drifting clouds, a few pale stars were shedding their dull light alike on West Vesey Place and on the rest of the world. Emily drew her wrap tightly about her, and when presently Mr. Dorset held open the door to the back seat of his car she shut her eyes and plunged into the pitch-blackness of the car's interior.

Tom Bascomb was a year older than Ned Meriwether and he was nearly two years older than Emily. He had been Ned's friend first. He and Ned had played baseball together on Saturdays before Emily ever set eyes on him. Yet according to Tom Bascomb himself, with whom several of us older boys talked just a few weeks after the night he went to the Dorsets', Emily always insisted that it was she who had known him first. On what she based this false claim Tom could not say. And on the two or three other occasions when we got Tom to talk about that night, he kept saying that he didn't understand what it was that had made Emily and Ned quarrel over which of them knew him first and knew him better.

We could have told him what it was, I think. But we didn't. It would have been too hard to say to him that at one time or another all of us in West Vesey had had our Tom Bascombs. Tom lived with his parents in an apartment house on a wide thoroughfare known as Division Boulevard, and his only real connection with West Vesey Place was that that street was included in his paper route. During the early morning hours he rode his bicycle along West Vesey and along other quiet streets like it, carefully aiming a neatly rolled paper at the dark loggia, at the colonnaded porch, or at the ornamented doorway of each of the palazzos and chateaux and manor houses that glowered at him in the dawn. He was well thought of as a paper boy. If by mistake one of his papers went astray and lit on an upstairs balcony or on the roof of a porch, Tom would always take more careful aim and throw another. Even if the paper only went into the shrubbery, Tom got off his bicycle and fished it out. He wasn't the kind of boy to whom it would have occurred that the old fogies and the rich kids in West Vesey could very well get out and scramble for their own papers.

Actually, a party at the Dorsets' house was more a grand tour of the house than a real party. There was a half hour spent over very light refreshments (fruit jello, English tea biscuits, lime punch). There was another half hour ostensibly given to general dancing in the basement ballroom (to the accompaniment of victrola music). But mainly there was the tour. As the party passed through the house, stopping sometimes to sit down in the principal rooms, the host and hostess provided entertainment in the form of an almost continuous dialogue between themselves. This dialogue was famous and was full of interest, being all about how much the Dorsets had given up for each other's sake and about how much higher the tone of Chatham society used to be than it was nowadays. They would invariably speak of their parents, who had died within a year of each other when Miss Louisa and Mr. Alfred were still in their teens; they even spoke of their wicked in-laws. When their parents died, the wicked in-laws had first tried to make them sell the house, then had tried to separate them and send them away to boarding schools, and had ended by trying to marry them off to "just anyone." Their two grandfathers had still been alive in those days and each had had a hand in the machinations, after the failure of which each grandfather had disinherited them. Mr. Alfred and Miss Louisa spoke also of how, a few years later, a procession of "young nobodies" had come of their own accord trying to steal the two of them away from each other. Both he and she would scowl at the very recollection of those "just anybodies" and those "nobodies," those "would-be suitors" who always turned out to be misguided fortune-hunters and had to be driven away.

The Dorsets' dialogue usually began in the living room the moment Mr. Dorset returned with his last collection of guests. (He sometimes had to make five or six trips in the car.) There, as in other rooms afterward, they were likely to begin with a reference to the room itself or perhaps to some piece of furniture in the room. For instance, the extraordinary length of the drawing room—or reception room, as the Dorsets called it—would lead them to speak of an even longer room which they had had torn away from the house. "It grieved us, we wept," Miss Dorset would say, "to have Mama's French drawing room torn away from us."

"But we tore it away from ourselves," her brother would add, "as we tore away our in-laws—because we could not afford them." Both of them spoke in a fine declamatory style, but they frequently interrupted themselves with a sad little laugh which expressed something quite different from what they were saying and which seemed to serve them as an aside not meant for our ears.

"That was one of our greatest sacrifices," Miss Dorset would say, referring still to her mother's French drawing room.

And her brother would say: "But we knew the day had passed in Chatham for entertainments worthy of that room."

"It was the room which Mama and Papa loved best, but we gave it up because we knew, from our upbringing, which things to give up."

From this they might go on to anecdotes about their childhood. Sometimes their parents had left them for months or even a whole year at a time with only the housekeeper or with trusted servants to see after them. "You could trust servants then," they explained. And: "In those days parents could do that sort of thing, because in those days there was a responsible body of people within which your young people could always find proper companionship."

In the library, to which the party always moved from the drawing room, Mr. Dorset was fond of exhibiting snapshots of the house taken before the south wing was pulled down. As the pictures were passed around, the dialogue continued. It was often there that they told the story of how the in-laws had tried to force them to sell the house. "For the sake of economy!" Mr. Dorset would exclaim, adding an ironic "Ha ha!"

"As though money—" he would begin.

"As though money ever took the place," his sister would come in, "of living with your own kind."

"Or of being well born," said Mr. Dorset.

After the billiard room, where everyone who wanted it was permitted one turn with the only cue that there seemed to be in the house, and after the dining room, where it was promised refreshments would be served later, the guests would be taken down to the ballroom—purportedly for dancing. Instead of everyone's being urged to dance, however, once they were assembled in the ballroom, Miss Dorset would announce that she and her brother understood the timidity which young people felt about dancing and that all that she and he intended to do was to set the party a good example. . . . It was only Miss Louisa and Mr. Alfred who danced. For perhaps thirty minutes, in a room without light excepting that from a few weak bulbs concealed among the flowers, the old couple danced; and they danced with such grace and there was such perfect harmony in all their movements that the guests stood about in stunned silence, as if hypnotized. The Dorsets waltzed, they two-stepped, they even fox-trotted, stopping only long enough between dances for Mr. Dorset, amid general applause, to change the victrola record.

But it was when their dance was ended that all the effects of the Dorsets' careful grooming that night would have vanished. And, alas, they made no effort to restore themselves. During the remainder of the evening Mr. Dorset went about with his bow tie hanging limply on his damp shirtfront, a gold collar button shining above it. A strand of gray hair, which normally covered his bald spot on top, now would have fallen on the wrong side of his part and hung like fringe about his ear. On his face and neck the thick layer of powder was streaked with perspiration. Miss Dorset was usually in an even more dishevelled state, depending somewhat upon the fashion of her dress that year. But always her powder was streaked, her lipstick entirely gone, her hair falling down on all sides, and her corsage dangling somewhere about the nape of her neck. In this condition they led the party upstairs again, not stopping until they had reached the second floor of the house.

On the second floor we—the guests—were shown the

rooms which the Dorsets' parents had once occupied (The Dorsets' own rooms were never shown). We saw, in glass museum cases along the hallway, the dresses and suits and hats and even the shoes which Miss Louisa and Mr. Alfred had worn to parties when they were very young. And now the dialogue, which had been left off while the Dorsets danced, was resumed. "Ah, the happy time," one of them would say, "was when we were *your* age!" And then, exhorting us to be happy and gay while we were still safe in the bosom of our own kind and before the world came crowding in on us with its ugly demands, the Dorsets would recall the happiness they had known when they were very young. This was their *pièce de résistance*. With many a wink and blush and giggle and shake of the forefinger—and of course standing before the whole party—they each would remind the other of his or her naughty behavior in some old-fashioned parlor game or of certain silly little flirtations which they had long ago caught each other in.

They were on their way downstairs again now, and by the time they had finished with this favorite subject they would be downstairs. They would be in the dark, flower-bedecked downstairs hall and just before entering the dining room for the promised refreshments: the fruit jello, the English tea biscuits, the lime punch.

And now for a moment Mr. Dorset bars the way to the dining room and prevents his sister from opening the closed door. "Now, my good friends," he says, "let us eat, drink and be merry!"

"For the night is yet young," says his sister.

"Tonight you must be gay and carefree," Mr. Dorset enjoins.

"Because in this house we are all friends," Miss Dorset says. "We are all young, we all love one another."

"And love can make us all young forever," her brother says.

"Remember!"

"Remember this evening always, sweet young people!"

"Remember!"

"Remember what our life is like here!"

And now Miss Dorset, with one hand on the knob of the great door which she is about to throw open, leans a little toward the guests and whispers hoarsely: "This is what it is like to be young forever!"

Ned Meriwether was waiting behind a big japonica shrub near the sidewalk when, about twenty minutes after he had last seen Emily, the queer old touring car drew up in front of the Dorsets' house. During the interval, the car had gone from the Meriwether house to gather a number of other guests, and so it was not only Emily and Tom who alighted on the sidewalk before the Dorsets' house. The group was just large enough to make it easy for Ned to slip out from his dark hiding place and join them without being noticed by Mr. Dorset. And now the group was escorted rather unceremoniously up to the door of the house, and Mr. Dorset departed to fetch more guests.

They were received at the door by Miss Dorset. Her eyesight was no doubt better than her brother's, but still there was really no danger of her detecting an uninvited guest. Those of us who had gone to that house in the years just before Ned and Emily came along, could remember that during a whole evening, when their house was full of young people, the Dorsets made no introductions and made no effort to distinguish which of their guests was which. They did not even make a count of heads. Perhaps they did vaguely recognize some of the faces, because sometimes when they had come delivering figs or paper flowers to a house they had of necessity encountered a young child there, and always they smiled sweetly at it, asked its age, and calculated on their old fingers how many years must pass before the child would be eligible for an invitation. Yet at those moments something in the way they had held up their fingers and in the way they had gazed *at* the little face instead of into it had revealed their lack of interest in the individual child. And later when the child was finally old enough to receive their invitation he found it was still no different with the Dorsets. Even in their own house it was evidently to the young people as a group that the Dorsets' hearts went out; while they had the boys and girls under their roof they herded them about like so many little thoroughbred calves. Even when Miss Dorset opened the front door she did so exactly as though she were opening a gate. She pulled it open very slowly, standing half behind it to keep out of harm's way. And the children, all huddled together, surged in.

How meticulously this Ned and Emily Meriwether must have laid their plans for that evening! And the whole business might have come out all right if only they could have foreseen the effect which one part of their plan —rather a last minute embellishment of it—would produce upon Ned himself. Barely ten minutes after they entered the house Ned was watching Tom as he took his seat on the piano bench beside Emily. Ned probably watched Tom closely, because certainly he knew what the next move was going to be. The moment Miss Louisa Dorset's back was turned Tom Bascomb slipped his arm gently about Emily's little waist and commenced kissing her all over her pretty face. It was almost as if he were kissing away tears.

This spectacle on the piano bench, and others like it which followed, had been an inspiration of the last day or so before the party. Or so Ned and Emily maintained afterward when defending themselves to their parents. But no matter when it was conceived, a part of their plan it was, and Ned must have believed himself fully prepared for it. Probably he expected to join in the round of giggling which it produced from the other guests. But now that the time had come—it is easy to imagine—the boy Ned Meriwether found himself not quite able to join in the fun. He watched with the others, but he was not quite infected by their laughter. He stood a little apart, and possibly he was hoping that Emily and Tom would not notice his failure to appreciate the success of their comedy. He was no doubt baffled by his own feelings, by the failure of his own enthusiasm, and by a growing desire to withdraw himself from the plot and from the party itself.

It is easy to imagine Ned's uneasiness and confusion that night. And I believe the account which I have given of Emily's impressions and her delicate little sensations while on the way to the party has the ring of truth about it, though actually the account was supplied by girls who knew her only slightly, who were not at the party, who could not possibly have seen her afterward. It may, after all, represent only what other girls imagined she would have felt. As for the account of how Mr. and Mrs. Meriwether spent the evening, it is their very own. And they did not hesitate to give it to anyone who would listen.

It was a long time, though, before many of us had a
clear picture of the main events of the evening. We heard
very soon that the parties for young people were to be no
more, that there had been a wild scramble and chase
through the Dorsets' house, and that it had ended by the
Dorsets locking some boy—whether Ned or Tom was not
easy to determine at first—in a queer sort of bathroom in
which the plumbing had been disconnected, and even the
fixtures removed, I believe. (Later I learned that there
was nothing literally sinister about the bathroom itself.
By having the pipes disconnected to this, and perhaps
other bathrooms, the Dorsets had obtained further reduc-
tions in their taxes.) But a clear picture of the whole evening wasn't to be had—not without considerable searching. For one thing, the Meriwether parents immediately,
within a week after the party, packed their son and daughter off to boarding schools. Accounts from the other children were contradictory and vague—perversely so, it
seemed. Parents reported to each other that the little girls
had nightmares which were worse even than those which
their older sisters had had. And the boys were secretive
and elusive, even with us older boys when we questioned
them about what had gone on.

One sketchy account of events leading up to the chase,
however, did go the rounds almost at once. Ned must have
written it back to some older boy in a letter, because it
contained information which no one but Ned could have
had. The account went like this: When Mr. Dorset returned from his last round-up of guests, he came hurrying
into the drawing room where the others were waiting and
said in a voice trembling with excitement: "Now, let us

all be seated, my young friends, and let us warm ourselves with some good talk."

At that moment everyone who was not already seated
made a dash for a place on one of the divans or love seats
or even in one of the broad window seats. (There were no
individual chairs in the room.) Everyone made a dash,
that is, except Ned. Ned did not move. He remained
standing beside a little table rubbing his fingers over its
polished surface. And from this moment he was clearly an
object of supicion in the eyes of his host and hostess. Soon
the party moved from the drawing room to the library,
but in whatever room they stopped Ned managed to iso-
late himself from the rest. He would sit or stand looking
down at his hands until once again an explosion of giggles
filled the room. Then he would look up just in time to see
Tom Bascomb's cheek against Emily's or his arm about
her waist.

For nearly two hours Ned didn't speak a word to anyone. He endured the Dorsets' dialogue, the paper flowers,
the perfumed air, the works of art. Whenever a burst of
giggling forced him to raise his eyes he would look up at
Tom and Emily and then turn his eyes away. Before looking down at his hands again he would let his eyes travel
slowly about the room until they came to rest on the figures of the two Dorsets. That, it seems, was how he happened to discover that the Dorsets understood, or thought
they understood, what the giggles meant. In the great mirror mounted over the library mantel he saw them exchanging half suppressed smiles. Their smiles lasted precisely as long as the giggling continued, and then, in the
mirror, Ned saw their faces change and grow solemn when

their eyes—their identical, tiny, dull, amber colored eyes —focused upon himself.

From the library the party continued on the regular tour of the house. At last when they had been to the ballroom and watched the Dorsets dance, had been upstairs to gaze upon the faded party clothes in the museum cases, they descended into the downstairs hall and were just before being turned into the dining room. The guests had already heard the Dorsets teasing each other about the silly little flirtations and about their naughtiness in parlor games when they were young and had listened to their exhortations to be gay and happy and carefree. Then just when Miss Dorset leaned toward them and whispered, "This is what it is like to be young forever," there rose a chorus of laughter, breathless and shrill, yet loud and intensely penetrating.

Ned Meriwether, standing on the bottom step of the stairway, lifted his eyes and looked over the heads of the party to see Tom and Emily half hidden in a bower of paper flowers and caught directly in a ray of mauve light. The two had squeezed themselves into a little niche there and stood squarely in front of the Rodin statuary. Tom had one arm placed about Emily's shoulders and he was kissing her lightly first on the lobe of one ear and then on the tip of her nose. Emily stood as rigid and pale as the plaster sculpture behind her and with just the faintest smile on her lips. Ned looked at the two of them and then turned his glance at once on the Dorsets.

He found Miss Louisa and Mr. Alfred gazing quite openly at Tom and Emily and frankly grinning at the spectacle. It was more than Ned could endure. "Don't you *know?*" he failed, as if in great physical pain. "Can't you

tell? Can't you see who they *are?* They're *brother* and
sister!"

From the other guests came one concerted gasp. And
then an instant later, mistaking Ned's outcry to be something he had planned all along and probably intended—
as they imagined—for the very cream of the jest, the
whole company burst once again into laughter—not a
chorus of laughter this time but a volley of loud guffaws
from the boys, and from the girls a cacophony of separately
articulated shrieks and trills.

None of the guests present that night could—or would
—give a satisfactory account of what happened next.
Everyone insisted that he had not even looked at the Dorsets, that he, or she, didn't know how Miss Louisa and
Mr. Alfred reacted at first. Yet this was precisely what
those of us who had gone there in the past *had* to know.
And when finally we did manage to get an account of it,
we knew that it was a very truthful and accurate one. Because we got it, of course, from Tom Bascomb.

Since Ned's outburst came after the dancing exhibition,
the Dorsets were in their most dishevelled state. Miss
Louisa's hair was fallen half over her face, and that long,
limp strand of Mr. Alfred's was dangling about his left
ear. Like that, they stood at the doorway to the dining
room grinning at Tom Bascomb's antics. And when Tom
Bascomb, hearing Ned's wail, whirled about, the grins
were still on the Dorsets' faces even though the guffaws
and the shrieks of laughter were now silenced. Tom said
that for several moments they continued to wear their
grins like masks and that you couldn't really tell how they

were taking it all until presently Miss Louisa's face, still wearing the grin, began turning all the queer colors of her paper flowers. Then the grin vanished from her lips and her mouth fell open and every bit of color went out of her face. She took a step backward and leaned against the doorjamb with her mouth still open and her eyes closed. If she hadn't been on her feet, Tom said he would have thought she was dead. Her brother didn't look at her, but his own grin had vanished just as hers did, and his face, all drawn and wrinkled, momentarily turned a dull copperish green.

Presently, though, he too went white, not white in faintness but in anger. His little brown eyes now shone like rosin. And he took several steps toward Ned Meriwether. "What we know is that you are not one of us," he croaked. "We have perceived that from the beginning! We don't know how you got here or who you are. But the important question is, What are you doing here among these nice children?"

The question seemed to restore life to Miss Louisa. Her amber eyes popped wide open. She stepped away from the door and began pinning up her hair which had fallen down on her shoulders, and at the same time addressing the guests who were huddled together in the center of the hall. "Who is he, children? He is an intruder, that we know. If you know who he is, you must tell us."

"Who *am* I? Why, I am Tom Bascomb!" shouted Ned, still from the bottom step of the stairway. "I am Tom Bascomb, your paper boy!"

Then he turned and fled up the stairs toward the second floor. In a moment Mr. Dorset was after him.

To the real Tom Bascomb it had seemed that Ned

honestly believed what he had been saying; and his own first impulse was to shout a denial. But being a level-headed boy and seeing how bad things were, Tom went instead to Miss Dorset and whispered to her that Tom Bascomb was a pretty tough guy and that she had better let *him* call the police for her. She told him where the telephone was in the side hall, and he started away.

But Miss Dorset changed her mind. She ran after Tom telling him not to call. Some of the guests mistook this for the beginning of another chase. Before the old lady could overtake Tom, however, Ned himself had appeared in the doorway toward which she and Tom were moving. He had come down the back stairway and he was calling out to Emily, "We're going *home,* Sis!"

A cheer went up from the whole party. Maybe it was this that caused Ned to lose his head, or maybe it was simply the sight of Miss Dorset rushing at him that did it. At any rate, the next moment he was running up the front stairs again, this time with Miss Dorset in pursuit.

When Tom returned from the telephone, all was quiet in the hall. The guests—everybody except Emily—had moved to the foot of the stairs and they were looking up and listening. From upstairs Tom could hear Ned saying, "All right. All right. All right." The old couple had him cornered.

Emily was still standing in the little niche among the flowers. And it is the image of Emily Meriwether standing among the paper flowers that tantalizes me whenever I think or hear someone speak of that evening. That, more than anything else, can make me wish that I had been there. I shall never cease to wonder what kind of thoughts were in her head to make her seem so oblivious to all that was going on while she stood there, and, for that matter, what had been in her mind all evening while she endured Tom Bascomb's caresses. When, in years since, I have had reason to wonder what some girl or woman is thinking— some Emily grown older—my mind nearly always returns to the image of that girl among the paper flowers. Tom said that when he returned from the telephone she looked very solemn and pale still but that her mind didn't seem to be on any of the present excitement. Immediately he went to her and said, "Your dad is on his way over, Emily." For it was the Meriwether parents he had telephoned, of course, and not the police.

It seemed to Tom that so far as he was concerned the party was now over. There was nothing more he could do. Mr. Dorset was upstairs guarding the door to the strange little room in which Ned was locked up. Miss Dorset was serving lime punch to the other guests in the dining room, all the while listening with one ear for the arrival of the police whom Tom pretended he had called. When the doorbell finally rang and Miss Dorset hurried to answer it, Tom slipped quietly out through the pantry and through the kitchen and left the house by the back door as the Meriwether parents entered by the front.

There was no difficulty in getting Edwin and Muriel Meriwether, the children's parents, to talk about what happened after they arrived that night. Both of them were sensible and clear-headed people, and they were not so conservative as some of our other neighbors in West Vesey. Being fond of gossip of any kind and fond of reasonably funny stories on themselves, they told how their children had deceived them earlier in the evening and how they had deceived themselves later. They tended to blame themselves more than the children for what had happened. They tried to protect the children from any harm or embarrassment that might result from it by sending them off to boarding school. In their talk they never referred directly to Tom's reprehensible conduct or to the possible motives that the children might have had for getting up their plan. They tried to spare their children and they tried to spare Tom, but fortunately it didn't occur to them to try to spare the poor old Dorsets.

When Miss Louisa opened the door, Mr. Meriwether said, "I'm Edwin Meriwether, Miss Dorset. I've come for my son, Ned."

"And for your daughter Emily, I hope," his wife whispered to him.

"And for my daughter Emily."

Before Miss Dorset could answer him Edwin Meriwether spied Mr. Dorset descending the stairs. With his wife, Muriel, sticking close to his side Edwin now strode over to the foot of the stairs. "Mr. Dorset," he began, "my son Ned—"

From behind them, Edwin and Muriel now heard Miss Dorset saying, "All the invited guests are gathered in the dining room." From where they were standing the two parents could see into the dining room. Suddenly they turned and hurried in there. Mr. Dorset and his sister of course followed them.

Muriel Meriwether went directly to Emily who was standing in a group of girls. "Emily, where is your brother?"

Emily said nothing, but one of the boys answered: "I think they've got him locked up upstairs somewhere."

"Oh, no!" said Miss Louisa, a hairpin in her mouth—

for she was still rather absent-mindedly working at her hair. "It is an intruder that my brother has upstairs."

Mr. Dorset began speaking in a confidential tone to Edwin. "My dear neighbor," he said, "our paper boy saw fit to intrude himself upon our company tonight. But we recognized him as an outsider from the start."

Muriel Meriwether asked: "Where *is* the paper boy? Where is the paper boy, Emily?"

Again one of the boys volunteered: "He went out through the back door, Mrs. Meriwether."

The eyes of Mr. Alfred and Miss Louisa searched the room for Tom. Finally their eyes met and they smiled coyly. "*All* the children are being mischievous tonight," said Miss Louisa, and it was quite as though she had said, "all *we* children." Then, still smiling, she said, "Your tie has come undone, Brother. Mr. and Mrs. Meriwether will hardly know what to think."

Mr. Alfred fumbled for a moment with his tie but soon gave it up. Now with a bashful glance at the Meriwether parents, and giving a nod in the direction of the children, he actually said, "I'm afraid we've all decided to play a trick on Mr. and Mrs. Meriwether."

Miss Louisa said to Emily: "We've hidden our brother somewhere, haven't we?"

Emily's mother said firmly: "Emily, tell me where Ned is."

"He's upstairs, Mother," said Emily in a whisper.

Emily's father said: "I wish you to take me to the boy upstairs, Mr. Dorset."

The coy, bashful expressions vanished from the faces of the two Dorsets. Their eyes were little dark pools of incredulity, growing narrower by the second. And both of them were now trying to put their hair in order. "Why, *we* know nice children when we see them," Miss Louisa said peevishly. There was a pleading quality in her voice, too. "We knew from the beginning that that boy upstairs didn't belong amongst us," she said. "Dear neighbors, it isn't just the money, you know, that makes the difference." All at once she sounded like a little girl about to burst into tears.

"It isn't just the money?" Edwin Meriwether repeated.

"Miss Dorset," said Muriel with new gentleness in her tone, as though she had just recognized that it was a little girl she was talking to, "there has been some kind of mistake—a misunderstanding."

Mr. Alfred Dorset said: "Oh, we wouldn't make a mistake of that kind! People *are* different. It isn't something you can put your finger on, but it isn't the money."

"I don't know what you're talking about," Edwin said, exasperated. "But I'm going upstairs and find that boy." He left the room with Mr. Dorset following him with quick little steps—steps like those of a small boy trying to keep up with a man.

Miss Louisa now sat down in one of the high-backed dining chairs which were lined up along the oak wainscot. She was trembling, and Muriel came and stood beside her. Neither of them spoke, and in almost no time Edwin Meriwether came downstairs again with Ned. Miss Louisa looked at Ned, and tears came into her eyes. "Where is my brother?" she asked accusingly, as though she thought possibly Ned and his father had locked Mr. Dorset in the bathroom.

"I believe he has retired," said Edwin. "He left us and disappeared into one of the rooms upstairs."

"Then I must go up to him," said Miss Louisa. For a moment she seemed unable to rise. At last she pushed herself up from the chair and walked from the room with the slow, steady gait of a somnambulist. Muriel Meriwether followed her into the hall and as she watched the old woman ascending the steps, leaning heavily on the rail, her impulse was to go and offer to assist her. But something made her turn back into the dining room. Perhaps she imagined that her daughter, Emily, might need her now.

The Dorsets did not reappear that night. After Miss Louisa went upstairs, Muriel promptly got on the telephone and called the parents of some of the other boys and girls. Within a quarter of an hour half a dozen parents had assembled. It was the first time in many years that any adult had set foot inside the Dorset house. It was the first time that any parent had ever inhaled the perfumed air or seen the masses of paper flowers and the illuminations and the statuary. In the guise of holding consultations over whether or not they should put out the lights and lock up the house the parents lingered much longer than was necessary before taking the young people home. Some of them even tasted the lime punch. But in the presence of their children they made no comment on what had happened and gave no indication of what their own impressions were—not even their impressions of the punch. At last it was decided that two of the men should see to putting out the lights everywhere on the first floor and down in the ballroom. They were a long time in finding the switches for the indirect lighting. In most cases they simply resorted to unscrewing the bulbs. Meanwhile the children went to the large cloak closet behind the stairway and got their wraps. When Ned and Emily Meriwether rejoined their parents at the front door to leave the house, Ned was wearing his own overcoat and held his own fedora in his hand.

Miss Louisa and Mr. Alfred Dorset lived on for nearly ten years after that night, but they gave up selling their figs and paper flowers and of course they never entertained young people again. I often wonder if growing up in Chatham can ever have seemed quite the same since. Some of the terror must have gone out of it. Half the dread of coming of age must have vanished with the dread of the Dorsets' parties.

After that night, their old car would sometimes be observed creeping about town, but it was never parked in front of their house any more. It stood usually at the side entrance where the Dorsets could climb in and out of it without being seen. They began keeping a servant too—mainly to run their errands for them, I imagine. Sometimes it would be a man, sometimes a woman, never the same one for more than a few months at a time. Both of the Dorsets died during the Second World War while many of us who had gone to their parties were away from Chatham. But the story went round—and I am inclined to believe it—that after they were dead and the house was sold, Tom Bascomb's coat and hat were found still hanging in the cloak closet behind the stairs.

Tom himself was a pilot in the war and was a considerable hero. He was such a success and made such a name for himself that he never came back to Chatham to live. He found bigger opportunities elsewhere I suppose, and I don't suppose he ever felt the ties to Chatham that people with Ned's kind of upbringing do. Ned was in the war too, of course. He was in the navy and after the war he did return to Chatham to live, though actually it was not until then that he had spent much time here since his parents bundled him off to boarding school. Emily came home and made her début just two or three years before the war, but she was already engaged to some boy in the East; she never comes back any more except to bring her children to see their grandparents for a few days during Christmas or at Easter.

I understand that Emily and Ned are pretty indifferent to each other's existence nowadays. I have been told this by Ned Meriwether's own wife. Ned's wife maintains that the night Ned and Emily went to the Dorsets' party marked the beginning of this indifference, that it marked the end of their childhood intimacy and the beginning of a shyness, a reserve, even an animosity between them that was destined to be a sorrow forever to the two sensible parents who had sat in the upstairs sitting room that night waiting until the telephone call came from Tom Bascomb.

Ned's wife is a girl he met while he was in the navy. She was a Wave, and her background isn't the same as his. Apparently she isn't too happy with life in what she refers to as "Chatham proper." She and Ned have recently moved out into a suburban development, which she doesn't like either and which she refers to as "greater Chatham." She asked me at a party one night how Chatham got its name (She was just making conversation and appealing to my interest in such things) and when I told

her that it was named for the Earl of Chatham and
pointed out that the city is located in Pitt County she
burst out laughing. "How very elegant," she said. "Why
has nobody ever told me that before?" But what interests
me most about Ned's wife is that after a few drinks she
likes to talk about Ned and Emily and Tom Bascomb and
the Dorsets. Tom Bascomb has become a kind of hero—
and I don't mean a wartime hero—in her eyes, though of
course not having grown up in Chatham she has never
seen him in her life. But she is a clever girl, and there are
times when she will say to me, "Tell me about Chatham.
Tell me about the Dorsets." And I try to tell her. I tell
her to remember that Chatham looks upon itself as a
rather old city. I tell her to remember that it was one of
the first English-speaking settlements west of the Alle-
ghenies and that by the end of the American Revolution,
when veterans began pouring westward over the Wilder-
ness Road or down the Ohio River, Chatham was often
referred to as a thriving village. Then she tells me that
I am being dull, because it is hard for her to concentrate
on any aspect of the story that doesn't center around Tom
Bascomb and that night at the Dorsets'.

But I make her listen. Or at least one time I did. The
Dorset family, I insisted on saying, was in Chatham even
in those earliest times right after the Revolution, but they
had come here under somewhat different circumstances
from those of the other early settlers. How could that
really matter, Ned's wife asked, after a hundred and fifty
years? How could distinctions between the first settlers
matter after the Irish had come to Chatham, after the
Germans, after the Italians? Well, in West Vesey Place it

could matter. It had to. If the distinction was false, it mattered all the more and it was all the more necessary to make it.

But let me interject here that Chatham is located in a state about whose history most Chatham citizens—not newcomers like Ned's wife, but old timers—have little interest and less knowledge. Most of us, for instance, are never even quite sure whether during the 1860's our state did secede or didn't secede. As for the city itself, some of us hold that it is geographically Northern and culturally Southern. Others say the reverse is true. We are all apt to want to feel misplaced in Chatham, and so we are not content merely to say that it is a border city. How you stand on this important question is apt to depend entirely on whether your family is one of those with a good Southern name or one that had its origin in New England, because those are the two main categories of old society families in Chatham.

But truly—I told Ned's wife—the Dorset family was never in either of those categories. The first Dorset had come, with his family and his possessions and even a little capital, direct from a city in the English Midlands to Chatham. The Dorsets came not as pioneers, but paying their way all the way. They had not bothered to stop for a generation or two to put down roots in Pennsylvania or Virginia or Massachusetts. And this was the distinction which some people wished always to make. Apparently those early Dorsets had cared no more for putting down roots in the soil of the New World than they had cared for whatever they had left behind in the Old. They were an obscure mercantile family who came to invest in a new western city. Within two generations the business—no, the industry!—which they established made them rich beyond any dreams they could have had in the beginning. For half a century they were looked upon, if any family ever was, as our first family.

And then the Dorsets left Chatham—practically all of them except the one old bachelor and the one old maid —left it just as they had come, not caring much about what they were leaving or where they were going. They were city people, and they were Americans. They knew that what they had in Chatham they could buy more of in other places. For them Chatham was an investment that had paid off. They went to live in Santa Barbara and Laguna Beach, in Newport and on Long Island. And the truth which it was so hard for the rest of us to admit was that, despite our families of Massachusetts and Virginia, we were all more like the Dorsets—those Dorsets who left Chatham—than we were unlike them. Their spirit was just a little closer to being the very essence of Chatham than ours was. The obvious difference was that we had to stay on here and pretend that our life had a meaning which it did not. And if it was only by a sort of chance that Miss Louisa and Mr. Alfred played the role of social arbiters among the young people for a number of years, still no one could honestly question their divine right to do so.

"It may have been their right," Ned's wife said at this point, "but just think what might have happened."

"It's not a matter of what might have happened," I said. "It is a matter of what did happen. Otherwise, what have you and I been talking about?"

"Otherwise," she said with an irrepressible shudder, "I would not be forever getting you off in a corner at these parties to talk about my husband and my husband's sister and how it is they care so little for each other's company nowadays?"

And I could think of nothing to say to that except that probably we had now pretty well covered our subject.

II
OTHER PLACES

A Friend and Protector

———✦———

Family friends would always say how devoted Jesse Munroe was to my uncle. And Jesse himself would tell me sometimes what he would do to anybody who harmed a hair on "that white gentleman's head." The poor fellow was much too humorless and lived much too much in the past—or in some other kind of removal from the present—to reflect that Uncle Andrew no longer had a hair on his head to be harmed. While he was telling me the things he would do, I'd often burst out laughing at the very thought of my uncle's baldness. Or that was what I told myself I was laughing about. At any rate, my outbursts didn't bother Jesse. He always went right ahead with his description of the violence he would do Uncle Andrew's assailant. And I, watching his obscene gestures and reminding my-

self of all the scrapes he had been in and of the serious
trouble my uncle had got him out of twenty years back, I
could almost believe he would do the things he said. More
than one time, in fact, his delineations became so real
and convincing it took my best fit of laughter to conceal
the shudders he sent through me.

He was a naturally fierce-looking little man with pur-
plish black skin and thick wiry hair which he wore not
clipped short like most Negro men's hair but long and
bushed up on his head. It was intended to give him
height, I used to suppose. But it contributed instead to a
general sinister effect, just as his long, narrow sideburns
did; and my Uncle Andrew would always insist that it
was this effect Jesse strived for. He wasn't, actually, such
a little man. He was of medium height. It was because he
was so stoop-shouldered and was so often seen beside my
Uncle Andrew that we, my aunt and I, thought of him as
little. He *was* extremely stoop-shouldered, though, and his
neck was so short that the lobes of his overlarge ears
seemed to reach almost to the collar of his white linen
jacket. Probably it was this peculiarity along with his
bushy hair and his perpetually bloodshot eyes that made
me say at first he was naturally fierce looking.

He wasn't *naturally* fierce looking. My Uncle Andrew
was right about that. It was something he had achieved.
And according to my uncle, the scrapes he was always
getting into didn't really amount to much. My Aunt Margaret, however—my "blood aunt," married to Uncle Andrew—used to shake her head bitterly and say that Negroes could get away with anything with Uncle Andrew
and that his ideas of "much" were very different from
hers. "Jesse Munroe can disappear into the bowels of

Beale Street," she would say in Jesse's presence, "knowing
that when he comes out all he did there will be a closed
chapter for 'Mr. Andrew'." Jesse would be clearing the
table or laying a fire in the living room, and while such
talk went on he would keep his eyes lowered except to
steal a glance now and then at my aunt.

I was a boy of fifteen when I used to observe this. I was
staying there in Memphis with my uncle and aunt just
after Mother died. The things Aunt Margaret said in
Jesse's presence made me feel very uncomfortable. And
it seemed unlike her. I used to wish Jesse would look at
Uncle Andrew instead of at her and spare himself the
sight of the expression on her face at those moments.

But it was foolish of me to waste sympathy on Jesse
Munroe, and even at the time I knew it was. For one
thing, despite all the evenings we spent talking back in
the pantry during the two years I lived there, he never
seemed to be really aware of me as a person. Each time we
talked it was almost as though it was the first time. There
was no getting to know him. Two years later when I had
finished high school and was not getting along with my
uncle and aunt as well as at first, I didn't live at their
house any more. But I would sometimes see Jesse at my
uncle's Front Street office where I then had a job and
where Jesse soon came to work as my uncle's special
flunky. Uncle Andrew was a cotton broker, and it wasn't
unusual for such a successful cotton man as he was to keep
a factotum like Jesse around the office. I would see Jesse
there, and he wouldn't even bother to speak to me. I am
certain that if nowadays he is in a condition to remember
anyone he doesn't remember me. I appeared on the scene
too late. By the time I came along Jesse's escapades and

my uncle's and aunt's reactions to them had become a regular pattern. It was too well established, over too many years, for my presence or my sympathy one way or the other to make any difference. It was the central and perhaps the only reality in Jesse's life. It had been so since before I was born and it would continue to be so, for a while at least, after I left the house.

My uncle and aunt had brought Jesse with them to Memphis when Uncle Andrew moved his office there from out at Braxton, which is the country town our family comes from. He was the only local Negro they brought with them, and since this was right after Jesse had received a suspended sentence for an alleged part in the murder of Aunt Margaret's washwoman's husband, it was assumed in Braxton that there had been some sensible understanding arrived at between Andrew Nelson and the presiding judge. Jesse was to have a suspended sentence; Uncle Andrew was to get him out of Braxton and keep him out. . . . Be that as it may, Jesse came away with them to Memphis and during the first year he hardly set foot outside their house and yard.

He was altogether too faithful and too hard-working to be tolerated by any of the trifling servants Aunt Margaret was able to hire in Memphis. For a while she couldn't keep a cook on the place. Then one finally came along who discovered how to get Jesse's goat, and this one stayed the normal time for a Memphis cook—that is, four or five years. She was Jesse's ruin, I suppose. She discovered the secret of how to get his goat, and passed it on to the maid and the furnace boy and the part-time chauffeur that Uncle Andrew kept. And they passed it on to those who came after them. They teased him unmerci-

fully, made life a misery for him. What they said to him
was that he was a country boy in the city, scared to go out
on the street. Now, there is a story, seemingly known to
all Negro citizens of Memphis, of a Mississippi country
boy who robs his old grandmother and comes to town
prepared to enjoy life. He takes a hotel room, and sits
in the window looking down at the crowds. But he can't
bring himself to go down and "mix with 'em." The story
has several versions, but usually it ends with the boy's
starving to death in his room because he is scared to go
down and take his chances on Beale Street. And this was
how they pictured Jesse. They went so far, even, as to
ridicule him that way in front of my aunt and uncle.

As a matter of fact, Jesse couldn't have been much more
than a boy in those days. And his nature may really have
been a timid one. Whatever other reasons there were for
his behavior, probably it was due partly to his being a
timid country boy. There was always something of the
puritan in him, too. I could see this when I was only fifteen. I never once heard him use any profanity, or any
rough language at all except when he was indicating
what he would do to my uncle's imaginary attacker—and
then it was more a matter of gestures than of words. When
the cook my aunt had during the time I was there would
sometimes make insinuating remarks about the dates I
began having and about the hours I kept toward the end
of my stay, Jesse would say: "You oughtn't talk that way
before this white boy." If I sometimes seemed to enjoy
the cook's teasing and even egged her on a little, he would
get up and leave the room. Perhaps the most old-fashioned
and country thing about him was that he still wore his
long underwear the year round. On Mondays, when he

generally had a terrible hang-over and was tapering off from the weekend, he would work all day in the garden. I would see him out there even on the hottest July day working with his shirt off but still wearing his long-sleeved undershirt. The other servants took his long underwear as another mark of his primness, and whenever they talked about the light he kept burning in his room all night they would say he never put it out except once a week when he took his bath and changed his long-johns.

Yet no matter how much fun they made of him to his face, when Jesse wasn't present the other servants admitted they would hate to run into him while he was off on one of his sprees, and they assured me that *they* didn't hang around the kind of places that he did. And laugh at him though they did, they respected him for the amount of work he could turn out and for the quality of it. He was a perfectionist in his work both in the house and in the yard, and especially in my uncle's vegetable garden.

The cook who found out how to get Jesse's goat shouldn't be blamed too much. She couldn't have known the harm she was doing. And surely Jesse couldn't have gone on forever never leaving the house. The time had to come. And once that teasing had started, Jesse had to *show* them. He didn't tell anyone when he first began going out. The other servants didn't live on the place regularly, and my uncle only discovered Jesse's absence by chance late one night when he wanted him for some trifle. He went out in the backyard and called up to his room above the garage. The light was on, but there was no answer. Uncle climbed the rickety outside stairs that went up to the room and banged on the door to wake him. Then he came down the stairs again and went in the house and conferred with Aunt Margaret. They were worried about Jesse, thinking something might have happened to him, and so Uncle Andrew went up and forced the lock on the door to Jesse's room.

The light was burning—a little twenty-watt bulb on a cord hanging in the middle of the room—and the room was as neat as a pin. But there was no Jesse. My aunt, who can always remember every detail of a moment like that, said that from the back door she could hear Uncle Andrew's footstep out there in the room above the garage. For a time that was all she heard. But then finally she heard Uncle Andrew break out into a kind of laughter that was characteristic of him. It expressed all the good nature in his being and at the same time a certain hateful spirit, too. From her description I am sure it was just like his laughter when he caught you napping at russian-bank or checkers or when he saw he had you beaten and began slapping down his cards or pushing his kings around.

Presently he came out on the stoop at the head of the stairs and, still chuckling in his throat, called down to Aunt Margaret: "Our chick has left the nest." Then, closing the door, he took out his pocket knife and managed to screw the lock in place again. When he joined Aunt Margaret at the kitchen door he told her not to say anything about the incident to Jesse, that it was none of their business if he wanted a night out now and again.

Aunt Margaret could never get Jesse to tell her when he was planning an evening out, and later when he began taking an occasional Sunday off he never gave advance warning of that either. Sunday morning would come and he would simply not be on the place. It was still the same when I came there to live. After a Sunday's absence-without-leave Jesse would be working my uncle's garden all day Monday. It was a big country vegetable garden right on Belvedere Street in Memphis. I have seen my aunt stand for a long period of time at one of the upstairs windows watching Jesse at work down there on a Monday morning, herself not moving a muscle until he looked up at her. Then she would shake her head sadly—exaggerating the shake so that he couldn't miss it—and turn her back to the window. When my uncle came home in the evening on one of those Mondays he would go straight to the garden and exclaim over the wonderful weeding and chopping the garden had had. Later, in the house, he would say it was worth having Jesse take French leave now and then in order to get that good day's work in the garden from him.

His real escapades and the scrapes he got into were in a different category from his occasional weekends. In the first place, they lasted longer. When he had already been missing for three or four days or even a week there would be a telephone call late at night or early some morning. Usually it would be an anonymous call, sometimes a man's voice, sometimes a woman's. If a name was given it was one that meant nothing to Uncle Andrew, and when Jesse had been rescued he invariably maintained he had never heard the name of the caller before. He would say he just wished he knew who it was, and always protested that he hadn't wanted Uncle Andrew to be bothered. The telephone call usually went about like this:

"You Mr. Andrew Nelson at Number 212 Belvedere Street?"

"Yes."

"Yo friend Jesse's in jail and he needs yo help."

Then the informer would hang up or, if questioned in time by Uncle Andrew, would give a name like "Henry White" or "Mary Jones" along with some made-up street number and a street nobody ever heard of. One time the voice said only: "Yo friend Jesse's been pisened. He's in room Number 9 at the New Charleston Hotel." Uncle Andrew had gone down to the New Charleston with a policeman and they found Jesse seriously ill and out of his head—probably from getting hold of bad whiskey. They took him to the John Gaston Hospital where he had to stay for nearly a week.

Usually, though, it wasn't just a matter of his being on a drunk. According to my aunt, he got into dreadful fights in which he slashed other Negroes with a knife and got cut up himself, though I never saw any of his scars. Probably they were all hidden beneath his long underwear. And besides by the time I came along they would have been old scars since by then his scrapes had, for a long time, been of a different kind. There had been a number of years when his troubles were all with women. There were women who fought over him, women who fought *him*, women who got him put in jail for bothering them, and women who got him put in jail for not helping support their children. Then, after this phase, he was involved off and on for several years in the numbers racket and the kind of gang warfare that goes along with that. Uncle Andrew would have to get the police and go down and rescue him from some room above a pool hall where the rival gang had him cornered.

My account of all this came of course from my aunt since my uncle never revealed the nature of Jesse's troubles to anyone but Aunt Margaret. She dragged it out of him because she felt she had a right to know. She may have exaggerated it all to me. But I used to think two of the points she made about it were good ones. She pointed out that the nature of his escapades grew successively worse, so that it was harder each time for Uncle Andrew to intervene. And she suspected that that gave Jesse considerable satisfaction. She also said that from the beginning all of Jesse's degrading adventures had had one thing in common: he never was able or willing to get out of any jam on his own. He would let any situation run on until there was no way he could be saved except through Uncle Andrew's intervention. "All he seems to want," she said, "is to have something worse than the time before for his 'Mr. Andrew' to save him from and dismiss as a mere nothing."

I felt at the time that this was very true, and it tended to make me agree with Uncle Andrew that Jesse Munroe's scrapes were not very important in themselves, and, in that sense, didn't "amount to much." In fact, my aunt's observation seemed so obviously true that it was hard to think of Jesse as anything but a spoiled child, which, I suppose, is the way Uncle Andrew did think of him.

The murder that Jesse had gotten mixed up in back in Braxton was as nasty a business as you hear about. Uncle Andrew would not have had a white man living above his garage who had had any connection with such a business. When *I* finally gave up my room at his house and went to live at the "Y," it was more because of *his* disapproval of my friends (and of the hours I kept) than it was because of my aunt's. And though I couldn't have said so to a living soul that I knew when I was a boy, I used to wish my uncle could have been half as tolerant of my own father, who was a weak man and got into various kinds of trouble, as he was of Jesse. My father was killed in an automobile crash when I was only a little fellow, but, for several years before, Uncle Andrew had refused to have anything to do with him personally, though he would always help him get jobs as long as they were away from Braxton and, always, on the condition that my mother and I would continue to live in Braxton with my grandparents. I was taught to believe that Uncle Andrew was right about all of this, and I still believe that he was in a way. Jesse hadn't, after all, had the advantages that my father had, and he may have been a victim of circumstances. But my father was a victim of circumstances, too, I think—as who isn't, for that matter? Even Uncle Andrew and Aunt Margaret were, in a way.

In that murder of Aunt Margaret's washwoman's husband I believe Jesse was accused of being an accessory after the fact. I don't think anyone accused him of having anything to do with the actual killing. The washwoman and a boy-friend of hers named Cleveland Blakemore had done-in her husband without help from anyone. They did it in a woods lot behind a roadhouse on the outskirts of town, where the husband found them together. At the trial I think the usual blunt instrument was produced as the murder weapon. Then they had transported the body to the washwoman's house where they dismembered it and attempted to burn the parts in the chimney. But it was a rainy night and the flue wouldn't draw. They ended by pulling out the charred remains and burying them in a cotton patch behind the washwoman's house, not in one grave but in a number of graves scattered about the cotton patch. (You may wonder why I bring in these awful details of the murder, and I wonder myself. I tell them out of some kind of compulsion and because I have known them ever since I was a small child in Braxton. I couldn't have told the story without somehow bringing them in. I find I have only been waiting for the right moment. And it seems to me now that I would never have had the interest I did in Jesse except that he was someone connected with those gory details of a crime I had heard about when I was very young and which had stuck in my mind during all the years when I was growing up in the house with my pretty, gentle mother and my aged grandparents.) At any rate, it was on a rainy winter morning just a few weeks after the murder that a Negro girl, hurrying to work, took a short cut through that cotton patch. In her haste she stumbled and fell into a hole where the pigs had rooted up what was left of the victim's left forearm and hand.

In the trial it was proved that Jesse had provided the transportation for the corpse from the woods lot to the washwoman's house. His defense contended that he just happened to be at the roadhouse that night, driving a funeral car which he had borrowed, without permission, from the undertaker's parlor where he worked as janitor, and sometimes as driver. (You can hear the voice of the prosecution: "It was the saddest funeral that car ever went to.") He was paid in advance for the trip, and it was represented to him (according to his defense) that the washwoman's husband was only dead drunk.

It was never proved conclusively that Jesse had any part in the dismemberment or in the efforts at burning. Witnesses who testified they had seen *two* men coming and going from the house to the cotton patch (in the heavy rain on that autumn night) were not reliable ones. Yet the testimony that Jesse's borrowed car was parked in front of the house during most of the night was given by Negro men and women of the highest character. Even Jesse's defense never denied his presence in there. But to me it seems quite as likely that, as his defense maintained, he was kept there at knife's point, or at least by the fear that if he attempted to go he might meet the same fate that the washwoman's husband had, quite as likely as that he willingly took part in what went on. My uncle of course felt that there was no question about it, that Jesse was an innocent country boy drawn into the business by the wash-woman and her friend, Cleveland Blakemore (who no doubt guessed he had taken the undertaker's car without permission) and that he wasn't to be blamed. Uncle Andrew even served as a character witness for Jesse at the trial, because he had known him before the murder when Jesse was janitor at his office as well as at the undertaker's.

I never heard any talk about the murder from Uncle Andrew and Aunt Margaret themselves. In private Aunt Margaret would tell me about some of the other troubles Jesse had been in and about how narrowly he had escaped long jail sentences. Only Uncle Andrew's ever widening connections among influential people in Memphis had been able to prevent those sentences. She said that my uncle was such a modest man that he naturally minimized Jesse's scrapes so as not to put too much importance on the things he was able to do to get him out of them.

But my uncle knew his wife well enough to know what she would have told me. Without ever giving me his version of any of the incidents he would say to me now and then that Aunt Margaret was much too severe and that she set too high standards for Jesse. And I did find it painful to hear the way she spoke to Jesse and to see the way she looked at him even after one of his milder weekends. In those days, so soon after my mother died, Aunt Margaret was always so kind and so considerate of my feelings and of my every want that it seemed out of character for her to be harsh and severe with anyone. Before that day I packed my things and moved out of her house, however, I came to doubt that it was so entirely out of character. If I had stayed there a day longer, I might have had even greater doubts. I think it is fortunate I left when I did. Our quarrel didn't amount to a lot. It was about my staying out all night one time without ever being willing to explain where I was. As soon as I was a little older and began to settle down to work and behave myself we made it up. Nowadays I'm on the best of terms with her and Uncle Andrew. And whenever I'm over at their place for a meal things seem very much the way they used to. Even the talk about Jesse goes very much the way it did when he was on the scene and in easy earshot.

When they talked about him together in the old days, especially when there was company around, it was all about his loyalty and devotion to Uncle Andrew. I agreed with every word they said on the subject, and if someone had said to me then that it was Aunt Margaret whom Jesse was most dependent upon and whose attention he most needed I would have said that person was crazy. How could anyone have supposed such a thing? And if I should advance such a theory nowadays to my uncle and aunt or to their friends they would imagine that I was expressing some long buried resentment against Uncle Andrew. Any new analysis made in the light of what happened to Jesse after he went to work in my uncle's Front Street office

would not interest them. They wouldn't be able to reverse a view based upon the impressions of all those years
when Jesse was with them, a view based upon impressions
received before any of them ever knew Jesse, impressions
inherited from their own uncles and aunts and parents
and grandparents.

I used to watch the expression on his black face when
he was waiting on Uncle Andrew at table or was helping
him into his overcoat when Uncle Andrew left for his
office in the morning. His careful attention to my uncle's
readiness for the next sleeve or for the next helping of
greens made you feel he considered it a privilege to be
doing all these little favors for a man who had done so
many large ones for him. His attentions to my uncle impressed everyone who came to the house. If there was a
party, he couldn't pass through the room, even with a tray
loaded with glasses, without stopping before Uncle Andrew to nod and mutter respectfully: "Mr. Andrew." This
itself was a memorable spectacle, and often was enough
to stop the party-talk of those who witnessed it: Uncle
Andrew, so tall and erect, so bald and clean-shaven, so
proudly beak-nosed and yet with such a benign expression
in those gray eyes that focused for one quick moment
upon Jesse. And Jesse, stooped and purple-black and
bushy-headed and red-eyed, clad in his white vestment and
all but genuflecting while he held the tray of glasses perfectly steady before my uncle. It lasted only a second, and
then Jesse's eyes would dart from one to another of the
men standing nearest Uncle Andrew as though looking
for some Cassius among them—some Judas. (And perhaps
thinking all the time only that my aunt's eyes were upon
him? denouncing him not merely as a sycophant and

hypocrite but as a man who would have to answer for his manifold sins before the dread seat of judgment on the Last Day?) When he had moved on with his tray, some guest who had not been to the house before was apt to comment on what a wicked-looking fellow he was. My uncle would laugh heartily and say that nothing would please Jesse more than to think this was the impression he gave. "He gets himself up to look awful mean and he likes to think of himself as a devil. But actually he's as harmless as that boy standing there," Uncle Andrew would say, pointing of course to me.

I would laugh self-consciously, not really liking to have my own harmlessness pointed out. And I wonder if Jesse, already on the other side of the room, sometimes heard my laughter then and detected a certain hollowness in it that was also there when he told me the things he would do to my uncle's imaginary assailant. Because often, when I stood looking at the guest made uncomfortable by Jesse's glance, I could not help thinking of those things. In my mind's eye I would see his gestures, see him seizing his throat, rolling his eyes about, making as if to slice off his ears and nose and indicating an even more debilitating operation. It may seem strange that I never imagined that those threats might be directed toward me personally, since I was my father's son and might easily have been supposed to bear a grudge against my uncle. But I felt that Jesse made it graphically clear that it was some Negro man like himself he had in mind as my uncle's assailant. When he was going through his routine he would usually be in the pantry and he would have placed himself in such relation to the mirror panel beside the swinging door there, that, by rolling his eyes, he could be certain to see the black visage of this man he was mutilating.

It was another coincidence, like their moving to Memphis just when Jesse had to be gotten out of Braxton, that my aunt and uncle decided to give up the house and move to an apartment at just the time when it was no longer feasible for them to have Jesse Munroe working at their house. Uncle Andrew was nearly seventy years old at the time. He was spending less time at his office, and he and Aunt Margaret wanted to be free to travel. During the two years I was with them, there were three occasions when Jesse was missing from the house for about a week and had to be rescued by my uncle. I didn't know then exactly what his current outside activities were. Even Aunt Margaret preferred not to discuss it with me. She would say only that in her estimation it was worse than anything before. Later I learned that he had become a kind of confidence man and that—as in the numbers racket—his chief troubles came from his competitors. He specialized, for a time, in preying upon green country boys who had come to Memphis with their little wads of money. After I had left the house he went to something still worse. He was delivering country girls whom he picked up on Beale Street into the hands of the Pontotoc Street madams.

It was the authorities from neighboring counties in West Tennessee and Mississippi who finally began to put pressure on the police. They threatened, so I have been told, to come in and take care of Jesse themselves. Uncle Andrew moved him to a little room on the top floor of the ramshackle old building that his cotton company was in. Jesse lived up there and acted as a kind of butler and bartender in my uncle's private office, which was a paneled, air-conditioned suite far in the rear of and very different-looking from the display rooms where the troughs of cotton samples were. The trouble was that his "Mr. Andrew" was not at the office very much any more, for Jesse to wait on. And so most of the time he stayed up in his little cubby hole on the top floor, and of course he got to drinking up my uncle's whiskey. He never left the building, never came down below the third floor which Uncle Andrew's offices were on, and he never talked to the other Negroes who worked there. I would pass him in the hallway sometimes and speak to him, but he wouldn't even look at me. At last, of course, he went crazy up there in my uncle's office. It may have been partly from drinking so much whiskey, but at least this time we knew it wasn't bad whiskey. . . . When the office force came and opened up that morning they found him locked up in Uncle Andrew's air-conditioned, sound-proofed suite and they could see through the glass doors the wreck he had made of everything in there. He had slashed the draperies and cut up the upholstery on the chairs. There were big spots and gashes on the walls where he had thrown things—mostly bottles of whiskey and gin, which of course had been broken and left lying all about the floor. He had pushed over the bar, the filing cabinets, the refrigerator, the electric water cooler, and even the air-conditioning unit. For a while nobody could tell where Jesse himself was. It wasn't till just before I got there that they spotted him crouched under Uncle Andrew's mahogany desk. From the beginning, though, they could hear him moaning and praying and calling out now and then for help. And even before I arrived someone had observed that it

wasn't for Uncle Andrew but for Aunt Margaret he was
calling.

I was parking my car down in the alley when one of the
secretaries who had already been up there rushed up to
me and told me what had happened. I hurried around to
the street side of the building and went up the stairs so
fast that I stumbled two or three times before I got to the
third floor. They made a place for me at the glass door
and told me that if I would stoop down I could see him
back in the inner office crouched under the desk. I saw
him there, and what I noticed first was that he didn't have
on his white jacket or his shirt but was still wearing his
long-sleeved winter underwear.

Fortunately, it happened that Uncle Andrew and Aunt
Margaret were not on one of their trips at the time.
Everyone at the office knew this, and they knew better
than to call the police. They would have known better
even if Uncle Andrew had not been in town. They waited
for me to come in and telephone Uncle Andrew. I went
up into the front display room and picked up the telephone. It was only eight-thirty, and I knew that Uncle
Andrew would probably still be in bed. He sounded half
asleep when he answered. I blurted out: "Uncle Andrew,
Jesse's cracked up pretty bad down here at the office and
has himself locked in your rooms."

"Yes," said Uncle Andrew, guardedly.

"He's made a mess of the place and is hiding under your
desk. He has a knife, I suppose. And he keeps calling for
Aunt Margaret. Do you think you'll come down, or—"

"Who is it speaking?" Uncle Andrew said, as though
anyone else at the office ever called him "uncle." He did
it out of habit. But it gave me an unpleasant feeling. I

was tempted to give some name like "Henry White" and hang up, but I said nothing. I just waited. Uncle Andrew was silent for a moment. Then I heard him clear his throat, and he said, "Do you think he'll be all right till I can get down there?"

"I think so," I said. "I don't know."

"I'll get Fred Morley and be down there in fifteen minutes," he said.

I don't know why but I said again: "He keeps calling for Aunt Margaret."

"I heard you," Uncle Andrew said. Then he said, "We'll be down in fifteen minutes."

I didn't know whether his "we" meant himself and Fred Morley, who was the family doctor, or whether it included Aunt Margaret. I don't know yet which he meant. But when he and Dr. Morley arrived, my aunt was with them, and I don't think I was ever so glad to see anyone. I kissed her when she came in.

I came near to kissing Uncle Andrew too. I was touched by how old he had looked as he came up the stairs—he and Aunt Margaret, and Dr. Morley, too—how old and yet how much the same. And I was touched by the fact that it hadn't occurred to any of the three not to come. However right or wrong their feelings toward Jesse were they were the same as they would have been thirty years before. In a way this seemed pretty wonderful to me. It did at the moment. I thought of the phrase my aunt was so fond of using about people: "true blue."

The office force, and two of the partners by now, were still bunched around the glass door peering in at Jesse and trying to hear the things he was saying. I stood at the top of the stairs watching the three old people ascend the two straight flights of steps that I had come stumbling up half an hour earlier—two flights that came up from the ground floor without a turn or a landing between floors. I thought how absurd it was that in these Front Street buildings, where so much Memphis money was made, such a thing as an elevator was unknown. Except for adding the little air-conditioned offices at the rear, nobody was allowed to do anything there that would change the old-fashioned, masculine character of the cotton man's world. This row of buildings, hardly two blocks long, with their plaster facade and unbroken line of windows looking out over the brown Mississippi River were a kind of last sanctuary—generally beyond the reach of the ladies and practically beyond the reach of the law.

When they got to the top of the stairs I kissed my aunt on her powdered cheek. She took my arm and stood a moment catching her breath before we moved out of the hallway. I thought to myself that she had put more powder on her face this morning than was usual for her. No doubt she had dressed in a great hurry, hardly looking in her glass. But I observed that underneath the powder her face was flushed from the climb, and her china blue eyes shone brightly. Instead of seeming older to me now, I felt she looked younger and prettier and more feminine than I had ever before seen her. It must have been just seeing her there in a Front Street office for the first time . . . . But I still remember the delicate pressure of her hand as she leaned on my arm.

Uncle Andrew went straight to the door of his office and shooed everyone else away. I don't know whether I saw him do this or not, but I know that's how it was. Presently I found myself in the middle display room standing beside Aunt Margaret while Dr. Morley made pleasantries to her about how the appearance of cotton offices never changed. He hadn't been inside one in more than a decade, and he wondered how long it had been for her. Uncle Andrew, meanwhile, in order to be sure that Jesse heard him through the glass door and above his moaning had to speak in a voice that resounded all over the third floor of the building. Yet he didn't seem to be shouting, and he managed to put into his voice all the reassurance and forgiveness that must have been there during their private interchanges in years past. It was like hearing a radio soap opera turned on unbearably loud in a drugstore or in some other public place. "Come open the door, Jesse. You know I'm your friend. Haven't I always done right by you? It doesn't matter about the mess you've made in there. I have insurance to cover everything, and I'm not going to let anybody harm you."

It didn't do any good, though. Even in the middle room we could hear Jesse calling out—more persistently now—for Aunt Margaret to help him. Yet Aunt Margaret still seemed to be listening to Dr. Morley. I couldn't understand it. I wanted to interrupt and ask her if she didn't hear Jesse? Why had she come if she wasn't even going in there and look at him through the glass door? Didn't she feel any compassion for the poor fellow? Surely she would suddenly turn her back on us and walk in there. That seemed how she would do it.

Then for a moment my attention was distracted from Aunt Margaret to myself—to how concerned I was about whether or not she would go to him, to how very much I cared about Jesse's suffering and his need to have my aunt come and look at him! I took my eyes off Aunt Margaret and was myself resolutely trying to observe what a Front Street cotton office was really like when I felt her hand on my arm again. Looking at her I saw that underneath the powder her color was still quite high. While Dr. Morley talked on she gazed at me with moist eyes which made her look still prettier than before. And now I perceived that she had been intending all the time to go to Jesse and give the poor brute whatever comfort she could. But I saw too that there were difficulties for her which I had not imagined. Suddenly she did as she *would* do. Without a word she turned her back on us and went back there and showed herself in the glass door.

That was all there was to it really. Or for Jesse it was. It seemed to be all the real help he needed or could accept. He didn't come out and open the door, but he was relatively quiet afterward, even after Aunt Margaret was finally led away by Uncle Andrew and Dr. Morley, and even after Dr. Morley's two men came and broke the glass in the door and went in for him. When Aunt Margaret had been led away it seemed to be my turn again, and so I went back there and stood watching him until the men came. Now and then he would start to crawl out from under the desk but each time would suddenly pull back and try to hide himself again, and then again the animal grunts and groans would begin. Obviously, he was still seeing the things he had thought were after him during the night. But though he made some feeble efforts at resistance, I think he had regained his senses sufficiently to be glad when Dr. Morley's men finally came in and took him.

That was the end of it for Jesse. And this is where I would like to leave off. It is the next part that it is hardest for me to tell. But the whole truth is that my aunt did more than just show herself to Jesse through the glass door. While she remained there her behavior was such that it made me understand for the first time that this was not merely the story of that purplish-black, kinky-headed Jesse's ruined life. It is the story of my aunt's pathetically unruined life, and my uncle's too, and even my own. I mean to say that at this moment I understood that Jesse's outside activities had been not only *his*, but *ours* too. My Uncle Andrew, with his double standard or triple standard—whichever it was—had most certainly forced Jesse's destruction upon him, and Aunt Margaret had made the complete destruction possible and desirable to him with her censorious words and looks. But they did it because they had to, because they were so dissatisfied with the pale *un*ruin of their own lives. They did it because something would not let them ruin their own lives as they wanted and felt a need to do—as I have often felt a need to do, myself. As who does not sometimes feel a need to do? Without knowing it, I think, Aunt Margaret wanted to see Jesse as he was that morning. And it occurs to me now that Dr. Morley understood this at the time.

The moment she left us to go to Jesse, the old doctor became silent. He and I stood on opposite sides of one of the troughs of cotton, each of us fumbling with samples we had picked up there. Dr. Morley carefully turned his back on the scene that was about to take place in the room beyond. I could not keep myself from watching it.

I think I had never seen my aunt hurry before. As soon as she had passed into the back display room she began running on tiptoe. Uncle Andrew heard her soft footfall.

As he turned around, their eyes must have met. I saw Uncle's face and saw, or imagined I saw, the expression in his gray eyes—one of utter dismay. Yet I don't think this had anything to do with Aunt Margaret. It was Jesse who was on his mind. He could not believe that he had failed to bring Jesse to his senses. I suspect that when Aunt Margaret looked into his eyes she got the impression that her husband didn't at that moment know who in the world she was. Maybe at that moment *she* couldn't have said who *he* was. I imagine their eyes meeting like the eyes of strangers, perhaps two white people passing each other on some desolate back street in the toughest part of niggertown, each wondering what dire circumstances could have brought so nice looking a person as the other to this unlikely neighborhood. . . . At last, when Aunt Margaret drew near the glass door, Uncle Andrew stepped aside and moved out of my view.

For a time she stood before the glass panel in silence. She was peering about the two rooms inside, looking for Jesse. At last, without ever seeing where he was, I suppose, she began speaking to him. Her words were not audible to me and almost certainly they weren't so to Jesse, who continued for some time to keep on with his moaning and praying, though seeing that she had come he didn't go on calling out for her. The voice she spoke to him in was utterly sweet and beautiful. I think she was quoting scripture to him part of the time—one of the Psalms, I believe. Instinctively, I began moving toward the doorway that joined the room I was in and the room she was in. It was the voice of that same Aunt Margaret who had spoken to me with so much kindness and sympathy and love in the days just after my mother died. I was barely able to keep from bursting into tears—tears of joy and exaltation.

Jesse didn't, as I have already said, come out and open the door. But at some point, which I didn't mark, he became quieter. Now there were only intermittent sobs and groans. After a while my aunt stopped speaking. She was searching again for his hiding place in there. Presently, Uncle Andrew appeared again. He came over to her and indicated that if she would stoop down she could see Jesse under the desk. He watched her very intently as she squatted there awkwardly before the door.

If it had seemed strange for me to see her running, a few minutes earlier, it seemed almost unbelievable now that I was seeing her squatting there that way on the floor. I watched her and I thought how unlike her it was. I think I know the very moment when she saw her friend Jesse. I could tell her body had suddenly gone perfectly rigid. She looked not like any woman I had ever seen but like some hideously angular piece of modern sculpture. And then, throwing her hands up to her face, she lost her balance. My uncle was quick and caught her before she fell. He brought her to her feet at once and as he did so he called out for assistance—not from me but from Dr. Morley. Dr. Morley brushed past me in the doorway, answering the call.

Even after she was on her feet she couldn't take her hands down from her face for several moments. When finally she did manage to do so, all her high color and all the brightness in her eyes had vanished. As they led her away it was hard to think of her as the same woman who had rested her hand on my sleeve only a little while ago.

Had she really wanted to see Jesse as he was this morning? I think she had. But I think the sight of the animal crouched underneath my uncle's desk—and probably peering out at her—had been more than she was actually prepared to look upon. As she was led off by her husband and her doctor, I felt certain that Aunt Margaret had suffered a shock from which she would never recover.

But how mistaken I was about her recovery soon became clear. I waited around until Dr. Morley's men arrived and I watched them go in and take Jesse. Then I wandered through the other display rooms up to the front office, where most of the real paperwork of the firm was done and where my own desk was. The front office was really a part of the front display room, divided from it only by a little railing with a swinging gate. I knew I would find my aunt up there and I supposed I would find her lying down on the old leather couch just inside the railing. I could even imagine how Dr. Morley and my uncle, and probably one of the office girls, would be hovering about and administering to her. Yet it was a different scene I came on. Dr. Morley was seated at my desk taking down information which he said would be necessary for him to have about Jesse. He was writing it on the back of an envelope. Aunt Margaret was seated in a chair drawn up beside him. She seemed completely herself again. Uncle, standing on the other side of the doctor, was trying to supply the required information. But Aunt Margaret kept correcting most of the facts that Uncle Andrew gave. While the doctor listened with perfect patience, the two of them disputed silly points like Jesse's probable age and the correct spelling of his surname,

whether it was "Munroe" or "Monroe," and what his
mother's maiden name had been. . . . It was hard to
believe that either Aunt Margaret or Uncle Andrew had
any idea of what was happening to Jesse at that very moment or any feeling about it.

Dr. Morley had Jesse committed to the state asylum
out at Bolivar. They locked him up for a while, then they
made a trusty of him. Dr. Morley says he seems very
happy and that he has made himself so useful that they
will almost certainly never let him go. I have never been
out there to see him, of course, and neither has Aunt
Margaret or Uncle Andrew. But I have dreams about
Jesse sometimes—absurd, wild dreams that are not like
anything that ever happened. One night recently when
I was at a dinner party at my uncle's and aunt's apartment and someone was recalling Jesse's devotion to my
uncle, I undertook to tell one of those dreams of mine.
But I broke it off in the middle and pretended that that
was all, because I saw that my aunt, at the far end of the
table, was looking as pale as if she had seen a ghost or as
if I had been telling a dream that *she* had had. As soon
as I stopped, the talk resumed its usual theme, and my
aunt seemed all right again. But when our eyes met a few
minutes later she sent me the same quick, disapproving
glance that my mother used to send me at my grandfather's table when I was relating some childish nightmare
I had had. "Don't bore people with what you dream," my
mother used to say after we had left the table and were
alone. "If you have nothing better than that to contribute,
leave the talking to someone else." Aunt Margaret's rude
glance said precisely that to me. But I must add that
when we were leaving the dining room my aunt rested her

hand rather firmly and yet tenderly on my arm as if to console and comfort me. She was by nature such a kind and gentle person that she could not bear to think she had hurt someone she loved.

A Walled Garden

———◆———

No, Memphis in autumn has not the moss-hung oaks of
Natchez. Nor, my dear young man, have we the exotic,
the really exotic orange and yellow and rust foliage of the
maples at Rye or Saratoga. When our five-month summer
season burns itself out, the foliage is left a cheerless
brown. Observe that Catawba tree beyond the wall; and
the leaves under your feet here on the terrace are mustard
and khaki colored; and the air, the atmosphere (who
would dare to breathe a deep breath!) is virtually a sea
of dust. But we do what we can. We've walled ourselves
in here with these evergreens and box and jasmine. You
must know, yourself, young man, that no beauty is native
to us but the verdure of early summer. And it's as though
I've had to take my finger, just so, and point out to

Frances the lack of sympathy that there is in the climate and in the eroded countryside of this region. I have had to build this garden and say, "See, my child, how nice and sympathetic everything can be." But now she does see it my way, you understand. You understand, my daughter has finally made her life with me in this little garden plot, and year by year she has come to realize how little else there is hereabouts to compare with it.

And you, you know nothing of flowers? A young man who doesn't know the zinnia from the aster! How curious that you and my daughter should have made friends. I don't know under what circumstances you two may have met. In her League work, no doubt. She *throws* herself so into whatever work she undertakes. Oh? Why, of course, I should have guessed. She simply *spent* herself on the Chest Drive this year. . . . But my daughter has most of her permanent friends among the flower-minded people. She makes so few friends nowadays outside of our little circle, sees so few people outside our own garden here, really, that I find it quite strange for there to be someone who doesn't know flowers.

No, nothing, we've come to feel, is ever very lovely, really lovely, I mean, in this part of the nation, nothing *but* this garden; and you can well imagine what even this little bandbox of a garden once was. I created it out of a virtual chaos of a backyard—Franny's playground, I might say. For three years I nursed that little magnolia there, for one whole summer did nothing but water the ivy on the east wall of the house; if only you could have seen the scrubby hedge and the unsightly servants' quarters of our neighbors that are beyond my serpentine wall (I suppose, at least, they're still there). In those days it was all very different, you understand, and Frances's father was about the house, and Frances was a child. But now in the spring we have what is truly a sweet garden here, modeled on my mother's at Rye; for three weeks in March our hyacinths are an inspiration to Frances and to me and to all those who come to us regularly; the larkspur and marigold are heavenly in May over there beside the roses.

But you do not know the zinnia from the aster, young man? How curious that you two should have become friends. And now you are impatient with her, and you mustn't be; I don't mean to be too indulgent, but she'll be along presently. Only recently she's become incredibly painstaking in her toilet again. Whereas in the last few years she's not cared so much for the popular fads of dress. Gardens and floral design have occupied her—with what guidance I could give—have been pretty much her life, really. Now in the old days, I confess, before her father was taken from us—I lost Mr. Harris in the dreadfully hot summer of '48 (People don't generally realize what a dreadful year that was—the worst year for perennials and annuals, alike, since Terrible '30. Things died that year that I didn't think would *ever* die. A dreadful summer)—why, she used then to run here and there with people of every sort, it seemed. I put no restraint upon her, understand. How many times I've said to my Franny, "You must make your own life, my child, as you would have it." Yes, in those days she used to run here and there with people of every sort and variety, it seemed to me. Where was it you say you met, for she goes so few places that are really *out* any more? But Mr. Harris would let me put no restraint upon her. I still remember the strongheadedness of her teens that had to be overcome and the testiness in her character when she was nearer to twenty than thirty. And you should have seen her as a tot of twelve when she would be somersaulting and rolling about on this very spot. Honestly, I see that child now, the mud on her middy-blouse and her straight yellow hair in her eyes.

When I used to come back from visiting my people at Rye, she would grit her teeth at me and give her confidence to the black cook. I would find my own child become a mad little animal. It was through this door here from the sun-room that I came one September afternoon —just such an afternoon as this, young man—still wearing my traveling suit, and called to my child across the yard for her to come and greet me. I had been away for the two miserable summer months, caring for my sick mother, but at the sight of me the little Indian turned and with a whoop she ran to hide in the scraggly privet hedge which was at the far end of the yard. I called her twice to come from out that filthiest of shrubs. "Frances Ann!" We used to call her by her full name when her father was alive. But she didn't stir. She crouched at the roots of the hedge and spied at her travel-worn mother between the leaves.

I pleaded with her at first quite indulgently and good-naturedly and described the new ruffled dress and the paper cut-outs I had brought from her grandmother at Rye. (I wasn't to have Mother much longer, and I knew it, and it was hard to come home to this kind of scene.) At last I threatened to withhold my presents until Thanksgiving or Christmas. The cook in the kitchen may have heard some change in my tone, for she came to the kitchen door over beyond the lattice work which we've since put up, and looked out first at me and then at the child. While I was threatening, my daughter crouched in the dirt and began to mumble things to herself which I could not hear, and the noises she made were like those of an angry little cat. It seems that it was a warmer afternoon than this one —but my garden does deceive—and I had been moving about in my heavy traveling suit. In my exasperation I stepped out into the rays of the sweltering sun, and into the yard which I so detested; and I uttered in a scream the child's full name, "Frances Ann Harris!" Just then the black cook stepped out onto the back porch, but I ordered her to return to the kitchen. I began to cross the yard toward Frances Ann—that scowling little creature who was *incredibly* the same Frances you've met—and simultaneously she began to crawl along the hedgerow toward the wire fence that divided my property from the neighbor's.

I believe it was the extreme heat that made me speak so very harshly and with such swiftness as to make my words incomprehensible. When I saw that the child had reached the fence and intended climbing it, I pulled off my hat, tearing my veil to pieces as I hurried my pace. I don't actually know what I was saying—I probably couldn't have told you even a moment later—and I didn't even feel any pain from the turn which I gave my ankle in the gulley across the middle of the yard. But the child kept her nervous little eyes on me and her lips continued to move now and again. Each time her lips moved I believed I must have raised my voice in more intense rage and greater horror at her ugliness. And so, young man, striding straight through the hedge I reached her before she had climbed to the top of the wire fencing. I think I took her by the arm above the elbow, about here, and I said something like, "I shall have to punish you, Frances

Ann." I did not jerk her. I didn't jerk her one bit, as she wished to make it appear, but rather, as soon as I touched her, she relaxed her hold on the wire and fell to the ground. But she lay there—in her canniness—only the briefest moment looking up and past me through the straight hair that hung over her face like an untrimmed mane. I had barely ordered her to rise when she sprang up and moved with such celerity that she soon was out of my reach again. I followed—running in those high heels— and this time I turned my other ankle in the gulley, and I fell there on the ground in that yard, this garden. You won't believe it—pardon, I must sit down. . . . I hope you don't think it too odd, my telling you all this. . . . You won't believe it: I lay there in the ditch and she didn't come to aid me with childish apologies and such, but instead she deliberately climbed into her swing that hung from the dirty old poplar that was here formerly (I have had it cut down and the roots dug up) and she be- gan to swing, not high and low, but only gently, and stared straight down at her mother through her long hair— which, you may be sure, young man, I had cut the very next day at my own beautician's and curled into a hun- dred ringlets.

The Little Cousins

———•❧•———

To the annual Veiled Prophet's Ball children were not
cordially invited. High up in the balcony, along with servants and poor relations, they were tolerated. Their presence was even sometimes suffered in the lower tiers and,
under certain circumstances, even down in the boxes. But,
generally speaking, children were expected to enjoy the
Prophet's parade the night before and be content to go to
bed without complaint on the night of the Ball. This was
twenty-five years ago, of course. There is no telling what
the practices are out there in St. Louis now. Children
have it much better everywhere nowadays. Perhaps they
flock to the Veiled Prophet's Ball by the hundred, and
even go to the Statler Hotel for breakfast afterward.

But I can't help hoping they don't. I hope they are

denied something. Else what do they have that's tangible
to hold against the grownups? My sister and I were denied
*every*thing. She more than I, since a boy naturally didn't
want so much—or so much of what it was St. Louis
seemed to offer us. Having less to complain of myself,
however, I undertook to suffer a good many things for
Corinna. And she suffered a few for me. We were motherless, and very close to each other at times.

What I suffered for Corinna I suffered in silence. But
the grand thing about Corinna was that she could always
find the right words for my feelings as well as her own.
The outrage I felt, for example, at our being always taken
down to Sportsman's Park to see the Browns play and
never the Cardinals left me grimly inarticulate. But
Corinna would say for me that it seemed "such an empty
glory" to have box seats at the Browns' games. "Any fool
had rather sit in the bleachers and watch the Cardinals,"
she said, "than have the very best box seats to see a
Browns game." She phrased things beautifully. At our
house we had always to serve Dr. Pep instead of Coca-
Cola. Of this Corinna said, "It makes us seem so provincial." But we both knew that with a father like ours we
just had to endure these embarrassments. According to
Corinna, Daddy was "blind to the disadvantage he put us
at"—disadvantage, that is, with our friends at Mary Institute and Country Day. What's more, she had divined at
an early age what it was that blinded Daddy: It was always some friend or other of his who owned or manu-
factured the product imposed on us. We even had Bessie
Calhoun because of one of his friends—Bessie, from
Selma, Alabama, instead of some stylish, white foreign
governess who might be teaching us French or German.

"Except for Bessie," Corinna said, "we would be bilingual, like the Altvaders and the Tomlinsons."

The year Corinna and I were finally taken to the Ball, the project was kept a secret from us until the last moment—or practically. I came in from school at five-thirty, and Corinna had got home two hours before that, as usual. At the side door, which Bessie made us use on all days but Sunday in order to save "her floors," Corinna was waiting for me with narrow eyes and pursed lips. "You and I are going to the V.P. tonight," she said, "but they couldn't permit us the pleasures of anticipation. Isn't that typical?" The news had been broken to her when she came in from school and told Bessie she was going down the block to play. Corinna was already twelve at this time, and though at school she would never deign to associate with girls in the lower grades, out of school she spent most of her time playing with the younger children in our block. The little girls adored her, and I used to watch her sometimes, mothering them and supervising their games. She never seemed happier than then, and she often spoke of the younger children as her "little cousins." This, I suppose, was in fond allusion to all the tales we had listened to from Daddy, and from Bessie, too, about the horde of first, second and third cousins they each had grown up among—Daddy in Kentucky, Bessie in Alabama. At any rate, when Bessie told her she had to stay in and do her homework that afternoon, Corinna wasn't satisfied until she had wrung the reason out of her, and then, of course, she was indignant.

"*Why* didn't you tell me before, Bessie?" she said. "Two other girls in my class were lording it over everybody else today because *they're* going."

"That's it," said Bessie. "I didn't want you lording it over everybody you saw today. That's not the way I'm bringing you up. And I didn't want you being flighty about your lessons."

Corinna knew that Daddy must have told her not to tell us. Or she knew at least that Bessie had got his approval. Yet Bessie always pretended to do everything absolutely on her own authority. And this made life more difficult. This made us forget that she was merely someone hired to take charge of us. It made us try to reason with her about things, made us pretend to be sick sometimes in order to break down her resistance, made us nag at her continually for all kinds of privileges. Bessie's utter disregard for what we considered justice and reason was something else that made us forget who she was, and she never showed any fear of our telling on her or going over her head. Her favorite answer to our "whys" was "Because I said so" or "Because I said to." And if one of us gobbled up his dessert and begged for a share of the other's, Bessie was as apt as not to make the other one share. She was illogical, and she was inconsistent. When we were disobedient, she would hand out terrible punishments—dessertless days and movieless weekends—but then sometimes she would forget, or weaken of her own accord at the last moment. You could not tell about her.

There was her brutal frankness, too. Though she was as blind as Daddy to any need of ours to have our egos bolstered—such as by serving our friends the right drink —and as blind as he to our deep moral and intellectual failings—failings that we ourselves were aware of and often confessed to each other—still she never failed to notice the least sign of vanity in either of us. Corinna was beginning to worry about her looks, and when she asked Bessie whether she thought she would grow up to be as beautiful as a certain Mary Elizabeth Caswell, Bessie said, "Your legs are too thin. You'll have to do a lot of filling out before you can talk about that." I was proud of my drawing ability, and I tried to get Bessie to say she thought I might grow up to be an artist. "Do you like nature?" she said, and I had to admit what she already knew: flowers and trees had little attraction for me. Bessie only shook her head and gave me a doubting look.

Yet when I was sick in bed with mumps or measles she would often read my palm, and, among other glories, she saw that I would be a great musician. I objected that the singing teacher at school said I couldn't even carry a tune. "What does *he* know about how you may change if you keep trying? *I* know how little teachers know." It was when we were sick that we discovered Bessie's real talents and saw how indulgent she could be when she had a mind to. This made us sick a good deal; and pretended illness was one of our moral failings that Bessie was blind to. I never knew her to doubt a headache or a stomach ache or even "a funny feeling all over." When we were sick, she played cards with us, told our fortunes, read to us.

She read to us a lot even when we were well. She had taught school in Alabama before she came north and went into service, but it wasn't the kind of stories we were used to in St. Louis schools that she read to us. She read "Unc' Edinburg's Drowndin' " and "No Haid Pawn," and her favorites were the *Post* stories by Octavus Roy Cohen. When she read us those stories, she would sometimes throw back her head and laugh and slap her thigh the way she never did about anything else. We loved hearing her read, but we didn't ourselves think the stories were so funny. "Never mind," said Bessie. "*You* don't have to think they're funny."

In conversation Bessie had only two real subjects, and one of them was Mary Elizabeth Caswell. Mary Elizabeth was the bane of Corinna's existence. Bessie had brought up Mary Elizabeth to the age of thirteen. When our mother died, Mr. Caswell had sent Bessie over to us—supposedly for only a few days. I was five at the time and Corinna was eight. Mr. Caswell came to our house on several occasions during those first days and had long conferences with Bessie; it was finally decided between them that she would stay with us. Probably Mr. Caswell felt that Daddy's need was greater than his own. Though Mary Elizabeth was motherless, too, it was already known that Mr. Caswell was going to marry again within a few months. Besides, not only was Mary Elizabeth a big girl then, but her mother had been of an old family in the city and there was an abundance of aunts and other female relatives to guide her. And so *we* got Bessie, with the result that Corinna had to "spend her life," as she said, listening to unfavorable comparisons of herself to Mary Elizabeth.

Bessie's other subject was her own family down in Alabama and, more particularly, her half-sister, Lilly Belle Patton. Lilly Belle was a saint. Bessie assured us that Lilly Belle was nothing like her, had none of her bad temper and selfish ways, was always doing for others and asked nothing for herself. Lilly Belle was the finest looking, the smartest, and the best-natured of all Bessie's mama's eleven children. Yet she hadn't insisted on going through high school, the way Bessie had, and she hadn't married.

Bessie not only went through school and took to teaching afterward but the money she made teaching she spent foolishly—not on her mama, who was pretty greedy about money anyway, but on first one husband and then another. But Lilly Belle was content to stay at home and help Mama, who was certainly never much help to herself. Lilly Belle took in washing and looked after her little half brothers and sisters, of which Bessie was next-to-youngest, and even "adopted-like" two orphaned cousins. She was a hard church worker, a beautiful seamstress and laundress, she was the best cook in the whole town of Selma, she kept a garden that was the envy of everyone.

Corinna and I never tired of hearing about Lilly Belle, but for Corinna the most interesting part always was Lilly Belle's courtship. Lilly Belle never felt she could go off and marry while the younger children were still at home to be looked after, and by the time the younger ones were up and gone ("gone to the bad, most of them") Mama was too old to leave at home alone. But Lilly Belle had a faithful suitor, who had been waiting for her through all the years. He was, in fact, still waiting, and Lilly Belle wasn't even engaged to him. Sometimes Bessie had letters from a neighbor friend telling her she ought to make Lilly Belle have pity on Mr. Barker. It seems that on summer evenings he and Lilly Belle kept company sitting together on her front porch. Neighbors would hear their voices over there, and sometimes they would hear Mr. Barker break down and cry as he begged her "at least to get engaged" to him. But Lilly Belle knew what was right; she had taken a vow not even to get *engaged* while Mama lived. Sometimes, too, there would be a letter that Lilly Belle had asked the neighbor friend to write Bessie, warning her that Mama was "low sick." Bessie always "reckoned" Mama was really going this time. And Corinna would be on tenterhooks about it for days. She would try to linger in the mornings till the postman came, and she would rush home from school in the afternoon to see if there was any news. "If Mama goes this time," she would ask, "will Lilly Belle really get engaged to Mr. Barker?" And Bessie would reply, "Of course she will. She hasn't kept him waiting for nothing."

The unfavorable comparisons that Bessie made between herself and Lilly Belle were much more severe than those she made between Corinna and Mary Elizabeth. Yet, quite naturally, Corinna was able to think of Lilly Belle as a heroine of pure romance, whereas she saw Mary Elizabeth as a "pampered, spoiled, stuck-up thing." The worst of it was, Corinna was subject to wearing hand-me-downs from Mary Elizabeth. There was no need for it, of course, but Mr. Caswell and Daddy were that close. Or perhaps Bessie Calhoun was still *that* close to the Caswell family. The dresses would just appear in Corinna's closet and be allowed to hang there for her to ignore until she could resist them no longer. Once she had taken them down and begun wearing them, they became her favorite dresses. She may have managed to forget who it was they had belonged to. Or, without admitting it to me and perhaps not to herself, she may have remembered how lovely Mary Elizabeth had looked in them; because Corinna had never lacked opportunity for observing Mary Elizabeth Caswell firsthand. The older girl and Corinna were in the same school together until Corinna was ten. After that, Mary Elizabeth went off to finishing school for two years, but even so she was home for all the holidays, and she and her father and the stepmother would be at our house for meals or we would be at their house. Daddy, during these two years, had begun going about with a very stylish-looking young widow, who was a close friend of Mr. Caswell's second wife. Corinna and I knew this lady then as Mrs. Richards. It was not to be long before she would become our stepmother—a fact that deserves mention only because it explains why our family and the Caswells were now thrown together still more than formerly.

Bessie Calhoun had a clear recollection of every mark Mary Elizabeth ever received in the lower grades at Mary Institute. "Because of Mary Elizabeth," said Corinna, "I have to live in mortal dread of not making the honor roll." At an early age, Mary Elizabeth could cook and sew in a way that promised to rival the arts of Lilly Belle. This information cost Corinna many precious hours that might have been spent with her "little cousins." And because Mary Elizabeth had had a little pansy garden of her own, Corinna was sent "grubbing in the earth" every spring. On the other hand, Mary Elizabeth was almost certainly not the reader that Corinna was, or not the reader of novels—the old best-sellers on the shelves of what had been our mother's sitting room. One day Corinna inquired after Mary Elizabeth's reading habits. Bessie didn't answer right away—something unusual for her. Her eyes wandered about the room for a moment, and then she looked Corinna straight in the eye and said, "At your age that child read the Bible, honey." Corinna opened her mouth in astonishment and then she closed it again without saying anything. This was one time when both she and I doubted Bessie's veracity, but Corinna let it pass. There was a limit to what she would undertake. She never raised the question again.

We knew perfectly well why we were being taken to the Veiled Prophet's Ball. This was the year that Mary Elizabeth Caswell was going to be presented. As a matter of fact, Corinna had nagged Daddy about it one Sunday afternoon in the early fall. Since Mary Elizabeth was to be one of the debutantes this year, didn't he think Bessie might take us to watch from the balcony? ("Mary Elizabeth ought to be good for *something* to us," she had said to me in private beforehand.) But Daddy replied, "Don't be silly. You couldn't either of you stay awake that late. You can come downtown and watch the parade from my office the night before. One school night out will be enough." And, of course, we did go down and watch the parade. In fact, we went downtown for dinner with Daddy and Mrs. Richards, and the Caswells and some other grown-ups joined us at the office afterward. They all had a party, with drinks and hors d'oeuvres, while we tossed confetti out the window and watched the floats go by. I hadn't even realized that Mary Elizabeth wasn't present until Mrs. Caswell came over to the window where we were and said, "Mary Elizabeth's out with some of her own crowd, Corinna. But she told me to give you her love and say she would be thinking about you tomorrow night. She's dying for you to see her dress."

Suddenly Corinna leaned so far out the window that I thought she was sure to fall, and I grabbed hold of her.

"Stop it, stupid," she hissed. "Here comes the Prophet's float. The parade's nearly over."

Just below us was passing the last of the countless tab-
leaux representing life in French colonial times and in
the days of the Louisiana Territory. We had seen Lewis
and Clark, Marquette and Joliet, Indians, fur traders,
French peasant girls, river bullies from the days of the
keelboat and the pirogue. The parade had begun, for some
reason, with Jean Lafitte in the Old Absinthe House at
New Orleans, and the final tableau was of Thomas Jefferson signing the Louisiana Purchase. Beyond Jefferson, in
his oversized wig and silk knee breeches, I could see the
Prophet's float approaching. But I knew that for me the
best part of the parade was already over. After so many
Indians and fur traders, after the French explorers, after
the pirates, the Prophet, with his veil-hidden face and all
his Eastern finery, was bound to seem an anticlimax. I
stood beside Corinna, hardly watching the royal float go
by. As she continued to lean far out over the window
ledge, I quietly took hold of the sash of her dress and,
without her knowing it, held on to it tightly as long as we
remained at the window.

The night of the Ball, we had an early dinner without
Daddy. He came in and went up to dress while we were
still at the table. After dinner, he sent for us to come to his
room, where he said that he wanted us to behave ourselves
that night "as never before." He was going out to dinner
with the Caswells and Mrs. Richards and some other
friends, but he would send the car and chauffeur to fetch
us to the Colosseum. He didn't tell us that Bessie wasn't
going to accompany us or that we would be sitting with
him in one of the boxes downstairs.
And Bessie herself withheld this information till the

very last. When it was finally divulged, we had already been so dazzled by another piece of news that the evening before us and these unexpected arrangements seemed of little consequence. When we were both dressed, we went into the sewing room, where Bessie always sat in the evening, to have her look us over.

"How do I look?" Corinna asked.

"You look fine," said Bessie. Then she saw Corinna eying herself in the mirror stand, and she added, "But no better than you should."

Corinna went up on her tiptoes and said, "I ought to have on heels."

"Behave yourself tonight, Corinna," Bessie said. "And see that *he* does." She didn't look at me, even. Then leaning back in her chair she said, "I've got something to tell both of you."

"What?" said Corinna.

"I want you to behave yourself next week, too."

"Oh, I thought it was something," said Corinna.

"It *is* something. They've sent for me down home. I'll be gone on the train before you get home tonight."

Corinna stared at Bessie in the mirror. "It's Mama?" she asked, breathless. "*Tell* me, Bessie!"

Bessie nodded. "She's dead. She's been dead for two days. I've just been waiting around here to get tonight over."

Corinna observed a moment of silence. She knew that Mama had been "no pleasure to herself or anybody else" for several years now. Further, she knew that she had never heard Bessie say one good word for her mama, and that no commiseration was expected. But still, the respectful silence would be appreciated and would assure her getting answers to the questions she was bound to ask presently. She sat down on a wooden stool by the mirror and placed her feet, in their patent leather slippers, close together. She sat there smoothing the black velvet skirt over her knees. "Lilly Belle?" she said. "Is she engaged to Mr. Barker yet?"

Bessie nodded again. "She already has Mr. Barker's ring on her finger."

Now it was safe for Corinna to look up. "Will it be a long engagement?" she asked, still restraining herself somewhat.

"I'm going to stay over for the wedding Sunday week."

Corinna sprang to her feet. "Bessie!" she said. "Let me lend you my Brownie so you can bring us some pictures!"

Bessie shook her head. "Never mind about that. Lilly Belle's not going to get herself married to Mr. Barker without some high-type photographer there."

"Bessie, I wish I could go with you! Remember *every*-thing."

"When did I forget anything, Corinna? Is there anything I haven't told you about Lilly Belle before this? I'll tell you one thing now. She's going to marry in her mourning, with a black veil to the floor."

Corinna sat down on the stool again, obviously stunned —more by the striking picture in her mind than by the impropriety. But presently she did ask, "Will that be quite proper, though, Bessie?"

"Of course it's proper, if black becomes you like it does Lilly Belle."

Corinna fixed her gaze on the wastebasket in the far corner of the room. "Do you think—" she began, speaking in a tone at once admiring and suspicious. "Do you think maybe she's kept Mr. Barker waiting just so she could marry in black?"

"How can you ask that, Corinna? Do you suppose Lilly Belle's as vain as *you* are?" Then she got up from her chair and said, "It's time for you-all to start downstairs. That car will be here."

It was only after we were out in the upstairs hall that we realized she wasn't going with us. At first, Corinna said she would refuse to go without her. It would be much more fun just to stay at home and talk, she said. "Yes," said Bessie heavily. "I can just see us sending word to your daddy and Mrs. Richards that you've decided to stay home and talk to Bessie."

"Then you'll *have* to come with us," Corinna said. "How can we go by ourselves?"

"Yes, 'have' to come with you," Bessie said. "Can't you just see me in my six-dollar silk sitting down there in the box with you-all and the Caswells." That was the first we knew of where we would be sitting.

We heard Mrs. Richards' voice downstairs; she had convinced Daddy that he couldn't merely have the chauffeur pick us up and have us arrive at the Colosseum by ourselves. And so there Daddy and Mrs. Richards were, waiting for us at the foot of the stairs. As Bessie helped Corinna into her Sunday coat, she said in an undertone, "Behave yourself, Corinna. Don't act silly. Remember this isn't just something gay tonight. I suspect you'll see folks crying. You know, it'll be like a wedding or funeral. There'll be something sad about seeing Mary Elizabeth and all of those other debutantes walking out in their white dresses."

Then we started down, with Bessie still watching from

the head of the stairs and Daddy and Mrs. Richards waiting below.

Only a scene as strange and brilliant as that in the Colosseum could have made Corinna forget Lilly Belle altogether. But perhaps the pleasures of anticipation made
her begin forgetting in the car. Or it might have been the
sight of Mrs. Richards in her furs at the foot of the stairs.
I had noticed before that night that with Mrs. Richards
Corinna could be counted on to act more grown up than
she did with anyone else. As we rode through town to the
Colosseum, she and Mrs. Richards conversed, it seemed to
me, with wonderful ease. Mrs. Richards had been a Special Maid at the Veiled Prophet's Court when she was a
debutante some fifteen years before. She described the excitement of it as though it had been only yesterday—how
you waited behind the curtains to hear the herald call out
your name, and then how you heard, or imagined you
heard, the gasps of surprise from the throngs whose admiring eyes would presently be focused on you as you
walked, trembling, the length of the Colosseum, and knelt
before the Prophet to be crowned, and then took your
place on the dais.

For me, the Colosseum was like the most unreal of
dreams. Before that night it had meant to me a wide
sawdust arena with metal girders overhead and sur-
rounded by gloomy, often half-empty tiers of seats. It was
where I was taken to watch the annual horse show, the
radio show, and the Boy Scout Jamboree. Now it had been
transformed, by untold yards of bunting and by acres of
white canvas on the floor, into a quite cheerful, if rather
bathroomy-looking, ballroom. At one end were the thrones

of the Prophet and his Queen-to-be, on a raised dais underneath a tasseled canopy, and they were flanked on either side by tiers of folding chairs provided for members of the Court. At the other end were the immense and immaculate white portières through which the entrances of all persons of the first importance would be made.

After a drill by the Prophet's Guard of Bengal Lancers, the Prophet himself, attired in splendid medieval-Oriental garments and with his face veiled, made his duly ceremonious entrance. I was so bedazzled by the drill of the Prophet's guards and then by the arrival of the pirates and fur traders and Indians I had seen on the floats the night before that I hardly noticed when the Matrons of Honor began filing past our front-row box. These ladies, perhaps forty of them, circled the whole arena and at last took the places reserved for them on the Prophet's left. Even when the debutantes themselves, in white dresses and long white gloves, began to file by, I found it hard not just to sit there peering between them for glimpses of the people in costumes, who now occupied their places in the Court.

It was Corinna who brought me down to earth and reminded me of where my attention ought to be directed. She didn't do it intentionally, with a nudge or a cross whisper, but by her erratic behavior. She was sitting on the edge of her chair and leaning halfway across my lap trying to see the faces of the debutantes, who were now emerging from a small gateway on our side of the arena. I felt that she ought to wait and see them when they passed before our box.

"Stop," I said, trying to push her from in front of me.

"Oh, hush," she said, not budging.

She and I were in the very front row, and I glanced over my shoulder to see if Daddy had noticed her behavior. I discovered that he, along with everybody else in the box, was beaming at her. I was glad they couldn't see her face, or couldn't see it as well as I could, or at any rate didn't know what her narrowed-eyes-and-pursed-lips expression meant. Everything suddenly became clear to me. I knew what all the adults' smiling indulgence meant. Mary Elizabeth Caswell was going to have a place of honor in the Prophet's Court, and they expected Corinna to be thrilled by this. But I knew what tortures Corinna was suffering. Probably she was wishing I had let her fall out of that window last night. For, after this, how could she hope to measure up to Mary Elizabeth? It was hopeless. Now I began watching the faces of the girls as intently as she.

When the last debutante had passed us, Mrs. Richards leaned forward, smiling, and said to Corinna, "I didn't see Mary Elizabeth, did you?" And, somehow, probably just because it *was* Mrs. Richards, Corinna managed to give her a very knowing, grown-up smile. When she turned around and faced the arena, she sat staring straight ahead with a glazed look.

After this came the separate entrances of the four Special Maids, each summoned individually to the Court of Love and Beauty by the Prophet's herald, each making her entrance between the great portières and walking the length of the arena with measured steps and drawing after her a wide satin train. How I prayed each time that the next would be Mary Elizabeth! But already I knew that Mary Elizabeth would be nothing less than the Queen. Corinna knew it, too. By the time that awful announcement came, Corinna was even able to turn and smile at Mr. and Mrs. Caswell.

"His Mysterious Majesty, the Veiled Prophet, commands me to summon to his court of Love and Beauty to reign as Queen for one year. . . . Miss Mary Elizabeth Caswell." That was all. The Queen's subjects came to their feet. Between the white portières Mary Elizabeth appeared, arrayed in her white silk coronation gown, its bodice and its wide skirts embroidered all over with pearls and sparkling beads; her slender arms held gracefully, if just a little too stiffly, away from her body and encased in pure white kid so perfectly and smoothly fitted that only the occasional trembling of Mary Elizabeth's hands could suggest there were real hands and arms beneath; and her hair, her head of golden blond hair, fairly shimmering under the brilliant lights that now shone down on her from somewhere up among the panoplied steel girders. The orchestra, perched in a lofty spot directly above the portières, began to play. To the strains of "Pomp and Circumstance," Mary Elizabeth moved across our vision, with four liveried pages holding up the expanse of her bejewelled train—moved across the white canvas floor of the Colosseum toward her throne.

When the brief coronation ceremony was finished, the Prophet took his Queen's hand and led her out onto the floor for their dance. After only a few measures, the guards broke their formation, each of them going to seek the hand of one of the debutantes as a dancing partner. The Ball had officially commenced.

Very soon, Daddy and Mrs. Richards went out on the floor, with the Caswells, to congratulate the Queen and to join in the dancing themselves. Corinna and I were urged to come along, but I rejected the idea even quicker than Corinna did. We would wait in the box and find a chance to congratulate Mary Elizabeth later.

In almost no time, the floor was crowded with dancers. All but those who sat in the balcony were free to participate. Corinna and I sat with our elbows on the rail of the box, staring into the crowd. It was curious to see the Prophet's guards dancing in their heavy shoes, and it was most curious to me to see in how many instances there was a person in costume dancing with someone in ordinary evening clothes. I was seeking among the dancers for Mary Elizabeth and the Prophet.

It was Corinna, of course, who spied Mary Elizabeth first. "There she is," she said in a perfectly flat voice, indicating where with a tilt of her head, being very careful not to point. "She's not dancing with the Prophet any more."

And then I saw her out there, not twenty feet from us, dancing with a dark-haired young man in white tie and tails. Just as I caught my first glimpse of her, another young man tapped this one on the shoulder, and she changed partners. She was, as Corinna might have phrased it, the cynosure of all eyes.

Corinna was on her feet. She cupped her hands to her mouth and shouted, "Lilly Belle's engaged!"

Mary Elizabeth couldn't hear her above the music. But she stopped dancing and started toward us, leading her partner by the hand. The other dancers respectfully made way for her. When she had come about half the distance, Corinna called out again, "Lilly Belle's engaged!"

"No!" Mary Elizabeth called back, and her voice and

her radiant countenance expressed astonishment and delight. "Is it Mr. Barker?"

"None other!" said Corinna in her most grown-up tone. Mary Elizabeth was hurrying toward us now, and I beheld the spectacle of Corinna and Mary Elizabeth Caswell throwing their arms about each other. In that moment all was forgiven—all those splendid accomplishments, and all those unfavorable comparisons: forgiven forever. That which had separated them for so long had now united them.

"But Bessie didn't tell me!" Mary Elizabeth was saying. "She was by, this very morning, to have a close-up look at my dress."

"It's gorgeous," said Corinna.

"Isn't it!" And now another embrace.

"She told me just before I left the house," said Corinna. (Told *me*, not *us?* Before *I*, not *we,* left the house? How selfish that sounded.) "The wedding's Sunday week. And Lilly Belle's going to marry in her mourning veil!"

"Oh, no! Stop it!" cried Mary Elizabeth, and she and Corinna shrieked with laughter.

"Bessie's taking the train to Alabama late tonight," Corinna said when she had got her breath again.

"Oh, that wonderful Bessie!" said Mary Elizabeth. "Isn't she splendid!"

"Have you seen her?"

"Seen her?"

"Up there," said Mary Elizabeth, pointing to the balcony opposite us. "I spotted her a while ago and waved to her."

"Why, she didn't tell me she was coming!" said Corinna. "Isn't that typical?"

The two girls tried to locate Bessie again but soon gave it up. Next, I heard Mary Elizabeth introducing us to her partner, referring to us as her two "little cousins," and realized that Bessie must have talked to her about us. She went on to say how brilliant Corinna was in school and how well I could draw and what "perfect lambs" we both were.

I didn't stop searching for Bessie when they did, and I didn't hear what they were saying any longer. My eyes traveled up one row of the balcony and down the next, searching for Bessie's green silk dress. The crowd up there was thinning out; the poor relations and the children and the servants were going home. Bessie had likely hurried off to catch her train. Already I felt that I might never see Bessie Calhoun again.

But I kept on looking for her until I could bear my lonely thoughts no longer. I put my arms on the railing before me, hid my face in them, and commenced to sob.

Instantly all attention was turned toward me, but I wouldn't look up or answer questions. In a matter of seconds Daddy and Mrs. Richards arrived.

"What is it, honey?" I heard Mrs. Richards say.

"He's just tired," Daddy said. "He's not used to being up so late. This is what it means, bringing children to something like this."

Then I was led to a seat at the rear of the box, where I wouldn't be so conspicuous. The Caswells had returned, too, now. I heard Mrs. Caswell say, "Poor little fellow," and this evoked fresh tears and deeper sobs.

"What is it, Son?" Daddy said. "You must try to tell me."

Finally I knew I had to say something—something that

would sound reasonable to him. I swallowed hard and lifted my face and found Daddy. I don't know whether or not I knew what I was going to say before I said it. What I said was "Bessie's mama is dead."

"How did you know that, Son?" Daddy asked.

"She told me just before I was leaving the house to-night," I said. Then I hid my face and tried to begin crying again, but I couldn't.

"How awful of her!" I heard Mrs. Richards say, threateningly. "How really unspeakably awful!"

I sat with my face in my hands. After a moment I felt someone's arm go around my shoulder. I didn't know or care whose it was. Probably it was my father's, though it may have been Mrs. Richards', or even Corinna's. Whosever it was, it didn't have the feel I wanted, and I purposely kept my face hidden until it had been removed.

Guests

———◆———

The house was not itself. Relatives were visiting from the country. It was an old couple this time, an old couple who could not sleep after the sun was up and who began yawning as soon as dinner was over in the evening. They were silent at table, leaving the burden of conversation to their host and hostess, and they declined all outside invitations issued in their honor. Cousin Johnny was on a strict diet. Yet wanting to be no trouble, both he and Cousin Annie refused to reveal any principle of his diet. If he couldn't eat what was being served, he would do without. They made their own beds, washed out their own tubs, avoided using salad forks and butter knives. Upon arriving, they even produced their own old-fashioned ivory napkin rings, and when either of them chanced to spill something on the table cloth, they begged the nearest Negro servant's pardon. As a result, everybody, including the servants, was very uncomfortable from the moment the old couple entered the house.

Edmund Harper, their host, was most uncomfortable of all. What's more, he had to conceal the fact from his wife, Henrietta, because otherwise he would be accused of "not seeing her through." Henrietta was a planner, an arranger, a straighten-outer—especially of other people's lives. Somehow she always managed to involve Edmund in her good works, and never more so than when it was a matter of relatives from the country. Cousin Johnny and Cousin Annie, for instance, had clearly not wanted to make this visit. In fact, they had struggled valiantly against Henrietta's siege. But they couldn't withstand Henrietta's battering for very long. Henrietta knew that neither of them had ever set foot in the capital city of Nashville; and she couldn't bear the thought of the poor old souls' not seeing Nashville before they died. It ended by Edmund's going with Henrietta in her car to bring the unwilling visitors "bodily" into Nashville.

Some weeks before the visit, Henrietta had written a letter suggesting that she might enter the old couple's house and do their packing for them—that is, if Cousin Annie didn't feel up to it. And this was what finally made Cousin Annie run up the white flag and pretend to accept Henrietta's terms. Come what might, the old lady's little clapboard Gothic citadel, with its bay windows and gingerbread porches, was *not* going to be entered. In its upright posture on the rockiest hill of Cousin Johnny's stock farm —a farm where the land was now mostly rented out and the stock disposed of, because of Cousin Johnny's advanced years—the house was like Cousin Annie's very soul, and it would be defended at all costs. The morning that Henrietta's new Chrysler car turned through the stone gateposts at the bottom of the hill, the old lady not only had herself and her husband thoroughly packed up, she had them fully dressed for their journey, their hats on their heads, and, with the door to the house already stoutly locked, they were seated side by side on the porch swing—rigid as two pieces of graveyard statuary. As the car pulled up the hill, turning cautiously between the scrub pines and the cedar trees, Edmund Harper saw Cousin Annie rise slowly, in one continuous, wraithlike movement, from her place in the swing. Once on her feet, she stood there still and erect as a sentinel. In the swing, which until now had remained motionless, Cousin Johnny permitted himself a quick, little solo flight, so short and tentative that he must barely have touched his toe to the porch floor. Edmund interpreted this motion as a favorable sign. But then, almost immediately, he saw the old lady's hand go out to one of the swing's chains. The mere touch of her gloved hand was enough to halt the swing, but for several moments she kept her hand there on the chain. And the figures of the two old people, thus arranged, made a kind of *tableau vivant*, which Edmund was to carry in his mind throughout the visit.

For twenty-five years, Edmund had been seeing Henrietta through such plans as the present one. Three country nieces had been presented to Nashville society from the Harper house. Countless nephews had stayed there while working their way through the University—or as far through it as it seemed practicable for them to try to go. And Henrietta scarcely ever returned from a visit back home without bringing news of some ailing connection who needed to see a Nashville specialist, needed a place to stay while seeing the specialist, needed a place to stay while convalescing from the inevitable operation. The worst of all this, for Edmund, was not what he was called upon to do during these visitations but what he was called upon to feel, and the moral support he was expected to give Henrietta. For something nearly always went wrong. Two of the three nieces had eloped with worthless louts from back home before their seasons in Nashville were half over. Most of the countless nephews had taken to a wild life, for which their parents tended to blame the influence of the Harper household more than that of university and fraternity life. Worse still, the convalescents always outstayed their welcome, and Edmund had to support Henrietta in taking a firm hand when it was time for each poor old creature to return to his or her nearest of kin in the country.

In a sense, though, these larger projects of Henrietta's had been less trying for Edmund than the smaller ones— the ones that she had gone in for in recent years. She had turned more and more to brightening the lives of people like Cousin Johnny and Cousin Annie, people whose lives didn't seem absolutely to require her touch. It was three and four day visits from the likes of Cousin Johnny and Cousin Annie that Edmund found it hardest to adjust to —visits from people not really too far removed from his own generation. He found a part of himself always reaching out and wanting to communicate with them and another part forever holding back, as though afraid of what *would* be communicated. And the same seemed to be true for the guests themselves, particularly for the men.

Cousin Johnny Kincaid was not, of course, a real con-

temporary of Edmund Harper's. There was a twelve
years difference in their ages. Edmund was fifty-eight, and
Cousin Johnny was seventy. It was a delicate difference. A
certain respect was due the older man, but it had to be
manifested in a way that would not offend him and make
him feel that he was an old man and that Edmund was
not. On the second day of the visit, when the old couple's
silence had already become pretty irksome to her, Henrietta telephoned Edmund at his office and said that she
had a simple suggestion to make. At breakfast she had noticed that Cousin Johnny seemed to wince every time Edmund addressed him as "Cousin" Johnny. She thought he
might be sensitive about his age. She suggested that that
night Edmund should try calling him just plain Johnny.

Now, this was the kind of thing that was always coming
up. It seemed that every year Henrietta had to dig deeper
into the kin and deeper into the country to find suitable
objects for her good works. The couples were invariably
rather distant kin of his or hers, people Edmund had
known all his life but not known very well. Either Edmund couldn't remember what he had called them as a
boy or he had literally never called them anything. But
the problem had never come into such focus as it did now.
On the telephone he didn't dispute Henrietta's point,
though it was inconceivable to him that Cousin Johnny
had ever in his seventy years winced over a small matter
of personal vanity—if that's what it was. Since, at the moment of the telephone call, Edmund's law partner was
with him in his office and since the firm's most moneyed
and currently most troubled client was also there, Edmund said only, "I'll see what I can do about it tonight."

And he wrote the word "Johnny" on the pad of paper in front of him.

"I can tell from your voice that you're terribly busy," Henrietta said apologetically.

"No, not particularly," Edmund said.

"I probably shouldn't have called about something so—"

"Oh, nonsense!" Edmund laughed. And he wound up the conversation in hearty tones meant to convince everybody in earshot of his imperturbability.

But it *was* a serious matter, of course. And when he put down the telephone he still sat for a moment staring rather intently at the instrument. As a matter of fact, he was trying to think the problem through right then and there. It was his habit of mind, as a good trial lawyer, to think any question through and find a positive answer to it as soon as it came up. It wasn't the truth of Henrietta's observation he was debating; he had long since accepted her contention that she was "more sensitive to people" than he was, and so he had to assume that she was right about something like this. Nor was it a question of his willingness to do what she asked of him. It was a simple matter of whether or not he could bring himself to call Cousin Johnny Kincaid just plain "Johnny." Then in a flash he saw he could. He could because—but he didn't go into that at the time. The immediate question was answered, and he was free now to return to his client's urgent affairs.

It wasn't till several hours later that he let himself think again about this silly piece of business that Henrietta had cooked up. He was driving home from work in his hardtop convertible, and the moment he opened the subject with himself, his mind took him back to the previous day. They were making the return trip from the country, with Cousin Annie and Cousin Johnny in the car. It was a seventy-five mile drive back into Nashville; they had to pass through sections of three counties. Since they were in Henrietta's car, she was doing the driving, and she was providing most of the conversation, too. Cousin Annie, wearing a plain black coat and an even plainer black hat, was in the front seat beside Henrietta. In the back seat of the big car the two long-legged men sat in opposite corners, each with one leg crossed stiffly over the other. They had traveled some twelve or fifteen miles when something made Edmund glance down at Cousin Johnny's foot. He found himself observing with great interest the high-topped shoe, the lisle sock held up by an elastic supporter, and, since it was still early April, the long underwear showing above the sock where the old man's trouser leg was pulled up.

Somehow to be thus reminded that there were still men who dressed in the old style was unaccountably pleasant to Edmund. At the same time it saddened him, too. For here was the kind of old man that he had once upon a time supposed he would himself someday become. And now he knew, of course, he never would. It seemed like being denied an experience without which life wouldn't be complete. It seemed almost the same as discovering that no matter how long he lived he would never *be* an old man. For how could you really *be* old and have it mean anything if you lived in a world where you weren't expected to dress and behave in a special way, in a world

where you went on dressing and trying to behave like
a young man or at least a middle-aged man till the very
end? It was bad enough to be childless and therefore
grandchildless, as he and Henrietta of course were, without also being denied any prospect of ever *feeling* or
being *treated* like a grandfather, something which Cousin
Johnny, also childless and grandchildless, must for a long
time now have felt and been treated like. Edmund found
the subject absorbing.

The foot gave an involuntary little kick, and Edmund
realized that this was probably what had drawn his attention to it in the first place. The twitch was presently
followed by another and then, at irregular intervals, by
another and another. This was bound to interest a mind
like Edmund's, especially in its present mood. With his
lawyer's eye he soon made out that the kicks occurred always when the car was passing a field where cattle grazed.
He wasn't surprised when Cousin Johnny finally came
right out with it: "Seems like the livestock gets fatter
every mile we pull in towards Nashville." But as soon as
he had said this the old man's eyes narrowed and he bit
his lower lip with such vehemence that it was plain he
wished it was his tongue he was biting. His utterance had
been as involuntary as any of those kicks his foot was giving.

It was as if Fate and Cousin Annie had been waiting together for such a slip from him. The car had just left a
fine stretch of low ground where he had seen the herd
that brought forth his comment. Now the car was climbing a long, wooded hill, and in a little clearing near the
summit Cousin Annie spied a herd of bunched-up,
scrawny, and altogether sorry-looking milk cows. For the

only time during the long trip, she turned around and showed her face to the two men in the back seat. And it was only the profile of her face, at that. She merely turned and stared out the window, on Cousin Johnny's side, at those cows in the clearing.

"Yes, but—" Cousin Johnny began, exactly as though the old lady had spoken. And then, Cousin Annie having already turned her back to him again, he broke off. That was the whole of the interchange between them. When Cousin Johnny spoke again, which was surprisingly soon, Edmund felt his words had no reference to what had passed between him and Cousin Annie. He said directly to Edmund, "I guess a fellow who's been concerned with cattle as long as I have won't ever see much out a car window but cows, no matter where he goes."

It was some kind of an apology. An apology for what? For a certain boorishness he felt he had been guilty of? An apology for his own narrow interest in life. Or was it, rather, an indication of the old man's awareness of the figure he must be cutting with Edmund?

Edmund's reply to the outburst and the apology was a ten-minute discourse on the history of stock farming in Middle Tennessee. Most of what he said came out of some research he had had one of the young men in his office do for a case he had tried a few years back. He wasn't showing off. He was honestly trying to reassure Cousin Johnny and to draw him out, because already Edmund's interest in this man and his desire to win his confidence and to find a common ground on which they could meet was considerable. But the discourse on cattle farming did not produce a single remark from Cousin Johnny.

A long silence followed. Then there was a period of

give-and-take between Henrietta and Cousin Annie about the illnesses and deaths of various relatives. After that, there was more silence. Cousin Johnny's lips seemed to have been permanently sealed. But in the last miles before Nashville, his caution must have been lulled by Henrietta's fresh chatter about the Nashville sights they would be seeing in the days just ahead. When a colossal city limits sign suddenly hove into view at the roadside, Cousin Johnny's mouth dropped open. "Why," he said. "It's a funny thing. When I was just married and was still just a young fellow, I almost came here to work." It was as if until then he hadn't known, or hadn't believed, where it was they were taking him. "In a shoe factory, it was. But my wife and I decided against it. I was to start at the bottom and maybe later go on the road for them."

How different the whole visit might have been if Cousin Johnny had not said that. Because, after that, Edmund Harper would have consented to almost any scheme of Henrietta's to promote understanding between him and his house guest. Why, what wonderful things mightn't they say to each other if only they could talk together man to man! In a flight of fancy that was utterly novel to him, Edmund visualized Cousin Johnny as he would have appeared today had he taken that job at the shoe factory. He saw him now as president of the shoe company after years of working up from the bottom, and saw himself as a country lawyer in Nashville on a visit with his rich relatives. Why, it was *Maud Muller* twice reversed! Moreover, that client Edmund was going to see in his office tomorrow morning and who had been in his office nearly every day for the past two weeks, that richest and currently most troubled of the firm's clients, was none other than the president of a shoe company, probably the very shoe company that Cousin Johnny would have gone to work for. . . . *That* was precisely how Cousin Johnny might have turned out. And to think it was only a difference of seventy-five miles.

Cousin Johnny's response to being called just plain "Johnny" was, to say the least, disconcerting. He did exactly what Henrietta said he had done when Edmund called him "Cousin Johnny." He winced. He drew in his chin—almost imperceptibly, though not quite—batted his eyes, and gave his head a quick little shake. And then, as Edmund hurried on to finish the long sentence which he had dropped his "Johnny" in the midst of, Cousin Johnny gazed past Edmund into a fire the houseboy had just now lit in the fireplace. Plainly he was trying to decide how he liked the sound of it—the sound of his Christian name on the lips of this man, this strange kind of man who could come in from work at four-thirty in the afternoon, disappear above stairs to change from a dark double-breasted suit to a plaid jacket and gray trousers, and then reappear and settle down to a long evening, without ever mentioning the work that had kept him all day.

Edmund had carefully waited, before springing that "Johnny" on the old man, till a moment when Henreitta and Cousin Annie were well on the other side of the living room. Afterward, he realized that Henrietta had been conspiring with him without his knowing it. She had lured Cousin Annie over there beyond the piano to see a scrapbook that she kept in the piano bench for just such moments. During the hour since Edmund came in the house, she hadn't mentioned the subject of their telephone conversation. But she knew well enough that he

was going to follow her suggestion. And he knew what
her attitude would be by now; they were in this together,
and she wanted to make his part as easy for him as possible—and as interesting. One quick glance told him
that however much he had tried to slur his articulation of
the name, Henrietta had heard it. As for Cousin Annie,
whose back was toward him, he could not at the moment
tell whether or not she heard. Probably he could not have
told if he had had a clear view of her face. And, for that
matter, the incident was to pass without his knowing
what conclusion Cousin Johnny had reached—whether he
did or didn't like the sound of it.

They went into dinner at six o'clock. At first the table
talk was livelier than it had been the previous night.
Cousin Annie, right away, spoke a number of complete
sentences which were not dragged out of her by direct
questions. She spoke with enthusiasm of the sights they
had taken in that day: the Parthenon, the capital building,
old Fort Nashboro. There was, in fact, every indication
that matters had taken a real turn for the better. Edmund
found himself wondering if Cousin Annie weren't going
to turn out to be like all the other country ladies who had
come here in recent years—vain, garrulous, and utterly
susceptible to the luxuries of Henrietta's commodious,
well staffed, elegantly appointed house. The bright look
on Henrietta's face at the opposite end of the table informed him that she was thinking the same thing. And
then, as though conscious of just how far into the woods
she had led them, Cousin Annie Kincaid began quietly
closing in.

"You mustn't think," she said, "that Mr. Kincaid and
I can't dine at whatever your accustomed dinner hour is."

This was very much in her usual vein—making known her awareness that they were dining earlier than was normal for the Harpers. Since the houseboy was removing the soup bowls at the time, it might have been supposed that what she said was meant for his ears and that she had phrased it with that in mind. But the old lady wasn't long in finding another occasion to refer to Cousin Johnny as "Mr. Kincaid." She did it a third and fourth time, even. Each time it was as if she feared they hadn't understood her before. Finally, though, she made it absolutely clear. During the meat course, while everyone except Cousin Johnny was working away at the roast lamb and baked potatoes, she drove the point home to her own satisfaction. "It isn't that Mr. Kincaid doesn't like roast lamb," she said, addressing herself to Edmund and speaking in the most old-fashioned country-genteel voice that Edmund had heard since he was a boy at home. "It isn't that he doesn't like roast lamb," she repeated. "It's that he dined alone with ladies at noon and so had to eat the greater share of an uncommonly fine cut of sirloin steak. He isn't, you understand, used to eating a great deal of meat." Now she turned to Henrietta. "He seldom eats any meat at all for supper. . . ." Edmund, remembering the other country ladies who had sat where Cousin Annie now sat, supposed that she would continue endlessly on this fascinating subject. But once she saw that she had the attention of both host and hostess, she suddenly turned to Cousin Johnny and said genially, "You seldom eat any meat at all for supper, do you, Mr. Kincaid?" It was the voice of a woman from an earlier generation than the Harpers', addressing her husband with the respect due a husband. How could anyone call him just plain Johnny after that?

The meat course was finished in almost total silence, but Edmund had two things to think about. After putting her question to Cousin Johnny, Cousin Annie had turned a triumphant gaze on Henrietta, indicating that she recognized who her real adversary was. That was one thing. The other thing was Cousin Johnny's response to being addressed as Mr. Kincaid. There was but one way to describe it. He winced. And there was but one conclusion that Edmund could draw: The poor fellow had lived so long in isolation that he would always wince when singled out in company and addressed directly by any name whatever.

Cousin Annie and Cousin Johnny retired within less than thirty minutes after dinner. As soon as they were safely upstairs, Edmund expected Henrietta to launch into Cousin Annie's performance. She did nothing of the kind. While he was setting up the card table and fetching the cards for a game of double solitaire, she turned on the television set and stood switching aimlessly from one channel to another—a practice she often criticized him for. She seemed to be avoiding conversation. Once they were seated at the table with the cards laid out and the television playing a favorite Western, Edmund said cozily, *"They* disapprove of cards, and *they* detest TV." These were two points that Cousin Annie had made clear the first night.

"I think they're awfully sweet, all the same," Henrietta said gently, smiling a little, and keeping her eyes on her cards.

"Oh, I like them," Edmund said defensively. "Everything they do or say takes me back forty years."

"They have real character."

"Yes," Edmund agreed. "It was pretty marvelous the way she let me have it at the table. She fairly rubbed my nose in it."

Henrietta looked up at him for the first time. "You mean—?"

"I mean the name business, of course. What else?"

"I don't know about that. I suppose she always calls him Mr. Kincaid."

"Well, what else did you think I meant?"

"Didn't you understand what she was saying? Of course I may be wrong."

"What on earth?"

"I'm afraid she was offended because you left Cousin Johnny to have lunch 'alone'—with the ladies. What else could you make of her emphasis?"

"She meant I should have come home to lunch today?"

"I don't know, darling. Maybe not."

"But you think I might come home tomorrow? Or take you all out somewhere?"

She smiled at him appreciatively. "Or better still," she offered, "take Cousin Johnny to lunch with some men downtown. I wonder if he wouldn't like that?"

"But would Cousin Annie let him?"

Henrietta leaned across the table and spoke in a conspiratorial whisper. "We could see," she said.

Edmund was silent. "Well, we'll see about it," he said finally, not promising anything but knowing in his heart that everything was already promised.

At the breakfast table next morning, Edmund sat admiring the graceful curve of Henrietta's wrist as she poured coffee from the silver urn into his cup. He had

asked for this third cup mostly for the sake of admiring
again the way she lifted the heavy urn and then let the
weight of it pull her wrist over in that pretty arc. And
the ruffles on the collar of Henrietta's breakfast gown
seemed particularly becoming to her, and Edmund admired the soft arrangement of her hair and the extraordinary freshness of her complexion. She really looked incredibly young. She was a beautiful woman in every sense,
and nothing about her this morning was more beautiful
than the way she had been so right about Cousin Annie.
Cousin Annie and Cousin Johnny had already finished
their breakfast, and the old lady had gone back upstairs
with her husband to prepare him for his morning at the
office with Edmund and his noonday luncheon at the
Hermitage Club. Edmund was now waiting for Cousin
Johnny to come down in his "other suit" and "good tie."

He wouldn't have thought it possible for it to turn out
this way. He was convinced all over again of how much
more sensitive to people Henrietta was than he was. And
he was so grateful to her. No sooner had he issued the invitation to Cousin Johnny than Cousin Annie became positively affable. And at once Cousin Johnny had begun nodding his head in agreement. Edmund noticed also that
the old man began pulling rather strenuously at his lower
lip, but all such lip pullings and winces and twitches Edmund was now willing to lump together as meaningless
nervous habits. He wasn't at all sure he wouldn't end by
having lunch alone with Cousin Johnny in a booth at
Jackson's Stable, where they could talk without interruption.

And what a relief it was, anyway, that the thing was
settled one way or the other. He had spent his last hour in

bed this morning tossing about and wishing that he didn't
have to raise the question and yet knowing that he wanted
to. Long before the cook came in to fix breakfast, he had
heard the old couple stirring in the guest room. It had
been this way the day before, too. The monotonous buzz
of the two old people's lowered voices seemed to pene-
trate the walls of the house in a way that no ordinary
speech would have done. At that hour they seemed to feel
that they must speak in the voice that one normally uses
only when there is someone dead in the house or when
something has gone awfully wrong. They were hard-of-
hearing, of course, and believed they were whispering!
Edmund had to smile at the thought of how carefully
they concealed the fact of their deafness in company. At
any rate, he woke to the drone of these old country people's voices. And with Cousin Johnny so much on his
mind, he couldn't go back to sleep again. He knew that
Henrietta was awake, too, and after a while he felt her
hand on his shoulder, and he turned his head on the pillow and looked at her. "It's awful to have to lie here
quietly like this, knowing that they're hungry," she whispered. There was very little light in the room but he
could see that while she spoke she lay perfectly relaxed,
with her eyes closed. "I'd give anything if there were some
way they could go on and have their breakfast," she continued, still in a whisper. "Yet to get up and offer to fix it
myself, or even to suggest they fix it for themselves, would
only make them more uncomfortable, considering how
they are. . . . What do you think?"

"I just don't know," Edmund said, trying to sound less
awake than he was.

Finally at seven o'clock they heard Cousin Johnny creep

down the steps to fetch the morning *Tennessean* and then creep back up to the guest room again. (He wouldn't for the world have made so free as to sit down in the living room to read the morning paper—not without being expressly asked. It was a wonder Cousin Annie would let him go down and get the paper at all.) Edmund knew, from yesterday, that from this point on the buzz of voices would be only intermittent until the time should come for the first sounds of activity down in the kitchen. Then the buzz would begin again and remain constant until someone knocked on the guest room door and announced breakfast. And that was the way it happened. Everything went just the way he knew it would until they were all four seated at the breakfast table and he had popped the question to Cousin Johnny. From then on everything was different.

Cousin Johnny had gone up to put on his other suit and his good tie, and Cousin Annie had gone with him. Presently Edmund, thinking he heard Cousin Johnny coming down the stairs, rose from the table and went round and kissed Henrietta's cheek. He meant to join Cousin Johnny in the hall and to take him directly to the car, which had already been brought up to the side door. But when he went out into the big front hall, it was Cousin Annie he saw. She had already come three quarters of the way down the stairs, and when she saw Edmund she stopped there, with her hand on the railing. Even before she spoke, Edmund felt his heartbeat quicken. "It's a pity you've had to wait around," she said. "He's so changeable." Edmund said nothing. Cousin Annie descended the rest of the flight. At the foot of the stairs she said, "He had already changed to his good clothes. But he doesn't, after all, want to miss the sights Henrietta and I will be seeing. He's getting back into his other things now."

Henrietta, hearing Cousin Annie's voice, had come to the dining room door. "Cousin Johnny's all right, isn't he?" she asked.

"Of course he's all right," said the old lady with a shade of resentment in her voice. "It's that he doesn't want to miss that Presbyterian church or Bellemeade Plantation." Then she made her way into the dining room where she had left her coffee to cool.

Edmund went off in the other direction, making *his* way across the hall and into the dark corridor that led to the side entrance. He knew that Henrietta was following him, but he couldn't trust himself to discuss the situation. He hoped to reach the outside door before she caught up with him and merely to wave to her from the car. But he had forgotten his hat and coat. When he was at the entry door he heard a coat hanger drop on the floor of the cloak closet, which opened off the corridor, and he knew that Henrietta was fetching his things for him. He had to wait there and submit to her helping him on with his coat. Still he would have left without saying anything had she not at the last minute put her hand on his arm and said, "Darling, you mustn't mind."

"I think I really *hate* that woman," he said.

"Oh, Edmund," Henrietta whispered, "it may really have been Cousin Johnny's decision. And what difference does it make? Why else do we have them here except to let them do whatever they will enjoy most?"

"Yes, why do we?" he said angrily.

Henrietta removed her hand from his arm and stepped back, away from him. With her eyes lowered she said,

"We've been over that." Then she looked up at him accusingly: He wasn't seeing her through.

They had been over it, certainly, some two or three years before this. And he had thought, as she had, that he would never ask this question again. As he raced along the corridor, he had known he would ask it if he let her overtake him. That's why he had made such a dash for the car. He might have reached into the closet and grabbed his hat—to hell with the coat!—but he hadn't had his wits about him. And for that you always had to pay.

Finally, though, he kissed Henrietta goodbye again, and he waved to her from the car.

All the way to town this morning, he went over and over the foolish business. It had never been so complicated before. She had always managed to involve him in her good works among the relatives—having discovered his weakness there, she had abandoned most of her other good works—but this time he was involved in a way or in a sense that Henrietta didn't dream of. Or maybe she did. He shouldn't underestimate her. Was it really only a difference in degree this time? In some degree he was always affected by these country visitors as though it were something more than a visit from relatives. With them he had often felt there ought to be more to say to each other than there ever seemed to be. But never about anyone, before Cousin Johnny, had he felt Here is such a person as I might have been, and I am such a one as he might have been.

Now he could not resist going back to what he considered the real beginning. It was Henrietta who had urged him to leave Ewingsburg, the county seat where they had grown up and where he first practiced law. He hadn't wanted to leave and had argued against it, and, despite the fine opportunities offered him by firms in Nashville, she hadn't begun urging him to go until they had been married for five years and had learned pretty definitely that there would never be any children. When he used to come home for lunch in Ewingsburg and would be lingering over his second cup of coffee, it got so he would catch Henrietta sometimes stealing furtive glances at him. She suspected him of being bored with his life. And yet when he talked of buying up more farm land and joining Uncle Alex and Uncle Nat in their lespedeza venture—aiming for the seed market—Henrietta thought he would be frittering away his life. He ought to be in a big place, she told him, where he could have a real career and be fully occupied.

And so they had gone to Nashville. And Edmund *was* fully occupied. And perhaps that was the trouble. Who could say. . . . Not that Henrietta wasn't occupied, too. She was an enthusiastic joiner of clubs and circles and committees. Why not? What better way of getting to know people? Edmund was entirely sympathetic. But she was never satisfied until she had tried to draw Edmund into each activity, and, since she always failed, she was seldom satisfied with the activity afterward. In the early days, she was always finding something new to interest her—and him. Edmund wondered if there would have been a Nashville for the likes of Cousin Johnny and Cousin Annie to see if Henrietta hadn't been so active in the work of preserving landmarks and setting up monuments. (Even his refusal to help iron out the inevitable legal snarls of that work had never completely destroyed her interest in it. Recently she had had a hand in preserving the First Presbyterian Church from the vandals who wanted to pull it down.) For a time she took a great interest in the home for delinquent girls. Her reports of the individual cases had interested him hugely, but not enough to make him consent to join her as a board member. He came very near to being drawn into her juvenile court work, but somehow he even escaped involvement there.

Then, after a number of years, she began bringing in those nieces for the debutante season. Two of the girls were from his side of the family, one from hers. But that didn't matter. They were all of them kinfolks from out home—the nieces, the nephews, the invalids, and finally, after so many years, the nearly contemporary old couples. They were his responsibility, his involvement as much as hers. There was no getting around it—not in Edmund's mind. And so they came, and they came, and they came. Finally he began to wonder if he and Henrietta weren't more alike than he had ever imagined. It occurred to him that she was really fonder of these visitors and of the people she went out to the country to "see about" than she was of the friends she had gone to such lengths to make in Nashville.

One day he spoke to her about it. And he suggested that perhaps they should think of moving back to Ewingsburg when the time came for him to retire from his practice. Henrietta had laughed at the idea. Why, she asked him, should they plan to bury themselves alive in their old age?

Well, then, he had another idea. (He was only trying to please her, wasn't he?) Why didn't they invite one of her favorites from among their not too affluent relatives, or maybe two of her favorites—"It's the kind of thing people used often to do," he said—to come and live with them on a permanent basis? Wouldn't that give her an even deeper satisfaction than doing only a little for this one and that one? (He didn't say: And then the house would always seem itself.) But in reply Henrietta expressed an astonishment just short of outrage. How could he imagine that this would be the case!

"But why not?" Edmund asked impatiently.

Henrietta shook her head bitterly. To think that he understood so little about what her life was like, she said. And then for the first time in years she mentioned her disappointment at not being able to have children. Edmund was confused. Could there possibly be any connection? Was she merely trying to play on his sympathy? He felt his cheeks growing warm, and could tell from the expression in her eyes that she saw his color rising. But looking deeper into her eyes he saw that she, too, was utterly confused. If there was any connection, then she was as confused about it as he was. She knew no better than he what it meant or why she had dragged it in. And he was sure that, whatever it was, they would never understand it now and that, having discovered it so late, they need not do so. Their course together was set, and he had no intention of trying to change it. But he felt a renewed interest in seeing to what strange places it might yet bring them.

Before he reached his office that second morning of the visit, he saw how salutary it had been for him to go over the whole story in his mind again. It was going to allow him to pass the remainder of the visit in comparative equanimity. From then on, it was as if he was an impartial witness to the contest between Henrietta and Cousin Annie. If, afterward, he had had to testify in court and explain why he did not intervene between them, he would have had to say that he thought it only a kind of game they were playing, and that he had had no idea of how deadly serious they were.

There was no telephone call from Henrietta that day. Edmund tried to reach her just after noon but learned from the maid that she and "the company" hadn't been at home for lunch. The maid happened to know the restaurant out on Hillsboro Pike where they had gone and happened to have the telephone number handy. Edmund could not help smiling as he jotted down the number. Henrietta knew he would be expecting a call from her, and knew that if it didn't come *he* would call—not because he would be afraid she was pouting or because he would feel a need to apologize. She was not a woman who pouted, and she always knew how sorry he was when they had had any kind of tiff. She was wonderful, really. He would find her tonight in the best of spirits. There would be no reference made to their exchange at the side door this morning. It was past, and she had already forgotten it. She was a wonderful woman, and nothing about her was more wonderful than her serenity and the way she was certain to have another suggestion to make to him today or tonight. The only trouble was that he knew what *this* suggestion would be, and it was important that he give her the opportunity of making it as soon as possible. He telephoned the restaurant, but the hostess said that Mrs. Harper and her party had just left.

Not infrequently Edmund stayed home from his office for one day of a visit that wasn't going too well. It was usually the last day. But his staying was by no means a pattern. He could never be certain it was the thing Henrietta wanted, and he always waited for her suggestion. Tomorrow would be the last day for Cousin Johnny and Cousin Annie, and though this was a case in which Henrietta was almost sure to suggest it, it wasn't going to be possible for him to stay. When he came in the house that night, Henrietta was still upstairs dressing. He considered this a stroke of good luck, because it would give her the opportunity he had in mind. Perhaps even it was for this that she happened still to be up there.

Henrietta's dressing for dinner, like Edmund's, consisted not of getting into more formal attire but of putting on something more comfortable and something more youthful than she ever wore away from home. When he came into her room, she was fresh from her bath, still moving about the room in her knee length slip and her high heeled mules. And right away she was bubbling with talk about the day's events, proving that she bore him no grudge, even saying the kind of things about Cousin Johnny and Cousin Annie that she had refused to say last night. "Once in the car when we were on our way out to Traveler's Rest—they were enchanted by Traveler's Rest and didn't care for Bellemeade or even the Hermitage—once I said—it was when we were talking about people from Ewingsburg who live here (and whom Cousin Annie has *refused* to let entertain them or even to see)—I said Bob Coppinger has gotten to look exactly like Laurence Olivier. 'Like who?' said Cousin Johnny from the

back seat. Cousin Annie was sitting in the front seat with
me and she turned around and said to him with the ut-
most contempt for my allusion, 'Some moving picture
star, I think, Mr. Kincaid.' (Yes, she has continued to call
him Mr. Kincaid all day today.) It was as if the old dear
had read my mind. I had been thinking that even though
she disapproves so of TV, we might be able to get them
out to see a Western movie tonight—something real old-
fashioned, like a movie. But after her remark I knew
there was no chance, and that it had been silly of me to
think there might be. I even marvel that she knows who
Olivier is. But she knows things. She knows things you'd
never in the world suppose she did. Let me tell you—
Here, give me a hand with these buttons, won't you?"

While she talked she had gone to her closet and pulled
out the dress she was going to wear. Edmund was marvel-
ing more at the pretty print of the dress material and at
the mysterious row of buttons down the back than at
Cousin Annie Kincaid's knowledge of movie stars. He
realized that the buttons seemed mysterious because they
were at once so unnecessary, so numerous and so large—
each the size of a silver dollar—and yet were so carefully
camouflaged, being covered with the same print the dress
was made of. He found it most absorbing, and intriguing,
and endearing. And suddenly he recognized the similarity
of the whole fashioning of this dress to that of dresses
Henrietta had worn when he was courting her. As he
stood behind her, buttoning those buttons that began at
the very low waistline and continued up to the rounded
neckline, he could not resist, midway, leaning forward and
kissing her on the back of her neck. Henrietta began to

give him the day's itinerary: the First Presbyterian Church, the plantation houses of Andrew Jackson, John Overton, the Harding family.

"Every place we went," she said, "I had a time making them get out and see the very thing they had come to see. But what I was going to tell you was that when we were on our way down town to see the church, Cousin Annie asked me to point out the James K. Polk Apartments and Vaux Hall! Could you have imagined she would have heard of either or remembered the names? When I told her both buildings had been torn down, she only said, 'I'm not surprised.' . . . What I think is that those were places where friends of hers who came to Nashville a million years ago must have had apartments. . . . We might have lived there ourselves if we had come ten or fifteen years before we did. Do you remember when the Braxtons lived there—at Vaux Hall?"

But now it was time for Edmund to rush off into his room and dress. "Well, do make it snappy, dear," Henrietta said. "Remember I've had them all day. You must have noticed I'm quite hoarse from doing all the talking."

At dinner, Edmund made a special point of carrying his full share of the conversation. Cousin Johnny, on the other hand, was completely silent tonight and ate absolutely nothing. Cousin Annie was kept busy eating two portions of everything so that nothing would be wasted on *their* account. It was the first time Cousin Annie had done this, but then it was the first time Cousin Johnny had gone without food altogether. Edmund wondered silently if the old man wasn't hungry and if they couldn't find him something in the kitchen he could eat. Yet he couldn't ask. He began speculating on how many other discomforts the old man might have suffered in the past two days. He noticed that he had come to the table tonight without his vest. And at some moment last night he had noticed how the old man's clothes seemed to hang on him and how he seemed thinner than when he first arrived. The answer was that he had left off his long underwear. It was the central heat in the house! *They* weren't used to it. And now Edmund recalled the scene in the living room when he came into the house this afternoon. Having been detained at the office to make last minute revisions of his brief for the shoe company case, Edmund had come home a little later than usual, but the houseboy was lighting the log fire in the living room at the usual hour. Edmund had, at the time, been scarcely conscious of one detail in the scene, but subconsciously he had made a note of it. At the moment of his entrance, the houseboy was on his knees fanning the flames of the fire, and across the room, seated beside Cousin Johnny and with him watching silently the houseboy's efforts, Cousin Annie was fanning herself with a little picture postcard of the Hermitage.

Until these details began to pile up in his mind, at the dinner table, Edmund had thought of Cousin Annie as waging a merely defensive war against Henrietta. Now he saw it wasn't so. She had had the offensive from the beginning and she was winning battle after battle. Every discomfort that Cousin Johnny suffered in silence, every dish he did without, every custom he had to conform to that was "bad for him" was a victory over Henrietta, and gave the old lady the deeper satisfaction just because Henrietta might not be aware of it.

But Edmund had no premonition of how far she might

be prepared to go—or perhaps already had gone—until after dinner, when Cousin Johnny and Cousin Annie were going up the stairs together. They ascended very slowly, and Edmund realized that her footsteps were every bit as heavy as Cousin Johnny's. He recalled having mistaken her for the old man on the stair this morning. Very likely it had been she, after all, who had come down to fetch the paper each morning. Was climbing the stairs perhaps bad for Cousin Johnny?—the stairs in this house and in all the landmarks he had been taken to see? And when he went upstairs this morning, had it really been that he *couldn't* come back down and go with Edmund to the office? Suddenly Edmund could visualize the old fellow lying on his back in the bed, or even on the floor, before the old lady helped him onto the bed and made him comfortable and then came downstairs to say that he had changed his mind.

When their guests had gone upstairs for the night and Edmund was setting up the card table in the living room, Henrietta still hadn't mentioned tomorrow and the possibility of his staying at home. But after they had arranged their cards and had begun to play, the suggestion wasn't long in coming. By now, however, his concern for Cousin Johnny had driven that problem out of Edmund's mind, and, because of this, his reply to Henrietta was more abrupt than it might otherwise have been.

"There's one thing I do hope," she had said with considerable force, "and that is that you are going to be able to stay at home tomorrow."

"I can't possibly." That was all he said. For a minute they sat looking at each other across the card table.

"But I've told them you'd be here," she said.

"I wish you had asked me earlier," he said, in a softer tone now.

Her voice was still full of confidence. "I *had* counted on it," she said. "And they have gone up to bed thinking you'll be here."

"Tomorrow is Friday," he said, as if speaking to a child. "I'll have to be in court all day. It's the shoe company case. There's no chance."

"Oh," said Henrietta. She knew that this meant there really was no chance.

"I'm truly sorry, Henrietta," he said. "Fortunately, there will be no court on Saturday. I'll be able to go with you to take them home. But there's nothing I can do about tomorrow."

"Of course there's not. I understand that," she said, smiling at him. She was already recovering from her disappointment. Quietly they began playing out their game of cards. During the rest of the time they sat there, it seemed to Edmund that Henrietta played her cards as though she were performing some magic that was going to change everything—in her favor. And he couldn't bring himself to tell her about the sudden insight he had had at the dinner table, or about the ridiculous but genuine and quite black apprehension that he wasn't able to rid himself of.

At some hour in the night he heard the old woman's voice distinctly. He tried to think he had only dreamed it and that some other noise had waked him. But then he heard her again and heard Cousin Johnny. The familiar, funereal tones were unmistakable. He only managed to get back to sleep by assuring himself that it meant it must be nearly morning, by reminding himself that he had to have his sleep if he was to have his wits about him in court today.

The next time he woke, he put on the light and looked at his watch. He was sleeping alone in his own room. The two previous nights he had been with Henrietta in her room, but tonight she hadn't suggested it. His pocket watch was lying on his bedside table, with the gold chain coiled about it. It had been his father's watch and had the circumference and the thickness of a doorknob. Before he fastened his eyes on the Roman numerals to which the filigreed hands pointed, he remembered noticing that Cousin Johnny's watch, which the old man took out and wound before going up to bed each night, was almost identical with this one of his father's. It occurred to him that Cousin Johnny's would be resting now on the bedside table in the guest room with its chain coiled around it. This neat coiling of the chain about the watch was a habit Edmund had picked up from his father and one that his father had no doubt picked up from his own father. When finally Edmund focused his attention on the face of the watch, he found the very hour of the night itself alarming. It was half past three. From that moment, he didn't hear Cousin Johnny's voice again; it was only the old lady he heard. He was certain now that the old man was really very sick. He waited, sitting on the side of the bed with the light on. There were silences, broken always and only by Cousin Annie's voice. At last he got up and switched off the light and felt his way through the bathroom into Henrietta's room.

"Do you suppose something is really wrong?" Henrietta said from her bed. He was hardly through the doorway, and the room was pitch dark. Something in the way she said it made him answer, "I suppose not."

"The light's been on in their room for some time. You can see it on the garage roof. Do you think you might just go and make sure—or I could."

"What good would it do? It would only make matters worse, considering how they are."

"Well, what do you think?" she said, meaning, "Then why are you here?"

"I couldn't sleep."

"Is it that case today?"

"No, but I thought I might sleep better in here." He was sitting on the side of her bed now. "Do you mind?" He didn't know what he would do if she said, yes, she minded. He knew only that he couldn't go back to his own room and bed before morning. He felt that it hadn't, after all, been the voices that waked him, and that there *had* been a dream—the kind of dream that could never be remembered afterward.

"Of course I don't mind, silly," she said. She sounded wide awake. "I've had a wonderfully funny thought," she said as he lay down beside her. "You might just go to their door and tell Cousin Annie that you won't be able to stay home today. Then maybe she would let *him* get some sleep."

"Can she be that awful?" Edmund said. "You don't suppose it's anything more than just that?"

"I suppose not," she answered, putting her arm around him. "You know what an evil influence you are on people." The touch of her arm was all he had needed. Once again he believed it was the voices that had waked him, and remembered that he must have his wits about him to-morrow.

At seven o'clock nobody went downstairs to fetch the paper. Edmund had left his watch in his room, but neighborhood noises and a distant whistle told him the time. He slept again, and next time he waked he knew it was the unnatural silence in the house that had waked him. He slipped out of bed and went into his room to dress. It was seven-thirty by his watch. He dressed hurriedly, but when he went to look in on Henrietta before going downstairs, he found her also fully dressed and standing with her hand on the knob to the hall door. She had put on lipstick but no other make-up. She looked pale and frightened. He crossed over to her and they went out into the hall together.

The door to the guest room was standing open but the blinds were still drawn and the room was in complete darkness. Presently Cousin Annie appeared out of the darkness, wearing the black dress she had worn on the trip in from the country and clutching some object in her hand. Edmund and Henrietta moved quickly toward her. As they drew near, Edmund saw it was Cousin Johnny's watch she held. When they stood before her in the doorway, Cousin Annie said, "He's gone."

"Gone?" Edmund echoed, and he almost added, "Where?" But in time he remembered the euphemism. She spoke as though they had all been waiting together through the night for the old man to be released from his mortal pain.

He felt Henrietta lean against him. He put his arms about her, and when she turned and hid her face on his

shirtfront, he had to support her to keep her from crumbling to the floor.

"You mustn't," said Cousin Annie. "I did everything
anyone could have done. We had known for some time he
hadn't long."

Henrietta's strength returned. She drew herself away
from him and faced Cousin Annie. "But why—how could
you let him come if—"

Edmund felt himself blushing. Was his wife really so
shameless?

But the old lady seemed to think the question quite in
order. She even completed the question for Henrietta. "If
it was unwise for him? Because he wanted so much to
come, to see what it was like here. . . . Like all of us, he
was foolish about some things."

The two women stood a moment looking at each other.
Without being blind to the genuine grief in Cousin Annie's countenance, Edmund detected the glint of victory
in the last glance she gave Henrietta before turning back
into the dark room.

Poor Cousin Johnny, Edmund thought to himself. . . .
Now Henrietta was following Cousin Annie in there, and
now he heard the old lady's first sobs and knew that she
had given way, as she had to, and was letting Henrietta
see after her. The battle was over, really. . . . But poor
Cousin Johnny, he kept thinking. Poor old fellow. . . .
Presently Henrietta led Cousin Annie out into the hall
again, and as the two women moved toward the door to
Henrietta's room, Henrietta gave him a look that recalled him to his senses and reminded him of his obliga-
tions. Already it was time for him to begin making the
arrangements. He would be at home after all today. The

court would grant a postponement under the circumstances. Cousin Johnny was gone, but *he* was still here to see Henrietta through and make the arrangements.

For a moment Edmund stood there staring into the dead man's room. The door should be shut, he supposed. And when he had done this, he would have to go and telephone a doctor. Cousin Annie didn't realize you couldn't die without a doctor nowadays. While he waited for the doctor to arrive, he would call an undertaker. No, he was being as bad as Cousin Annie. It wouldn't do to call an undertaker before a doctor had been there. He stepped forward and placed his hand on the door knob. And then, as though it was what he had intended all along, he went inside the room and closed the door behind him.

He waited just inside the door till his eyes got used to the dark. Then he went over to the foot of the bed where she had the old man laid out. At last they were alone—he and Cousin Johnny. There was only just enough light for him to make out that she had him completely dressed, and with something that must be a handkerchief covering his face. No doubt he was wearing the very clothes—his other suit and good tie—that he would have worn to lunch at Jackson's Stable. And would she have put him in his long underwear? Edmund speculated, not idly, and not, certainly, with humor. And the vest? And the lisle socks and the elastic supporters? Yes, she would have. That was how Cousin Johnny would be taken back to Ewingsburg for burial, was how he would be taken away from Edmund's house where he had died. Suddenly, at the thought of it, Edmund was seized with a dreadful terror of their taking the old man away. Wasn't there

some way he could postpone it? But postponing it
wouldn't be enough. What if he should lock the door to
the guest room and refuse to let them have the body! He
had heard of cases in which grief had driven people to
such madness, and surely his present anguish was grief
—if not exactly grief for Cousin Johnny. What if he
should refuse to let them have the old man's body!

He stood peering through the darkness at the white
handkerchief over the old man's face, the face whose features he already found it hard to remember distinctly. And
he was wondering at his own simplicity—indulging in such a
fantasy, giving way to such unnatural and morbid feelings!
And at such a time. Soon Henrietta or Cousin Annie—or
the two of them, even—might come and discover him
there. That wasn't likely, but soon he would have to go
back to them and he must begin preparing himself for his
return. He knew that the first step must be to begin thinking of Cousin Johnny more realistically, not as a part of
himself that was being taken away forever but once again
as a visitor from the country who had died in his guest
room. And, all at once, it seemed to Edmund the most
natural thing in the world for him to speak to his dead
house guest.

"Well, Cousin Johnny, you're gone," he said. That was
all he said aloud. But, placing his two hands on the
smooth footrail of the bed as though it were the familiar
rail of a jury box, he went on silently: "What was it we
were going to talk about, Cousin Johnny, in that talk of
ours? Was it our wives and their wars within wars and
what made them that way. . . . We certainly ought to
have got round to that. But it wasn't our wives who divided us. It was somehow our both being from the country

that did it. You had done one thing about being from the country and I had done another. You buried yourself alive on that farm of yours, I buried myself in my work here. But something in the life out there didn't satisfy you the way it should. The country wasn't itself any more. And something was wrong for me here. By 'country' we mean the old world, don't we, Cousin Johnny—the old ways, the old life, where people had real grandfathers and real children, and where love was something that could endure the light of day—something real, not merely a hand one holds in the dark so that sleep will come. Our trouble was, Cousin Johnny, we were lost without our old realities. We couldn't discover what it is people keep alive for without them. Surely there must be something. Other people seem to know some reason why it is better to be alive than dead this April morning. I will have to find it out. There must be something."

1939

Twenty years ago, in 1939, I was in my senior year at Kenyon College. I was restless, and wasn't sure I wanted to stay on and finish college. My roommate at Kenyon was Jim Prewitt. Jim was restless, too. That fall, he and I drove to New York City to spend our Thanksgiving holiday. Probably both of us felt restless and uneasy for the same reasons that everyone else did in 1939, or for just the obvious reasons that college seniors always do, but we imagined our reasons to be highly individual and beyond the understanding of the other students.

It was four o'clock on Wednesday afternoon when we left Gambier, the little Ohio village that gives Kenyon its post office address. We had had to wait till the four o'clock mail was put in the Gambier post office, because each of us was expecting a check from home. My check came. Jim's did not. But mine was enough to get us to New York, and Jim's would be enough to get us back. "Enough to get back, *if* we come back!" That became our motto for the trip. We had both expressed the thought in precisely the same words and at precisely the same moment as we came out of the post office. And during the short time it took us to dash back across the village street, with its wide green in the center, and climb the steps up to our room in Douglass House and then dash down again with our suitcases to the car, we found half a dozen excuses for repeating our motto.

The day was freakishly warm, and all of our housemates were gathered on the front stoop when we made our departure. In their presence, we took new pleasure in proclaiming our motto and repeating it over and over while we threw our things into the car. The other boys didn't respond, however, as we hoped they would. They leaned against the iron railing of the stoop, or sat on the stone steps leaning against one another, and refused to admit any interest in our "childish" insinuation: *if* we came back. All seven of them were there and all seven were in agreement on the "utter stupidity" of our long Thanksgiving trip as well as that of our present behavior. But they didn't know our incentive, and they couldn't be expected to understand.

For two years, Jim and I had shared a room on the second floor of old Douglass House. I say "old" because at Kenyon in those days there was still a tendency to prefix that adjective to the name of everything of any worth on the campus or in the village. Oldness had for so many years been the most respected attribute of the college that

it was natural for its prestige to linger on a few years after what we considered the new dispensation and the intellectual awaking. Old Douglass House *was* an oldish
house, but it had only been given over for use as a dormitory the year that Jim and I—and most of our friends—
came to Kenyon. The nine of us moved into it just a few
weeks after its former occupants—a retired professor and
his wife, I believe—had moved out. And we were to live
there during our three years at Kenyon (all of us having
transferred from other colleges as sophomores)—to live
there without ever caring to inquire into the age or history of the house. We were not the kind of students who
cared about such things. We were hardly aware, even, of
just how quaint the house was, with its steep white gables
laced with gingerbread-work, and its Gothic windows and
their arched window blinds. Our unawareness—Jim's and
mine—was probably never more profound than on that
late afternoon in November, when we set out for New
York. Our plan was to spend two days in Manhattan and
then go on to Boston for a day with Jim's family, and our
only awareness was of that plan.

During the previous summer, Jim Prewitt had become
engaged to a glorious, talented girl with long flaxen hair,
whom he had met at a student writers' conference somewhere out West. And I, more attached to things at home
in St. Louis than Jim was to things in Boston—*I* had been
"accepted" by an equally glorious dark-eyed girl in whose
veins ran the Creole blood of old-time St. Louis. By a happy
coincidence both of these glorious girls were now in New
York City. Carol Crawford, with her flaxen hair fixed in a
bun on the back of her neck and a four-hundred-page
manuscript in her suitcase, had headed East from the fate-

ful writers' conference in search of a publisher for her novel. Nancy Gibault had left St. Louis in September to study painting at the National Academy. The two girls were as yet unacquainted, and it was partly to the correcting of this that Jim and I meant to dedicate our Thanksgiving holiday.

The other boys at Douglass House didn't know our incentive, and when we said goodbye to them there on the front steps I really felt a little sorry for them. Altogether, they were a sad, shabby, shaggy-looking lot. All of us who lived at Douglass House were, I suppose. You have probably seen students who look the way we did—especially if you have ever visited Bard College or Black Mountain or Rollins or almost any other college nowadays. Such students seem to affect a kind of hungry, unkempt look. And yet they don't really know what kind of impression they want to make; they only know that there are certain kinds they *don't* want to make.

Generally speaking, we at Douglass House were reviled by the rest of the student body, all of whom lived in the vine-covered dormitories facing the campus, and by a certain proportion of the faculty. I am sure we were thought of as a group as closely knit as any other in the college. We were even considered a sort of fraternity. But we didn't see ourselves that way. We would have none of that. Under that high gabled roof, we were all independents and meant to remain so. Housing us "transfers" together this way had been the inspiration of the Dean or the President under the necessity of solving a problem of overflow in the dormitories. Yet we did not object to his solution, and of our own accord we ate together in the Commons, we hiked together about the countryside, we went together to see girls in nearby Mount Vernon, we enrolled in the same classes, flocked more or less after the same professors, and met every Thursday night at the Creative Writing class, which we all acknowledged as our reason for being at Kenyon. But think of ourselves as a club, or as dependent upon each other for companionship or for anything else, we would not. There were times when each of us talked of leaving Kenyon and going back to the college or university from which he had come— back to Ann Arbor or Olivet, back to Chapel Hill, to Vanderbilt, to Southwestern, or back to Harvard or Yale. It was a moderately polite way each of us had of telling the others that *they* were a bunch of Kenyon boys but that *he* knew something of a less cloistered existence and was not to be confused with their kind. We were so jealous of every aspect of our independence and individuality that one time, I remember, Bruce Gordon nearly fought with Bill Anderson because Bill, for some strange reason, had managed to tune in, with his radio, on a Hindemith sonata that Bruce was playing on the electric phonograph in his own room.

Most of us had separate rooms. Only Jim Prewitt and I shared a room, and ours was three or four times as big as most dormitory cubicles. It opened off the hall on the second floor, but it was on a somewhat lower level than the hall. And so when you entered the door, you found yourself at the head of a little flight of steps, with the top of your head almost against the ceiling. This made the room seem even larger than it was, as did the scarcity and peculiar arrangement of the furniture. Our beds, with our desks beside them, were placed in diagonally opposite corners, and we each had a wobbly five-foot bookshelf set up at the foot of his bed, like a hospital screen. The only thing we shared was a little three-legged oak table in the very center of the room, on which were a hot plate and an electric coffepot, and from which two long black extension cords reached up to the light fixture overhead.

The car that Jim and I were driving to New York did not belong to either of us. It didn't at that time belong to anybody, really, and I don't know what ever became of it. At the end of our holiday, we left it parked on Marlborough Street in Boston, with the ignition key lost somewhere in the gutter. I suppose Jim's parents finally disposed of the car in some way or other. It had come into our hands the spring before, when its last owner had abandoned it behind the college library and left the keys on Jim's desk up in our room. He, the last owner, had been one of us in Douglass House for a while—though it was, indeed, for a very short while. He was a poor boy who had been at Harvard the year that Jim was there, before Jim transferred to Kenyon, and he was enormously ambitious and possessed enough creative energy to produce in a month the quantity of writing that most of us were hoping to produce in a lifetime. He was a very handsome fellow, with a shock of yellow hair and the physique of a good trackman. On him the cheapest department store clothes looked as though they were tailor-made, and he could never have looked like the rest of us, no matter how hard he might have tried. I am not sure that he ever actually matriculated at Kenyon, but he was there in Douglass House for about two months, clicking away on first one typewriter and then another (since he had none of his own); I shall never forget the bulk of manuscript that he turned out during his stay, most of which he left behind in the house or in the trunk of the car. The sight of it depressed me then, and it depresses me now to think of it. His neatly typed manuscripts were in every room in the house—novels, poetic dramas, drawing-room comedies, lyrics, epic poems, short stories, scenarios. He wasn't at all like the rest of us. And except for his car he has no place in this account of our trip to New York. Yet since I have digressed this far, there is something more that I some- how feel I ought to say about him.

Kenyon was to him only a convenient place to rest awhile (for writing was not work to him) on his long but certain journey from Harvard College to Hollywood. He used to say to us that he wished he could do the way we were doing and really dig in at Kenyon for a year or so and get his degree. The place appealed to him, he said, with its luxuriant countryside, and its old stone buildings send- ing up turrets and steeples and spires above the treetops. If he stayed, he would join a fraternity, so he said, and walk the Middle Path with the other fraternity boys on Tuesday nights, singing fraternity songs and songs of old Kenyon. He said he envied us—and yet he hadn't himself time to stay at Kenyon. He was there for two months, and while he was there he was universally admired by the boys in Douglass House. But when he had gone, we all hated him. Perhaps we were jealous. For in no time at all stories and poems of his began appearing in the quarter- lies as well as in the popular magazines. Pretty soon one of his plays had a good run on Broadway, and I believe he had a novel out even before that. He didn't actually go to Hollywood till after the war, but get there at last he did, and now, I am told, he has a house in the San Fernando Valley and has the two requisite swimming pools, too.

To us at Kenyon he left his car. It was a car given to him by an elderly benefactor in Cambridge, but a car that had been finally and quite suddenly rendered worthless in his eyes by a publisher's advance, which sent him flying out of our world by the first plane he could get passage on. He left us the car without any regret, left it in the same spirit that American tourists left their cars on the docks at European ports when war broke out that same year. In effect, he tossed us his keys from the first-class deck of the giant ship he had boarded at the end of his plane trip, glad to know that he would never need the old rattletrap again and glad to be out of the mess that all of us were in for life.

I have said that I somehow felt obliged to include everything I have about our car's last real owner. And now I know why I felt so. Without that digression it would have been impossible to explain what the other boys were thinking—or what we thought they were thinking—when we left them hanging about the front stoop that afternoon. They were thinking that there was a chance Jim and I had had an "offer" of some kind, that we had "sold out" and were headed in the same direction that our repudiated brother had taken last spring. Perhaps they did not actually think that, but that was how we interpreted the sullen and brooding expressions on their faces when we were preparing to leave that afternoon.

Of course, what their brooding expressions meant made no difference to Jim or me. And we said so to each other as, with Jim at the wheel, we backed out of the little alley-way beside the House and turned into the village street.

We cared not a hoot in hell for what they thought of us or of our trip to New York. Further, we cared no more— Jim and I—for each other's approval or disapproval, and we reminded each other of this then and there.

We were all independents in Douglass House. There was no spirit of camaraderie among us. We were not the kind of students who cared about such things as camaraderie. Besides, we felt that there was more than enough of that spirit abroad at Kenyon, among the students who lived in the regular dormitories and whose fraternity lodges were scattered about the wooded hillside beyond the village. In those days, the student body at Kenyon was almost as picturesque as the old vine-clad buildings and the rolling countryside itself. So it seemed to us, at least. We used to sit on the front stoop or in the upstairs windows of Douglass House and watch the fops and dandies of the campus go strolling and strutting by on their way to the post office or the bank, or to Jean Val Dean's short-order joint. Those three establishments, along with Dicky Doolittle's filling station, Jim Lynch's barber shop, Jim Hayes' grocery store, Tom Wilson's Home Market, and Mrs. Titus' lunchroom and bakery (the Kokosing Restaurant), constituted the business district of Gambier. And it was in their midst that Douglass House was situated. Actually, those places of business were strung along just one block of the village's main thoroughfare. Each was housed in its separate little store building or in a converted dwelling house, and in the spring and in the fall, while the leaves were still on the low hanging branches of the trees, a stranger in town would hardly notice that they were places of business at all.

From the windows of Douglass House, between the bakery and the barber shop, we could look down on the dormitory students who passed along the sidewalk, and could make our comment on what we considered their silly affectations—on their provincial manners and their foppish, collegiate clothing. In midwinter, when all the leaves were off the trees, we could see out into the parkway that divided the street into two lanes—and in the center of the parkway was the Middle Path. For us, the Middle Path was the epitome of everything about Kenyon that we wanted no part of. It was a broad gravel walkway extending not merely the length of the village green; it had its beginning, rather, at the far end of the campus, at the worn doorstep of the dormitory known as Old Kenyon, and ran the length of the campus, on through the village, then through the wooded area where most of the faculty houses were, and ended at the door of Bexley Hall, Kenyon's Episcopal seminary. In the late afternoon, boys on horseback rode along it as they returned from the Polo Field. At noon, sometimes, boys who had just come up from Kenyon's private airfield appeared on the Middle Path still wearing their helmets and goggles. And after dinner every Tuesday night the fraternity boys marched up and down the Path singing their fraternity songs and singing fine old songs about early days at Kenyon and about its founder, Bishop Philander Chase:

The first of Kenyon's goodly race
Was that great man Philander Chase.
He climbed the hill and said a prayer
And founded Kenyon College there.

He dug up stones, he chopped down trees,
He sailed across the stormy seas,

And begged at ev'ry noble's door,
And also that of Hannah Moore.

He built the college, built the dam,
He milked the cow, he smoked the ham;
He taught the classes, rang the bell,
And spanked the naughty freshmen well.

At Douglass House we wanted none of that. We had all come to Kenyon because we were bent upon becoming writers of some kind or other and the new President of the college had just appointed a famous and distinguished poet to the staff of the English Department. Kenyon was, in our opinion, an obscure little college that had for more than a hundred years slept the sweet, sound sleep that only a small Episcopal college can ever afford to sleep. It was a quaint and pretty spot. We recognized that, but we held that against it. That was not what we were looking for. We even collected stories about other people who had resisted the beauties of the campus and the surrounding countryside. A famous English critic had stopped here on his way home from a long stay in the Orient, and when asked if he did not admire our landscape he replied, "No. It's too rich for my blood." We all felt it was too rich for ours, too. Another English visitor was asked if the college buildings did not remind him of Oxford, and by way of reply he permitted his mouth to fall open while he stared in blank amazement at his questioner.

Despite our feeling that the countryside was too rich for our blood, we came to know it a great deal better—or at least in more detail—than did the polo players or the fliers or the members of the champion tennis team. For we were nearly all of us walkers. We walked the country roads for miles in every direction, talking every step of the way about ourselves or about our writing, or if we exhausted those two dearer subjects, we talked about whatever we were reading at the time. We read W. H. Auden and Yvor Winters and Wyndham Lewis and Joyce and Christopher Dawson. We read *The Wings of the Dove* (aloud!) and *The Cosmological Eye* and *The Last Puritan* and *In Dreams Begin Responsibilities*. (Of course, I am speaking only of books that didn't come within the range of the formal courses we were taking in the college.) On our walks through the country—never more than two or three of us together—we talked and talked, but I think none of us ever listened to anyone's talk but his own. Our talk seemed always to come to nothing. But our walking took us past the sheep farms and orchards and past some of the old stone farmhouses that are scattered throughout that township. It brought us to the old quarry from which most of the stone for the college buildings and for the farmhouses had been taken, and brought us to Quarry Chapel, a long since deserted and "deconsecrated" chapel, standing on a hill two miles from the college and symbolizing there the failure of Episcopalianism to take root among the Ohio country-people. Sometimes we walked along the railroad track through the valley at the foot of the college hill, and I remember more than once coming upon two or three tramps warming themselves by a little fire they had built or even cooking a meal over it. We would see them maybe a hundred yards ahead, and we would get close enough to hear them laughing and talking together. But as soon as they noticed us we would turn back and walk in the

other direction, for we pitied them and felt that our
presence was an intrusion. And yet, looking back on it, I
remember how happy those tramps always seemed. And
how sad and serious we were.

Jim and I headed due east from Gambier on the road
to Coshocton and Pittsburgh. Darkness overtook us long
before we ever reached the Pennsylvania state line. We
were in Pittsburgh by about 9 P.M., and then there lay
ahead of us the whole long night of driving. Nothing
could have better suited our mood than the prospect of
this ride through the dark, wooded countryside of Pennsylvania on that autumn night. This being before the
days of the turnpike—or at least before its completion—
the roads wound about the great domelike hills of that
region and through the deep valleys in a way that answered some need we both felt. We spoke of it many times
during the night, and Jim said he felt he knew for the
first time the meaning of "verdurous glooms and winding
mossy ways." The two of us were setting out on this trip
not in search of the kind of quick success in the world that
had so degraded our former friend in our eyes; we
sought, rather, a taste—or foretaste—of "life's deeper
and more real experience," the kind that dormitory life
seemed to deprive us of. We expressed these yearnings in
just those words that I have put in quotation marks, not
feeling the need for any show of delicate restraint. We, at
twenty, had no abhorrence of raw ideas or explicit state-
ment. We didn't hesitate to say what we wanted to be and
what we felt we must have in order to become that. We
wanted to be writers, and we knew well enough that before we could write we had to have "mature and adult ex-

perience." And, by God, we *said* so to each other, there in the car as we sped through towns like Turtle Creek and Greensburg and Acme.

I have observed in recent years that boys the age we were then and with our inclinations tend to value ideas of this sort above all else. They are apt to find their own crude obsession with mere ideas the greatest barrier to producing the works of art they are after. I have observed this from the vantage ground of the college professor's desk, behind which the irony of fate has placed me from time to time. From there, I have also had the chance to observe something about *girls* of an artistic bent or temperament, and for that reason I am able to tell you more about the two girls we were going to see in New York than I could possibly have known then.

At the time—that is, during the dark hours of the drive East—each of us carried in his mind an image of the girl who had inspired him to make this journey. In each case, the image of the girl's face and form was more or less accurate. In my mind was the image of a brunette with dark eyes and a heart-shaped face. In Jim's was that of a blonde, somewhat above average height, with green eyes and perhaps a few freckles on her nose. That, in general, was how we pictured them, but neither of us would have been dogmatic about the accuracy of his picture. Perhaps Carol Crawford didn't have any freckles. Jim wasn't sure. And maybe her eyes were more blue than green. As for me, I wouldn't have contradicted anyone who said Nancy Gibault's face was actually slightly elongated, rather than heart-shaped, or that her hair had a decided reddish cast to it. Our impressions of this kind were only more or less accurate, and we would have been the first to admit it.

But as to the talent and the character and the original mind of the two glorious girls, we would have brooked no questioning of our concepts. Just after we passed through Acme, Pennsylvania, our talk turned from ourselves to these girls—from our inner yearnings for mature and adult experience to the particular objects toward which we were being led by these yearnings. We agreed that the quality we most valued in Nancy and Carol was their "critical" and "objective" view of life, their unwillingness to accept the standards of "the world." I remember telling Jim that Nancy Gibault could always take a genuinely "disinterested" view of any matter—"disinterested in the best sense of the word." And Jim assured me that, whatever else I might perceive about Carol, I would sense at once the originality of her mind and "the absence of anything commonplace or banal in her intellectual makeup."

It seems hard to believe now, but that was how we spoke to each other about our girls. That was what we thought we believed and felt about them then. And despite our change of opinions by the time we headed back to Kenyon, despite our complete and permanent disenchantment, despite their unkind treatment of us—as worldly and as commonplace as could be—I know now that those two girls were as near the concepts we had of them to begin with as any two girls their age might be, or should be. And I believe now that the decisions *they* made about *us* were the right decisions for *them* to make. I have only the vaguest notion of how Nancy Gibault has fared in later life. I know only that she went back to St. Louis the following spring and was married that sum-

mer to Lon Havemeyer. But as for Carol Crawford, everybody with any interest in literary matters knows what became of her. Her novels are read everywhere. They have
even been translated into Javanese. She is, in her way,
even more successful than the boy who made the long pull
from Harvard College to Hollywood.

Probably I seem to be saying too much about things
that I understood only long after the events of my story.
But the need for the above digression seemed no less urgent to me than did that concerning the former owner of
our car. In his case, the digression dealt mostly with
events of a slightly earlier time. Here it has dealt with a
wisdom acquired at a much later time. And now I find
that I am still not quite finished with speaking of that
later time and wisdom. Before seeing me again in the car
that November night in 1939, picture me for just a moment—much changed in appearance and looking at you
through gold-rimmed spectacles—behind the lectern in a
classroom. I stand before the class as a kind of journey-
man writer, a type of whom Trollope might have ap-
proved, but one who has known neither the financial
success of the facile Harvard boy nor the reputation of
Carol Crawford. Yet this man behind the lectern is a man
who seems happy in the knowledge that he knows—or
thinks he knows—what he is about. And from behind his
lectern he is saying that any story that is written in the
form of a memoir should give offense to no one, because
before a writer can make a person he has known fit into
such a story—or any story, for that matter—he must do
more than change the real name of that person. He must
inevitably do such violence to that person's character that
the so-called original is forever lost to the story.

The last lap of Jim's and my all-night drive was the toughest. The night had begun as an unseasonably warm one. I recall that there were even a good many insects splattered on our windshield in the hours just after dark. But by the time we had got through Pittsburgh the sky was overcast and the temperature had begun to drop. Soon after 1 A.M. we noticed the first big, soft flakes of snow. I was driving at the time, and Jim was doing most of the talking. I raised one finger from the steering wheel to point out the snow to Jim, and he shook his head unhappily. But he went on talking. We had maintained our steady stream of talk during the first hours of the night partly to keep whoever was at the wheel from going to sleep, but from this point on it was more for the purpose of making us forget the threatening weather. We knew that a really heavy snowstorm could throw our holiday schedule completely out of gear. All night long we talked. Sometimes the snow fell thick and fast, but there were times, too, when it stopped altogether. There was a short period just before dawn when the snow turned to rain— a cold rain, worse than the snow, since it began to freeze on our windshield. By this time, however, we had passed through Philadelphia and we knew that somehow or other we would make it on to New York.

We had left Kenyon at four o'clock in the afternoon, and at eight the next morning we came to the first traffic rotary outside New York, in New Jersey. Half an hour later we saw the skyline of the city, and at the sight of it we both fell silent. I think we were both conscious at that moment not so much of having arrived at our destination as of having only then put Kenyon College behind us. I remember feeling that if I glanced over my shoulder I

might still see on the horizon the tower of Pierce Hall
and the spires of Old Kenyon Dormitory. And in my
mind's eye I saw the other Douglass House boys—all
seven of them—still lingering on the stone steps of the
front stoop, leaning against the iron railing and against
one another, staring after us. But more than that, after
the image had gone I realized suddenly that I had pictured not seven but *nine* figures there before the house,
and that among the other faces I had glimpsed my own
face and that of Jim Prewitt. It seemed to me that we had
been staring after ourselves with the same fixed, brooding
expression in our eyes that I saw in the eyes of the other
boys.

Nancy Gibault was staying in a sort of girls' hotel, or
rooming house, on 114th Street. Before she came down
from her room that Thanksgiving morning, she kept me
waiting in the lobby for nearly forty-five minutes. No
doubt she had planned this as a way of preparing me for
worse things to come. As I sat there, I had ample time to
reflect upon various dire possibilities. I wondered if she
had been out terribly late the night before and, if so,
with whom. I thought of the possibility that she was
angry with me for not letting her know what day I would
get there. (I had had to wait on my check from home, and
there had not been time to let her know exactly when we
would arrive.) I reflected, even, that there was a remote
chance she had not wanted me to come at all. What didn't
occur to me was the possibility that *all* of these things
were true. I sat in that dreary, overheated waiting room,
still wearing my overcoat and holding my hat in my lap.
When Nancy finally came down, she burst into laughter

at the sight of me. I rose slowly from my chair and said angrily, "What are you laughing at? At how long I've waited?"

"No, my dear," she said, crossing the room to where I stood. "I was laughing at the way you were sitting there in your overcoat with your hat in your lap like a little boy."

"I'm sweating like a horse," I said, and began unbuttoning my coat. By this time Nancy was standing directly in front of me, and I leaned forward to kiss her. She drew back with an expression of revulsion on her face.

"Keep your coat on!" she commanded. Then she began giggling and backing away from me. "If you expect me to be seen with you," she said, "you'll go back to wherever you're staying and shave that fuzz off your lip."

For three weeks I had been growing my first mustache.

I had not yet been to the hotel where Jim and I planned to stay. It was a place that Jim knew about, only three or four blocks from where Nancy was living, and I now set out for it on foot, carrying my suitcase. Our car had broken down just after we came up out of the Holland Tunnel. It had been knocking fiercely for the last hour of the trip, and we learned from the garage man with whom we left it that the crankcase was broken. It seems we had burned out a bearing, because we had forgotten to put any oil in the crankcase. I don't think we realized at the time how lucky we were to find a garage open on Thanksgiving morning and, more than that, one that would have the car ready to run again by the following night.

After I had shaved, I went back to Nancy's place. She

had gone upstairs again, but this time she did not keep me waiting so long. She came down wearing a small black hat and carrying a chesterfield coat. Back in St. Louis, she had seldom worn a hat when we went out together, and the sight of her in one now made me feel uncomfortable. We sat down together near the front bay window of that depressing room where I had waited so long, and we talked there for an hour, until it was time to meet Jim and Carol for lunch.

While we talked that morning, Nancy did not tell me that Lon Havemeyer was in town from St. Louis, much less that she had spent all her waking hours with him during the past week. I could not have expected her to tell me at once that she was now engaged to marry him, instead of me, but I did feel afterward that she could have begun at once by telling me that she had been seeing Lon and that he was still in town. It would have kept me from feeling quite so much at sea during the first hours I was with her. Lon was at least seven or eight years older than Nancy, and for five or six years he had been escorting debutantes to parties in St. Louis. His family were of German origin and were as new to society there as members of Nancy's family were old to it. The Havemeyers were also as rich nowadays as the Gibaults were poor. Just after Nancy graduated from Mary Institute, Lon had begun paying her attentions. They went about together a good deal while I was away at college, but between Nancy and me it had always been a great joke. To us, Lon was the essence of all that we were determined to get away from there at home. I don't know what he was really like. I had heard an older cousin of Nancy's say that Lon Havemeyer managed to give the impression of not being dry behind the ears but that the truth was he was "as slick as a newborn babe." But I never exchanged two sentences with him in my life—not even during the miserable day and a half that I was to tag along with him and Nancy in New York.

It may be that Nancy had not known that she was in love with Lon or that she was going to marry him until she saw me there, with the fuzz on my upper lip, that morning. Certainly I must have been an awful sight. Even after I had shaved my mustache, I was still the seedy-looking undergraduate in search of "mature experience." It must have been a frightful embarrassment to her to have to go traipsing about the city with me on Thanksgiving Day. My hair was long, my clothes, though quite genteel, were unpressed, and even rather dirty, and for some reason I was wearing a pair of heavy brogans. Nancy had never seen me out of St. Louis before, and since she had seen me last, she had seen Manhattan. To be fair to her, though, she had seen something more important than that. She had, for better or for worse, seen herself.

We had lunch with Jim and Carol at a little joint over near Columbia, and it was only after we had left them that Nancy told me Lon Havemeyer was in town and waiting that very moment to go with us to the Metropolitan Museum. I burst out laughing when she told me, and she laughed a little, too. I don't remember when I fully realized the significance of Lon's presence in New York. It wasn't that afternoon, or that night, even. It was sometime during the next day, which was Friday. I suppose that I should have realized it earlier and that I just wouldn't. From the time we met Lon on the museum steps, he was with us almost continuously until the last half hour before I took my leave of Nancy the following night. Sometimes I would laugh to myself at the thought of this big German oaf's trailing along with us through the galleries in the afternoon and then to the ballet that night. But I was also angry at Nancy from the start for having let him horn in on our holiday together, and at various moments I pulled her aside and expressed my anger. She would only look at me helplessly, shrug, and say, "I couldn't help it. You really have got to try to see that I couldn't help it."

After the ballet, we joined a group of people who seemed to be business acquaintances of Lon's and went to a Russian nightclub—on Fourteenth Street, I think. (I don't know exactly where it was, for I was lost in New York and kept asking Nancy what part of town we were in.) The next morning, about ten, Nancy and I took the subway down to the neighborhood of Fifty-seventh Street, where we met Lon for breakfast. Later we looked at pictures in some of the galleries. I don't know what became of the afternoon. We saw an awful play that night. I know it was awful, but I don't remember what it was. The events of that second day are almost entirely blotted from my memory. I only know that the mixture of anger and humiliation I felt kept me from ducking out long before the evening was over—a mixture of anger and humiliation and something else, something that I had begun to feel the day before when Nancy and I were having lunch with Jim and Carol Crawford.

Friday night, I was somehow or other permitted to take Nancy home alone from the theatre. We went in a taxi, and neither of us spoke until a few blocks before we reached 114th Street. Finally I said, "Nancy." And Nancy burst into tears.

"You won't understand, and you will never forgive me," she said through her tears, "but I am so terribly in love with him."

I didn't say anything till we had gone another block. Then I said, "How have things gone at the art school?"

Nancy blew her nose and turned her face to me, as she had not done when she spoke before. "Well, I've learned that I'm not an artist. They've made me see that."

"Oh," I said. Then, "Does that make it necessary to—"

"It makes everything in the world look different. If I could only have known in time to write you."

"When did you know?"

"I don't know. I don't know when I knew."

"Well, it's a good thing you came to New York," I said. "You almost made a bad mistake."

"No," she said. "You mustn't think I feel that about you."

"Oh, not about me," I said quickly. "About being an artist. When we were at lunch yesterday, you know, with Jim and his girl, it came over me suddenly that you weren't an artist. Just by looking at you I could tell."

"What a cruel thing to say," she said quietly. All the emotion had gone out of her voice. "Only a child could be so cruel," she said.

When the taxi stopped in front of her place, I opened the door for her but didn't get out, and neither of us said goodbye. I told the driver to wait until she was inside and then gave him the address of my hotel. When, five minutes later, I was getting out and paying the driver, I didn't know how much to tip him. I gave him fifteen cents. He sat with his motor running for a moment, and then, just before he pulled away, he threw the dime and the nickel out on the sidewalk and called out to me at the top of his voice, "You brat!"

The meeting between Nancy and Carol was supposed to be one of the high points of our trip. The four of us ate lunch together that first day sitting in the front booth of a little place that was crowded with Columbia University students. Because this was at noon on Thanksgiving Day, probably not too many restaurants in that neighborhood were open. But I felt that every student in the dark little lunchroom was exulting in his freedom from a certain turkey dinner somewhere, and from some particular family gathering. We four had to sit in the very front booth, which was actually no booth at all but a table and two benches set right in the window. Some people happened to be getting up from that table just as we came in, and Carol, who had brought us here, said, "Quick! We must take this one." Nancy had raised up on her tiptoes and craned her neck, looking for a booth not quite so exposed.

"I think there may be some people leaving back there," she said.

"No," said Carol in a whisper. "Quick! In here." And when we had sat down, she said, "There are some dreadful people I know back there. I'd rather die than have to talk to them."

Nancy and I sat with our backs almost against the plateglass window. There was scarcely room for the two of us on the bench we shared. I am sure the same was true for

Jim and Carol, and they faced us across a table so narrow that when our sandwiches were brought, the four plates could only be arranged in one straight row. There wasn't much conversation while we ate, though Jim and I tried to make a few jokes about our drive through the snow and about how the car broke down. Once, in the middle of something Jim was saying, Carol suddenly ducked her head almost under the table. "Oh, God!" she gasped. "Just my luck!" Jim sat up straighter and started peering out into the street. Nancy and I looked over our shoulders. There was a man walking along the sidewalk on the other side of the broad street.

"You mean that man way over there?" Nancy asked.

"Holy God, yes," hissed Carol. "Do please stop gaping at him."

Nancy giggled. "Is he dreadful, too?" she asked.

Carol straightened and took a sip of her coffee. "No, he's not exactly dreadful. He's the critic Melville Bland." And after a moment: "He's a full professor at Columbia. I was supposed to have dinner today with him and his stupid wife—she's the playwright Dorothy Lewis and really *awfully* stupid—at some chichi place in the East Sixties, and I told them an awful lie about my going out to Connecticut for the day. I'd rather be shot than talk to either of them for five minutes."

I was sitting directly across the table from Carol. While we were there, I had ample opportunity to observe her, without her seeming to notice that I was doing so. My opportunity came each time anyone entered the restaurant or left it. For nobody could approach the glass-front door, either from the street or from inside, without Carol's fastening her eyes upon that person and seeming to take in every detail of his or her appearance. Here, I said to myself, is a real novelist observing people—*objectively* and *critically*. And I was favorably impressed by her obvious concern with literary personages; it showed how committed she was to a life of writing. Carol seemed to me just the girl that Jim had described. Her blonde hair was not really flaxen. (It was golden, which is prettier but which doesn't sound as interesting as flaxen.) It was long and carelessly arranged. I believe Jim was right about its being fixed in a knot on the back of her neck. Her whole appearance showed that she cared as little about it as either Jim or I did about ours. . . . Perhaps *this* was what one's girl really ought to look like.

When we got up to leave, Nancy lingered at the table to put on fresh lipstick. Carol wandered to the newspaper stand beside the front door. Jim and I went together to pay our bills at the counter. As we waited for our change, I said an amiable, pointless "Well?"

"Well what?" Jim said petulantly.

"Well, they've met," I said.

"Yeah," he said. "They've met." He grinned and gave his head a little shake. "But Nancy's just another society girl, old man," he said. "I had expected something more than that." He suddenly looked very unhappy, and rather angry, too. I felt the blood rising in my cheeks and knew in a moment that I had turned quite red. Jim was much heavier than I was, and I would have been no match for him in any real fight, but my impulse was to hit him squarely in the face with my open hand. He must have guessed what I had in mind, for with one movement he jerked off his horn-rimmed glasses and jammed them into the pocket of his jacket.

At that moment, the man behind the counter said, "Do you want this change or not, fellows?"

We took our change and then glared at each other again. I had now had time to wonder what had come over Jim. Out of the corner of my eye I caught a glimpse of Carol at the newsstand and took in for the first time, in that quick glance, that she was wearing huaraches and a peasant skirt and blouse, and that what she now had thrown around her shoulders was not a topcoat but a long green cape. "At least," I said aloud to Jim, "Nancy's not the usual bohemian. She's not the run-of-the-mill arty type."

I fully expected Jim to take a swing at me after that. But, instead, a peculiar expression came over his face and he stood for a moment staring at Carol over there by the newsstand. I recognized the expression as the same one I had seen on his face sometimes in the classroom when his interpretation of a line of poetry had been questioned. He was reconsidering.

When Nancy joined us, Jim spoke to her very politely. But once we were out in the street there was no more conversation between the two couples. We parted at the first street corner, and in parting there was no mention of our joining forces again. That was the last time I ever saw Carol Crawford, and I am sure that Jim and Nancy never met again. At the corner, Nancy and I turned in the direction of her place on 114th Street. We walked for nearly a block without either of us speaking. Then I said, "Since when did you take to wearing a hat everywhere?"

Nancy didn't answer. When we got to her place, she went upstairs for a few minutes, and it was when she came down again that she told me Lon Havemeyer was going to join us at the Metropolitan. Looking back on it, I feel that it may have been only when I asked that question about her hat that Nancy decided definitely about how much Lon and I were going to be seeing of each other during the next thirty-six hours. It is possible, at least, that she called him on the telephone while she was upstairs.

I didn't know about it then, of course, but the reception that Jim Prewitt found awaiting him that morning had, in a sense, been worse even than mine. I didn't know about it and Jim didn't tell me until the following spring, just a few weeks before our graduation from Kenyon. By that time, it all seemed to us like something in the remote past, and Jim made no effort to give me a complete picture of his two days with Carol. The thing he said most about was his reception upon arriving.

He must have arrived at Carol's apartment, somewhere on Morningside Heights, at almost the same moment that I arrived at Nancy's place. He was not, however, kept waiting for forty-five minutes. He was met at the door by a man whom he described as a flabby middle-aged man wearing a patch over one eye, a T shirt, and denim trousers. The man did not introduce himself or ask for Jim's name. He only jerked his head to one side, to indicate that Jim should come in. Even before the door opened, Jim had heard strains of the Brandenburg Concerto from within. Now, as he stepped into the little entryway, the music seemed almost deafening, and when he was led into the room where the phonograph was playing, he could not resist the impulse to make a wry face and clap his hands over his ears.

But although there were half a dozen people in the room, nobody saw the gesture or the face he made. The man with the patch over his eye had preceded him into the room, and everyone else was sitting with eyes cast down or actually closed. Carol sat on the floor tailor-fashion, with an elbow on each knee and her face in her hands. The man with the patch went to her and touched the sole of one of her huaraches with his foot. When she looked up and saw Jim, she gave him no immediate sign of recognition. First she eyed him from head to foot with an air of disapproval. Jim's attire that day, unlike my own, was extremely conventional (though I won't say he ever looked conventional for a moment). At Kenyon, he was usually the most slovenly and ragged-looking of us all. He really went about in tatters, sometimes even with the soles hanging loose from his shoes. But in his closet, off our room, there were always to be found his "good" shoes, his "good" suit, his "good" coat, his "good" hat, all of which had been purchased for him at Brooks Brothers by his mother. Today he had on his "good" things. Probably it was that that made Carol stare at him as she did. At last she gave him a friendly but slightly casual smile, placed a silencing forefinger over her lips, and motioned for him to come sit down beside her and listen to the deafening tones of the concerto.

While the automatic phonograph was changing records, Carol introduced Jim to the other people in the room. She introduced him and everyone else—men and women alike—by their surnames only: "Prewitt, this is Carlson. Meyer, this is Prewitt." Everyone nodded, and the music began again at the same volume. After the Bach there was a Mozart symphony. Finally Jim, without warning, seized Carol by the wrist, forcibly led her from the room, and closed the door after them. He was prepared to tell her precisely what he thought of his reception, but he had no chance to. "Listen to me," Carol began at once—belligerently, threateningly, all but shaking her finger in his face. "I have sold my novel. It was definitely accepted three days ago and is going to be published in the spring. And two sections from it are going to be printed as stories in the *Partisan Review*."

From that moment, Jim and Carol were no more alone than Nancy and I were. Nearly everywhere they went, they went with the group that had been in Carol's apartment that morning. After lunch with us that first noon, they rejoined the same party at someone else's apartment, down in Greenwich Village. When Jim told me about it, he said he could never be sure whose apartment he was in, for they always behaved just as they did at Carol's. He said that once or twice he even found himself answering a knock at the door in some strange apartment and jerking his head at whoever stood outside. The man with the patch over his eye turned out to be a musicologist and composer. The others in the party were writers whose work Jim had read in New Directions Anthologies and in various little magazines, but they seemed to have no interest in anything he had to say about what they had written, and he noticed that their favorite way of disparaging any piece of writing was to say "it's *so* naïve, *so* undergraduate." After Jim got our car from the garage late Friday afternoon, they all decided to drive to New Jersey to see some "established writer" over there, but when they arrived at his house the "established writer" would not receive them.

Jim said there were actually a few times when he managed to get Carol away from her friends. But her book—the book that had been accepted by a publisher—was Carol's Lon Havemeyer, and her book was always with them.

Poor Carol Crawford! How unfair it is to describe her as she was that Thanksgiving weekend in 1939. Ever since she was a little girl on a dairy farm in Wisconsin she had dreamed of becoming a writer and going to live in New York City. She had not merely dreamed of it. She had worked toward it every waking hour of her life, taking jobs after school in the wintertime, and full-time jobs in the summer, always saving the money to put herself through the state University. She had made herself the best student—the prize pupil—in every grade of grammar school and high school. At the University she had managed to win every scholarship in sight. Through all those years she had had but one ambition, and yet I could not have met her at a worse moment in her life. Poor girl, she had just learned that she *was* a writer.

Driving to Boston on Saturday, Jim and I took turns at the wheel again. But now there was no talk about ourselves or about much of anything else. One of us drove while the other slept. Before we reached Boston, in mid-afternoon, it was snowing again. By night, there was a terrible blizzard in Boston.

As soon as we arrived, Jim's father announced that he would not hear of our trying to drive back to Kenyon in such weather and in such a car. Mrs. Prewitt got on the telephone and obtained a train schedule that would start us on our way early the next morning and put us in Cleveland sometime the next night. (From Cleveland we would take a bus to Gambier.) After dinner at the Prewitts' house, I went with Jim over to Cambridge to see some of his prep-school friends who were still at Harvard. The dinner with his parents had been painful enough, since he and I were hardly speaking to each other, but the evening with him and his friends was even worse for me. In the room of one of these friends, they spent the time drinking beer and talking about the undergraduate politics at Harvard and about the Shelley Poetry Prize. One of the friends was editor of the *Crimson,* I believe, and another was editor of the *Advocate*—or perhaps he was just on the staff. I sat in the corner pretending to read old copies of the *Advocate.* It was the first time I had been to Boston or to Cambridge, and ordinarily I would have been interested in forming my own impressions of how people like the Prewitts lived and of what Harvard students were like. But, as things were, I only sat cursing the fate that had made it necessary for me to come on to Boston instead of returning directly to Kenyon. That is, my own money having been exhausted, I was dependent upon the money Jim would get from his parents to pay for the return trip.

Shortly before seven o'clock Sunday morning, I followed Jim down two flights of stairs from his room on the third floor of his family's house. A taxi was waiting for us in the street outside. We were just barely going to make the train. In the hall I shook hands with each of his parents, and he kissed them goodbye. We dashed out the front door and down the steps to the street. Just as we were about to climb into the taxi, Mrs. Prewitt came rushing out, bare-headed and without a wrap, calling to us that we had forgotten to leave the key to the car, which was parked there in front of the house. I dug down into my pocket and pulled out the key along with a pocketful of change. But as I turned back toward Mrs. Prewitt I stumbled on the curb, and the key and the change went flying in every direction and were lost from sight in the deep snow that lay on the ground that morning. Jim and Mrs. Prewitt and I began to search for the key, but Mr. Prewitt called from the doorway that we should go ahead, that we would miss our train. We hopped in the taxi, and it pulled away. When I looked back through the rear window I saw Mrs. Prewitt still searching in the snow and Mr. Prewitt moving slowly down the steps from the house, shaking his head.

On the train that morning Jim and I didn't exchange a word or a glance. We sat in the same coach but in different seats, and we did not go into the diner together for lunch. It wasn't until almost dinnertime that the coach became so crowded that I had either to share my seat with a stranger or to go and sit beside Jim. The day had been long, I had done all the thinking I wanted to do about the way things had turned out in New York. Further, toward the middle of the afternoon I had begun writing in my notebook, and I now had several pages of uncommonly fine prose fiction, which I did not feel averse to reading aloud to someone.

I sat down beside Jim and noticed at once that *his* notebook was open, too. On the white, unlined page that lay open in his lap I saw the twenty or thirty lines of verse he had been working on. It was in pencil, quite smudged from many erasures, and was set down in Jim's own vigorous brand of progressive-school printing.

"What do you have there?" I said indifferently.

"You want to hear it?" he said with equal indifference.

"I guess so," I said. I glanced over at the poem's title, which was "For the Schoolboys of Douglass House," and immediately wished I had not got myself into this. The one thing I didn't want to hear was a preachment from him on his "mature experience" over the holiday. He began reading, and what he read was very nearly this (I have copied this part of the poem down as it later appeared in *Hika,* our undergraduate magazine at Kenyon):

> *Today while we are admissibly ungrown,*
> *Now when we are each half boy, half man,*
> *Let us each contrast himself with himself,*
> *And weighing the halves well, let us each regard*
> *In what manner he has not become a man.*
>
> *Today let us expose, and count as good,*
> *What is mature. And childish peccadillos*
> *Let us laugh out of our didactic house—*
> *The rident punishment one with reward*
> *For him bringing lack of manliness to light.*

But I could take no more than the first two stanzas. And I knew how to stop him. I touched my hand to his sleeve and whispered, "Shades of W. B. Yeats." And I commenced reciting

"Now that we're almost settled in our house
I'll name the friends that cannot sup with us
Beside a fire of turf in th' ancient tower . . ."

Before I knew it, Jim had snatched my notebook from
my hands, and began reading aloud from it:

"She had told him—Janet Monet had, for some in-
scrutable reason which she herself could not fathom,
and which, had he known—as she so positively and
with such likely assurance thought he knew—that if he
came on to New York in the weeks ensuing her so un-
benign father's funeral, she could not entertain him
alone. . . ."

Then he closed my notebook and returned it to me. "I
can put it into rhyme for you, Mr. Henry James," he
said. "It goes like this:

"She knew that he knew that her father was dead.
And she knew that he knew what a life he had led—"

While he was reciting, with a broad grin on his face
and his eyes closed, I left him and went up into the diner
to eat dinner. The next time we met was in the smoking
compartment, at eight o'clock, an hour before we got into
Cleveland.

It was I who wandered into the smoking compartment
first. I went there not to smoke, for neither Jim nor I
started smoking till after we left college, but in the hope

that it might be empty, which, oddly enough, it was at that moment. I sat down by the window, at the end of the long leather seat. But I had scarcely settled myself there and begun staring out into the dark when the green curtain in the doorway was drawn back. I saw the light it let in reflected in the windowpane, and I turned around. Jim was standing in the doorway with the green curtain draped back over his head and shoulders. I don't know why, but it was only then that I realized that Jim, too, had been jilted. Perhaps it was the expression on his face —an expression of disappointment at not finding the smoking compartment empty, at being deprived of his one last chance for solitude before returning to Douglass House. And now—more than I had all day—I hated the sight of him. My lips parted to speak, but he literally took the sarcastic words out of my mouth.

"Ah, you'll get over it, little friend," he said.

Suddenly I was off the leather seat and lunging toward him. And he had snatched off his glasses, with the same swift gesture he had used in the restaurant, and tossed them onto the seat. The train was moving at great speed and must have taken a sharp turn just then. I felt myself thrown forward with more force than I could possibly have mustered in the three or four steps I took. When I hit him, it was not with my fists, or even my open hands, but with my shoulder, as though I was blocking in a game of football. He staggered back through the doorway and into the narrow passage, and for a moment the green curtain separated us. Then he came back. He came at me just as I had come at him, with his arms half folded over his chest. The blow he struck me with his shoulders sent me into the corner of the leather seat again. But I, too, came back.

Apparently neither of us felt any impulse to strike the other with his fist or to take hold and wrestle. On the contrary, I think we felt a mutual abhorrence and revulsion toward any kind of physical contact between us, and if our fight had taken any other form than the one it did, I think that murder would almost certainly have been committed in the smoking compartment that night. We shoved each other about the little room for nearly half an hour, with ever increasing violence, our purpose always seeming to be to get the other through the narrow doorway and into the passage—out of sight behind the green curtain.

From time to time, after our first exchange of shoves, various would-be smokers appeared in the doorway. But they invariably beat a quick retreat. At last one of them found the conductor and sent him in to stop us. By then it was all over, however. The conductor stood in the doorway a moment before he spoke, and we stared at him from opposite corners of the room. He was an old man with an inquiring and rather friendly look on his face. He looked like a man who might have fought gamecocks in his day, and I think he must have waited that moment in the doorway in the hope of seeing something of the spectacle that had been described to him. But by then each of us was drenched in sweat, and I know from a later examination of my arms and chest and back that I was covered with bruises.

When the old conductor was satisfied that there was not going to be another rush from either of us, he glanced about the room to see if we had done any damage. We had not even upset the spittoon. Even Jim's glasses were safe on the leather seat. "If you boys want to stay on this train," the conductor said finally, "you'll hightail it back to your places before I pull that emergency cord."

We were only thirty minutes out of Cleveland then, but when I got back to my seat in the coach I fell asleep at once. It was a blissful kind of sleep, despite the fact that I woke up every five minutes or so and peered out into the night to see if I could see the lights of Cleveland yet. Each time, as I dropped off to sleep again, I would say to myself what a fine sort of sleep it was, and each time it seemed that the wheels of the train were saying: *Not yet, not yet, not yet.*

After Cleveland there was a four-hour ride by bus to Gambier. Sitting side by side in the bus, Jim and I kept up a continuous flow of uninhibited and even confidential talk about ourselves, about our writing, and even about the possibility of going to graduate school next year if the Army didn't take us. I don't think we were silent a moment until we were off the bus and, as we paced along the Middle Path, came in sight of Douglass House. It was 1 A.M., but through the bare branches of the trees we saw a light burning in the front dormer of our room. Immediately our talk was hushed, and we stopped dead still. Then, though we were as yet two hundred feet from the house and there was a blanket of snow on the ground, we began running on tiptoe and whispering our conjectures about what was going on in our room. We took the steps of the front stoop two at a time, and when we opened the front door, we were met by the odor of something cooking —bacon, or perhaps ham. We went up the long flight to the second floor on tiptoe, being careful not to bump our suitcases against the wall or the banisters. The door to our room was the first one at the top of the stairs. Jim seized the knob and threw the door open. The seven whom we had left lolling around the stoop on Wednesday were sprawled about our big room in various stages of undress, and all of them were eating. Bruce Gordon and Bill Anderson were in the center of the room, leaning over my hot plate.

Jim and I pushed through the doorway and stood on the doorstep looking down at them. I have never before or since seen seven such sober—no, such frightened-looking—people. Most eyes were directed at me, because it was my hot plate. But when Jim stepped down into the room, the two boys lounging back on his bed quickly stood up.

I remember my first feeling of outrage. The sacred privacy of that room under the eaves of Douglass House had been violated; this on top of what had happened in New York seemed for a moment more than flesh and blood could bear. Then, all of a sudden, Jim Prewitt and I began to laugh. Jim dropped his suitcase and went over to where the cooking was going on and said, "Give me something to eat. I haven't eaten all day."

I stood for a while leaning against the wall just inside the door. I was thinking of the tramps we had seen cooking down along the railroad track in the valley. Finally I said, "What a bunch of hoboes!" Everyone laughed—a little nervously, perhaps, but with a certain heartiness, too.

I continued to stand just inside the door, and presently I leaned my head against the wall and shut my eyes. My head swam for a moment. I had the sensation of being on the train again, swaying from side to side. It was hard to believe that I was really back in Douglass House and that the trip was over. I don't know how long I stood there that way. I was dead for sleep, and as I stood there with my eyes closed I could still hear the train wheels saying *Not yet, not yet, not yet.*

Je Suis Perdu

———◆◆———

L'Allegro

The sound of their laughter came to him along the narrow passage that split the apartment in two. It was the laughter of his wife and his little daughter, and he could tell they were laughing at something the baby had done or had tried to say. Shutting off the water in the washbasin, he cracked the door and listened. There was simply no mistaking a certain note in the little girl's giggles. Her naturally deep little voice could never be brought to such a high pitch except by her baby brother's "being funny." And on such a day as this, the day for packing the last suitcases and for setting the furnished apartment in order, the day before the day when they would really pull up stakes in Paris and take the boat train for Cherbourg— on such a day, only the baby could evoke from its mother

that resonant, relaxed, almost abandoned kind of laughter.
. . . *They* were in the dining room just sitting down to
breakfast. *He* had eaten when he got up with the baby
an hour before, and was now in the *salle de bain* preparing to shave.

The *salle de bain,* which was at one end of the long
central passage, was the only room in the apartment that
always went by its French name. For good reason, too: It
lacked the one all-important convenience that an American expects of what he will willingly call a bathroom. It
possessed a bathtub and a washbasin, and it had a bidet,
which was wonderful for washing the baby in. But the
missing convenience was in a closet close by the entrance
to the apartment, at the very opposite end of the passage
from the *salle de bain.* Altogether it was a devilish arrangement. But the separation of conveniences was not itself so devilish as the particular location of each. For instance just now, with only a towel wrapped around his
middle and with his face already lathered, he hesitated to
throw open the door and take part in a long-distance conversation with the rest of the family, because at any moment he expected to hear the maid's key rattling in the
old-fashioned lock of the entry door down the passage.
Instead, he had to remain inside the *salle de bain* with his
hand on the doorknob and his gaze on the blank washbasin mirror (still misted over from the hot bath he had
just got out of); had to stand there and be content merely
with hearing the sound of merriment in yonder, not able
—no matter how hard he strained—to determine the
precise cause of it.

At last, he could resist no longer. He pushed the door

half open and called out to them, "What is it? What's the baby up to?"

His daughter's voice piped from the dining room, "Come see, Daddy! Come see him!" And in the next instant she had bounced out of the dining room into the passage, and she continued bouncing up and down there as if she were on a pogo stick. She was a tall little girl for her seven years, and she looked positively lanky in her straight white nightgown and with her yellow hair not yet combed this morning but drawn roughly into a ponytail high on the back of her head.

And then his wife's voice: "It's incredible, honey! You really must come! And quick, before he stops! He's a perfect little monkey!"

But already it was too late. The maid's key rattled noisily in the lock. As he quickly stepped backward into the *salle de bain* and pulled the door to, he called to them in a stage whisper, "Bring me my bathrobe."

Through the door he heard his wife's answer: "You know your bathrobe's packed. You said you wouldn't need it again. Put on your clothes."

His trousers and his shirt and underwear hung on one door hook, beside his pajamas on another. His first impulse was to slip into his clothes and go and see what it was the baby was doing. But on second thought there seemed too many arguments against this. His face was already lathered. He much, much preferred shaving as he now was, wearing only his towel. But still more compelling was the argument that it was to be a very special shave this morning. *This morning the mustache was going to go!*

Months back he had made a secret pact with himself to the effect that if the work he came over here to do was really finished when the year was up, then the mustache he had begun growing the day he arrived would *go* the day he left. From the beginning his wife had pretended to loathe it, though he knew she rather favored the idea as long as they were here, and only dreaded, as he did, the prospect of his going home with that brush on his upper lip. But he had not even mentioned the possibility of shaving the mustache. And as he wiped the mist from the mirror and then slipped a fresh blade into his razor he smiled in anticipation of the carrying on there would be over its removal.

In the passage now there was the clacking sound of the maid's footsteps. He could hear her taking all her usual steps—putting away the milk and bread that she had picked up on her way to work, crossing to the cloak closet, and placing her worn suede jacket and her silk scarf on a hanger—just as though this were not her last day on the job; or rather, last day with *them* in the apartment, because she was coming the following day, faithful and obliging soul, to wax the floors and hang the clean curtains she herself had washed. Their blessed, hard-working Marie. According to his wife, their having had Marie constituted their greatest luck and their greatest luxury this year. He scarcely ever saw her himself, and sometimes he had passed her down on the Boulevard without recognizing her until, belatedly, he realized that it had been her scarf and her jacket, and his baby in the carriage she pushed. But he had gradually assumed his wife's view that their getting hold of Marie had been the real pinnacle of all their good luck about living arrangements.

Their apartment was a fourth-floor walkup, overlooking the Boulevard Saint-Michel and just two doors from the Rue des Écoles; with its genuine *chauffage central* and its Swedish kitchen, and even a study for him. It was everything they could have wished for. At first they had thought they ought not to afford such an apartment as this one, but because of the children they decided it was worth the price to them. And after his work on the book got off to a good start and he saw that the first draft would almost certainly get finished this year, they decided that it would be a shame not to make the most of the year; that is, not to have some degree of freedom from housekeeping and looking after the children. And so they spoke to the concierge, who recommended Marie to them, saying that she was a mature woman who knew what it was to work but who might have to be forgiven a good deal of ignorance since she had not lived always in Paris. They had found nothing to forgive in Marie. Even her haggard appearance his wife had come to speak of as her "ascetic look." Even her reluctance to try to understand a single word of English represented, as did the noisy rattling of the door key, her extreme consideration for their privacy. Every morning at half-past eight, her key rattled in the lock to their door. She was with them all day, sometimes taking the children to the park, always going out to do more marketing, never off her feet, never idle a moment until she had prepared their evening meal and left them, to ride the Metro across Paris again—almost to Saint-Denis—and prepare another evening meal for her own husband and son.

Yet this maid of theirs was, in his mind, only a symbol of how they had been served this year. It was hard to think of anything that had not worked out in their favor. They had ended by even liking their landlady, who, although she lived but a block away up the Boulevard Saint-Michel, had been no bother to them whatever, and had just yesterday actually returned the full amount of their deposit on the furniture. Their luck had, of course, been phenomenal. After one week in the Hôtel des Saints-Pères, someone there had told them about M. Pavlushkoff, "the honest real-estate agent." They had put their problem in the hands of this splendid White Russian—this amiable, honest, intelligent, efficient man, with his office (to signalize his greatest virtue, his sensibility) in the beautiful Place des Vosges. Once M. Pavlushkoff had found them their apartment they never saw him again, but periodically he would telephone them to inquire if all went well and if he could assist them in any way. And once in a desperate hour—near midnight—they telephoned him, to ask for the name of a doctor. In less than half an hour M. Pavlushkoff had sent dear old Dr. Marceau to them.

And Dr. Marceau himself had been another of their angels. The concierge had fetched round another doctor for them the previous afternoon, and he had made the little girl's ailment out to be something very grave and mysterious. He had prescribed some kind of febrifuge and the burning of eucalyptus leaves in her room. But Dr. Marceau immediately diagnosed measles (which they had believed it to be all along, with half her class at L'École Père Castor already out of school with it). Next day, Dr. Marceau had returned to give the baby an injection that made the little fellow's case a light one; and later on he saw them through the children's siege of chicken pox.

Both the children were completely charmed by the old
Doctor. Even on that first visit, when the little girl had
not yet taken possession of the French language, she found
the Doctor irresistible. He had bent over her and listened
to her heart not through a stethoscope but with only a
piece of Kleenex spread out between her bare chest and
his big pink ear. As he listened, sticking the top of his
bald head directly in her face, he quite unintentionally
tickled her nose with the pretty ruffle of white hair that
ringed his pate. Instantly the little girl's eyes met her
mother's. From her sickbed she burst into giggles and
came near to causing her mother to do the same. After
that, whenever the Doctor came to see her, or to see her
little brother, she would insist upon his listening to her
heart. It would be hard to say whether Dr. Marceau was
ever aware of why the little girl giggled, but he always
said in French that she had the heart of a lioness, and he
always stopped and kissed her on the forehead when he
was leaving.

That's what the whole year had been like. There was
that, and there had been the project—the work on his
book, which was about certain Confederate statesmen and
agents who, with their families, were in Paris at the end
of the Civil War, and who had to decide whether to go
home and live under the new regime or remain permanently in Europe.

As far as his research was concerned, he had soon found
that there was nothing to be got hold of at the Biblio-
thèque Nationale or anywhere else in Paris that was not
available at home. And yet how stimulating to his imagination it was just to walk along the Rue de l'Université in
the late afternoon, or along the Rue de Varenne, or over

on the other side of the Seine along the Rue de Rivoli and the Rue Saint-Antoine, hunting out the old addresses of the people he was writing about. And of course how stimulating to his work it was just being in Paris, no matter what his subject. Certain of his cronies back home at the University had accused him of selecting his subject merely as an excuse to come to Paris. . . . He couldn't be sure himself what part that had played in it. But it didn't matter. *He had had the idea, and he had done the work.*

With his face smoothly shaven, and dressed in his clean clothes, he was in such gay spirits that he was tempted to go into the dining room and announce that he was dedicating this book to M. Pavlushkoff, to Dr. Marceau, to Marie, to all his French collaborators.

He found the family in the dining room, still lingering over breakfast, the little girl still in her nightgown, his wife in her nylon housecoat. At sight of his naked upper lip his wife's face lit up. Without rising from her chair, she threw out her arms, saying, *"I* must have the first kiss! How beautiful you are!"

The little girl burst into laughter again. "Mama!" she exclaimed. "Don't *say* that! *Men* aren't beautiful, *are* they, Daddy?" She still had not noticed that the mustache was gone.

It was only a token kiss he got from his wife. She was afraid that Marie might come in at any moment to take their breakfast dishes. Keeping her eyes on the door to the passage, she began pushing him away almost before their lips met. And so he turned to his daughter, trying to give her a kiss. Still she hadn't grasped what had brought on her parents' foolishness, and she wriggled away from him and out of her chair, laughing and fairly shrieking out, "What's the matter with him, Mama?"

"Just look!" whispered his wife; and at first he thought of course she meant look at him. "Look at the baby, for heaven's sake," she said.

The baby was in his playpen in the corner of the dining room. With his hands clasped on the top of his head and his fat little legs stuck out before him, he was using his heels to turn himself round and round, pivoting on his bottom.

"How remarkable!" the baby's daddy now heard himself saying.

"Watch his eyes," said the mother. "Watch how he rolls them."

"Why, he *is* rolling them! How really remarkable!" He glanced joyfully at his wife.

"That's only the half of it," she said. "In a minute he'll begin going around the other way and rolling his eyes in the other direction."

"It's amazing," he said, speaking very earnestly and staring at the baby. "He already has better coordination than I've *ever* had or ever *hope* to have. I've noticed it in other things he's done recently. What a lucky break!"

And presently the baby, having made three complete turns to the right, did begin revolving the other way round and rolling his eyes in the other direction. The two parents and the little girl were laughing together now and exchanging intermittent glances in order to share the moment fully. The most comical aspect of it was the serious expression on the baby's face, particularly at the moment when, facing them and stopping quite still, he

shifted the direction of his eye rolling. At this moment
the little girl's voice moved up at least one octave. She
never showed any natural jealousy of her baby brother,
but at such times as this she often seemed to be determined to outdo her parents in their amusement and in
their admiration of the baby. Just now she was so con-
vulsed with laughter that she staggered back to her chair
and threw herself into it and leaned against the table.
As she did so, one of her flailing hands struck her milk
glass, which was still half full. The milk poured out over
the placemat and then traced little white rivulets over
the dark surface of the table.

Both parents pounced upon the child at once: "Honey!
Honey! Watch out! Watch what you're doing!"

The little girl crimsoned. Her lips trembled as she said
under her breath, "Je regrette."

"If you had drunk your milk this wouldn't have happened," said the mother, dabbing at the milk with a
paper napkin.

"Regardless of that," said the father with unusual se-
verity in his voice, "she has no business throwing herself
about so and going into such paroxysms over nothing."
But he knew, really, that it was not the threshing about
that irritated him so much as it was the lapse into French.
And it was almost as though his wife understood this and
wished to point it out. For, discovering that a few drops
of milk had trickled down one table leg and onto the carpet, she turned and herself called out in French to the
maid to come and bring a cloth. His own mastery of
French speech, he reflected, was the thing that *hadn't*
gone well this year. After all, as he was in the habit of
telling himself, *he* hadn't had the opportunity to converse

with Marie a large part of each day, or to attend a pri-
mary school where the teacher and the other pupils spoke
no English, and he hadn't—with his responsibilities to
his work and his family—been able to hang about the
cafés like some student. It was a consoling thought. Right-
eously, he put aside his irritation.

But now his little daughter, sitting erect in her chair,
repeated aloud: "Je regrette. Je regrette." This time it
affected him differently. It was impossible to tell whether
she was using the French phrase deliberately or whether
she wasn't even aware of doing so. But whether deliberate
or not, it had its effect on her father. For a time it caused
him to stare at his daughter with the same kind of interest
that he had watched his son with a few moments before.
And all the while his mind was busily tying the present
incident to one that had occurred several weeks before.
He had taken the little girl to see an old Charlie Chaplin
film one afternoon at a little movie theatre around the
corner from them on the Rue des Écoles. They had stayed
on after the feature to see the newsreel, and then after
the newsreel, along with a fairly large proportion of the
audience, they had risen in the dark to make their way
out. The ushers at the rear of the theatre were not able
to restrain the crowd that was waiting for seats; and so
there was the inevitable mêlée in the aisles. When finally
he came out into the lighted lobby he assumed that his
little girl was still sticking close behind him, and he began getting into his mackinaw without even looking back
to see that she was there. Yes, it was thoughtless of him,
all right; but it was what he had done. As he tugged at
the belt of the bulky mackinaw he became aware of a
small voice crying out above the noise of the canned

music back in the theatre. What interested him first was
merely the fact that he did understand the cry: *"Je suis
perdue! Je suis perdue!"* Actually he didn't recognize it
as his daughter's voice until rather casually and quite by
chance he glanced behind him and saw that she was not
there. He threw himself against the crowd that was still
emerging from the exit, all the while mumbling apologies to them in his Tennessee French which he was sure
they would not understand (though himself understanding perfectly their oaths and expletives) and still hearing
from the darkness ahead her repeated cry: *"Je suis perdue!"* When he found her she was standing against the
side wall of the theatre, perfectly rigid. Reaching down
in the darkness to take her hand he found her hand made
into a tight little fist. By the time he got her out into the
light of the lobby her hand in his felt quite relaxed.
Along the way she had begun to cry a little, but already
she was smiling at him through her tears. "I thought I
was lost, Daddy," she said to him. He had been so relieved
at finding her and at seeing her smiling so soon that he
had not even tried to explain how it had happened, much
less describe the chilling sensations that had been his at
that moment when he realized it was the voice of his own
child calling out to him, in French, that she was lost.

Now, in the dining room of their apartment, he was
looking into the same flushed little face and suddenly he
saw that the eyelashes were wet with tears. He was overcome with shame.

His wife must have discovered the tears at the same
moment. He glanced at her and saw that she, too, was
now filled with pity for the child and was probably think-

ing, as he was, that they were all of them keyed up this morning of their last day before starting home.

"Oh, it's all right, sweetie," said his wife, putting her hand on the top of the blond little head and pointing out the milk to Marie. "Accidents will happen."

Squatting down beside his daughter, he said, "Don't you notice anything different?" And he stuck his forefinger across his upper lip.

"Oh, Mama, it's gone!" she squealed. Placing her two little hands on his shoulders, she bent forward and kissed him on the mouth. "Mama, you're right," she exclaimed. "He *is* beautiful!"

After that, the spilt milk and the baby's gyrations were events of ancient history—dismissed and utterly forgotten.

A few minutes later, the little girl and Marie were beside the playpen chattering to the baby in French. His wife had wandered off into the bedroom, where she would dress and then throw herself into a final fury of packing. She had already asked him to make himself scarce this day, to keep out of the way of women's work. *His* duties, she had said, would begin when it came time to leave for the boat train tomorrow morning. Now he followed her into the bedroom to put on a tie and a jacket before setting out on his day's expedition.

She had taken off her housecoat and was standing in her slip before the big armoire, searching there among the few dresses that hadn't already been packed for something she might wear today. He stopped in front of the mirror above the chest of drawers and began slipping a tie into his collar. He was thinking of just how he would spend his

nothing unplanned nothing spontaneous

last day. Not, certainly, with any of his acquaintances. He had said goodbye to everyone he wanted to say goodbye to. No, he would enjoy the luxury of being by himself, of buying a paper and reading it over coffee somewhere, of wandering perhaps one more time through the Luxembourg Gardens—the wonderful luxury of walking in Paris on a June day without purpose or direction.

When he had finished with his tie, he discovered that his wife was now watching his face in the mirror. She was smiling, and as their eyes met she said, "I'm glad you shaved it but I shall miss it a little, along with everything else." And before she began pulling her dress over her head she blew him a kiss.

Il Penserosa

The feeling came over him in the Luxembourg Gardens at the very moment he was passing the Medici Grotto at the end of its little lagoon. He simply could not imagine what it was that had been able to depress his spirits so devastatingly on a day that had begun so well. Looking back at the grotto, he wanted to think that his depression had been induced by the ugliness and the triteness of the sculpture about the fountain there, but he knew that the fountain had nothing to do with it. He was so eager to dispel this sudden gloom and return to his earlier mood, however, that he turned to walk back to the spot and see what else might have struck his eye. Above all, it was important for it to be something outside himself that had crushed his fine spirits this way, and that was thus threatening to spoil his day.

He didn't actually return to the spot, but he did linger a

moment by the corner of the Palace, beside a flower bed where two workmen—surreptitiously it seemed to him— were sinking little clay pots of already blooming geranium plants into the black soil, trying to make it look as though the plants honestly grew and bloomed there. From here he eyed other strollers along the path and beside the lagoon, hoping to discover in one of them something tragic or pathetic which he might hold responsible for the change he had felt come over him. He would have much preferred finding an object, something not human, to pin it on, but, that failing, he was now willing to settle for any unhappy or unpleasant-looking person—a stranger, of course, someone who had no claim of any kind on him. But every child and its nurse, each shabby student with satchel and notebooks, every old gentleman or old lady waiting for his terrier or her poodle to perform in the center of the footpath appeared relatively happy (in their limited French way, of course, he found himself thinking)—as happy, almost, as he must have appeared not five minutes earlier. He even tried looking farther back on the path toward the gate into the Rue de Vaugirard, but it availed him nothing. Then his thoughts took him beyond the gate, and he remembered the miserable twenty minutes he had just been forced to spend trying to read his paper and enjoy his coffee in the Café Tournon, while a bearded fellow-American explained to him what was wrong with their country and why Americans were "universally unpopular" abroad.

But even this wouldn't do. For he was as used to the ubiquitous bearded American and his café explanations of everything as he was to the ugly Italian grotto; and he disliked them to just the same degree and found them equally incapable of disturbing him in this way. He gave up the search now, and as he strode out into the brightness of the big sunken garden he quietly conceded the truth of the matter: the feeling was not evoked by his surroundings at all but had sprung from something inside himself. Further, it was not worth all this searching; it wasn't important; it would pass soon. Why, as soon as it had run its course with him he would not even remember the feeling again until. . . . until it would come upon him again in the same unreasonable way, perhaps in six months, or in a few days, or in a year. When the mood was not on him, he could never believe in it. For instance, while he had been shaving this morning he truly did not know or, rather, he *knew not* that he was ever in his life subject to such fits of melancholy and gloom. . . . But still the mood *was* on him now. And actually he understood the source well enough.

It sprang from the same thing his earlier cheerful mood had come from—his own consciousness of how well everything had gone for him this year, and last year, and always, really. It was precisely this, he told himself, that depressed him. At the present moment he could almost wish that he hadn't finished the work on his book. He was able to wish this (or almost wish it) because he knew it was so typical of him to have accomplished just precisely what he had come to accomplish—and so American of him. Generally speaking, he didn't dislike being himself or being American, but to recognize that he was so definitely the man he was, so definitely the combination he was, and that certain experiences and accomplishments were now typical of him was to recognize how he was getting along in the world and how the time was moving by. He was only thirty-eight.

But the bad thought was that he was no longer *going to be* this or that. He *was*. It was a matter of *being*. And to *be* meant, or seemed to mean at such a moment, to *be over with*. Yet this, too, was a tiresome, recurrent thought of his —very literary, he considered it, and a platitude.

He went on with his walk. The Jardin du Luxembourg was perfection this morning, with its own special kind of sky and air and its wall of flat-topped chestnuts with their own delicate shade of green foliage, and he tried to feel guilty about his wife's being stuck back there in the apartment, packing their possessions, trying to fit everything that had not gone into the foot lockers and the duffelbags into six small pieces of luggage. But the guiltiness he tried for wouldn't materialize. Instead, he had a nasty little feeling of envy at her packing. And so he had to return to his efforts at delighting in the singular charm of the park on a day like this. "There is nothing else like it in Paris," he said, moving his lips, "which is to say there is nothing else like it in the world." And this pleased him just as long as it took for his lips to form the words.

It wasn't yet midmorning, but the little boys—both the ragged and the absurdly over-dressed-up ones—had already formed their circle about the boat basin in the center, and, balancing themselves on the masonry there, were sending their sailboats out over the bright water. This was almost a cheering sight to him. But not quite. For it was, after all, a regular seasonal feature of the place, like the puppet shows and the potted palm trees, and it was hardly less artificial in its effect.

He was rounding the lower garden of the park now; had passed the steps that lead up toward the Boulevard Saint-Michel entrance and toward that overpowering monster the Panthéon. (There were monsters and monstrous things everywhere he turned now.) He was walking just below the clumsy balustrade of the upper garden; and now, across the boat basin, across the potted flower beds and the potted palms, above the heads of the fun-loving, freedom-loving, stiff-necked, and pallid-faced Parisians, he saw the façade of the old Palace itself. It also loomed large and menacing. There was no look of fun or freedom about it. It did not smile down upon the garden. Rather, out of that pile of ponderous, dirty stone, all speckled with pigeon droppings, twenty-eyes glared at him over the iron fencing, which seemed surely to have been put there to protect the people from the monster—not the monster from the people. It was those vast, terrible, blank windows, like the whitened eyes of a blind horse, that made the building hideous. How could anyone ever have found it a thing of beauty? How could. . . . Then suddenly: "Oh, do stop it!" he said to himself. But he couldn't stop it. Wasn't it from one of those awful windows that the great David, as a prisoner of the Revolution, had painted his only landscape? That unpleasant man David, that future emperor of art, that personification of the final dead end to a long-dying tradition! "Oh, do stop it!" he said again to himself. "Can't you stop it?"

 But still he couldn't. The Palace *was* a tomb. The park was a formal cemetery. He was where everything was finished and over with. Too much had already happened here, and whatever else might come would be only anti-climactic. And nothing could be so anticlimactic as an American living on the left bank of the Seine and taking a morning walk in the Jardin du Luxembourg. He remembered two novels whose first chapters took for their setting this very spot. Nothing was so deadening to a place as literature! And wasn't it true, after all, that their year in that fourth-floor walkup had been a dismal, lonely one? Regardless of his having got his work done, of his having had his afternoons free to wander not only through the streets where his heroes had once lived but also through the Louvre and the Musée Cluny and through the old crumbling *hôtels* of the Marais? Regardless of the friends they had made and even of the occasional gay evening on the town. Wasn't it really so that he had just not been willing to admit this truth until this moment? Wasn't it so, really, that he had come to Paris too late? That this was a city for the very young and the very rich, and that he, being neither, might as well not have come? What was he but a poor plodding fellow approaching middle age, doing all right, getting along with his work well enough, providing for his family; and the years were moving by. . . .

Suddenly he turned his back on the boat basin and the Palace, and started at a brisk pace up the ramp that leads toward the great gilded south gate. And immediately he saw his daughter in the crowd! She was moving toward him, walking under the trees.

He saw her before she saw him. This gave him time to gather his wits, and to recall that his wife, as soon as she got *him* out of the apartment, was determined to get *them* out, too, so that there would be no one to interfere with her packing. And now, during the moment that *she* did not see him, he managed to find something that he could be cross with her about. She was ambling along, absent-mindedly leaning on the baby's carriage—that *awful* habit of hers—and making it all but impossible for

Marie to push the carriage. She had come out from under the trees now, and as she skipped and danced along, her two bouncing blond ponytails, which Marie had fixed, one directly above each ear, were literally dazzling in the sunlight. "Daddy," she said, as she came within his shadow on the gravel path. Her eyes were just exactly the color of the park's own blue heaven. His wife's mother had said it didn't seem quite normal for a girl to have such "positive blue" eyes. And her long little face with the chin just a tiny bit crooked, like his own!

He took her hand, and they went down the ramp toward the row of chairs on their left. "If we sit down, you'll have to pay," she warned him.

"That's all right," he said.

"I'll sit on your lap if you'll give me the ten francs for the extra chair."

"And if I won't?"

"Oh, I'll sit on your lap anyway, since you've shaved that mustache."

The old woman who collected for chairs was hot on their heels. He paid for the single chair and tipped her the price of another.

"I saw how much you gave her," his daughter said reproachfully. "But it's all right. She's one of the nice ones."

"Oh, they're all nice when you get to know them," he said, laughing.

She nodded. "And isn't it a lovely park, Daddy? I think it is."

"It's too bad we're going home so soon, isn't it?" he said.

"Daddy, we just *got* here!" she protested.

"I mean going back to America, silly," he said.

"I thought you meant to the apartment. . . . But we're *not* going back to America *today*."

"No, but tomorrow."

"Well, what difference does *that* make?"

He saw Marie approaching with the carriage. "Let's give our chair to Marie, since I have to be on my way," he said.

"Then you have to leave now?" she asked forlornly.

He gave her a big squeeze with his arms and held her a moment longer on his knee. He was wondering where his dark mood had gone. It was not just gone. He felt it had never been. And why had he lied to himself about this year? It *had* been a fine year. But still he kept thinking also of how she had interrupted his mood. And as soon as she was off his knee, he began to feel resentful again of the interruption and of the mysterious power she had over him. He found that he wanted the mood of despondency to return, and he knew it wouldn't for a long while. It was something she had taken from him, something she had taken from him before and would take from him again and again—she and the little fellow in the carriage there, and their mother, too, even before they were born. They would never allow him to have it for days and days at a time, as he once did. He felt he had been cheated. But this was not a mood, it was only a thought. He felt a great loss—except he didn't really feel it, he only thought of it. And he felt, he *knew* that he had after all gotten to Paris too late . . . after he had already established steady habits of work . . . after he had acknowledged claims that others had on him . . . after there were ideas and truths and work and people that he loved better even than himself.

Heads of Houses

— ◆ —

I. THE FOREIGN PARTS AND THE
FORGET-ME-NOTS

Kitty's old bachelor brother gave Dwight a hand with the
baggage as far as the car, but Dwight would accept no more
help than that. He had his own method of fitting everything into the trunk. His Olivetti and his portable record-
player went on the inside, where they would be most
protected. The overnight bag and the children's box of play-
things went on the outside, where they would be handy in
case of an overnight stop. It was very neat the way he did
it. And he had long since learned how to hoist the two
heaviest pieces into the rack on top of the car with almost
no effort, and knew how to wedge them in up there so that
they hardly needed the elastic straps he had bought in Italy
last summer. He was a big, lanky man, with a lean jaw that
listed to one side, and normally his movements were so de-

liberate, and yet so faltering, that anyone who did not mistake him for a sleepwalker recognized him at once for a college professor. But he never appeared less professorial, and never felt less so, than when he was loading the baggage on top of his little car. As he worked at it now, he was proud of his speed and efficiency, and was not at all unhappy to have his father-in-law watching from the porch of the big summer cottage.

From the porch, Kitty's father watched Dwight's packing activities with a cold and critical eye. Only gypsies, Judge Parker felt, rode about the country with their possessions tied all over the outside of their cars. Such baggage this was, too! His son-in-law seemed purposely to have chosen the two most disreputable-looking pieces to exhibit to the public eye. Perhaps he had selected these two because they had more of the European stickers on them than any of the other bags—not to mention the number of steamship stickers proclaiming that the Dwight Clarks always traveled Tourist Class!

Yet the exposed baggage was not half so irritating to Judge Parker as the little foreign car itself. The car would have been bad enough if it had been one of the showy, sporty models, but Dwight's car had a practical-foreign look to it that told the mountain people, over in the village, as well as the summer people from Nashville and Memphis, over in the resort grounds and at the Hotel, how committed Dwight was to whatever it was he thought he was committed to. The trouble was, it was a *big* little car. At first glance, you couldn't quite tell what was wrong with it. Yet it was little enough to have to have a baggage rack on top; and inside it there was too little room for Dwight and Kitty to take along even the one basket of fruit that

Kitty's mother had bought for them yesterday. Judge Parker pushed himself as far back in his rocker as he safely could. For a moment he managed to put the banister railing between his eyes and the car. He meant *not* to be irritated. He had been warned by his wife to be careful about what he said to his son-in-law this morning. After all, the long summer visit from the children was nearly over now.

Busy at work, Dwight was conscious of having more audience than just Dad Parker—an unseen, and unseeing, audience inside the cottage. Certain noises he made, he knew, telegraphed his progress to Kitty. She was upstairs—in the half story, that is, where everybody but Dad and Mother Parker slept—making sure both children used the bathroom before breakfast. (She knew he would not allow them time for the bathroom after breakfast.) And the same noises—the slamming down of the trunk lid, for instance, and even the scraping of the heavy bags over the little railing to the rack (the *galerie,* Dwight called it fondly)—would reach the ears of brother Henry, now stationed inside the screen door, considerately keeping hands off another man's work. The ears of Mother Parker would be reached, too, all the way back in the kitchen. Or, since breakfast must be about ready now, Mother Parker might be on the back porch, where the table was laid, waiting ever so patiently. Perhaps she was rearranging the fruit in the handmade basket, which she had bought at the arts-crafts shop, and which she was sure she could find space for in the car after everything else was in. . . . Everybody, in short, was keeping out of the way and being very patient and considerate. It really seemed to Dwight Clark that he and his little family might make their getaway, on this September morning, without harsh words from any quarter. He counted it

almost a miracle that such a summer could be concluded
without an open quarrel of any kind. Along toward the
end of July, midway in the visit, he had thought it certain
Kitty would not last. But now it was nearly over.

When the last strap over the bags was in place, Dwight
stepped away from the car and admired his work. He even
paused long enough to give a loving glance to the little
black car itself, his English Ford, bought in France two
summers ago. Such a sensible car it was, for a man who
wanted other things out of life than just a car. No fins, no
chromium, no high-test gasoline for him! And soon now
he and Kitty would be settled inside it, and they would be
on their way again, with just their own children, and
headed back toward their own life: to the life at the University, to life in their sensible little prefab, with their
own pictures and their own makeshift furniture (he could
hardly wait for the sight of his books on the brick-and-
board shelves!), to their plans for scrimping through another winter in order to go abroad again next summer—
their life. Suddenly, he had a vision of them in Spain next
summer, speeding along through Castile in the little black
automobile, with the baggage piled high and casting its
shadow on the hot roadside. He stepped toward the car
again, with one long arm extended as if he were going to
caress it. Instead, he gave the elastic straps—his Italian
straps, he liked to call them—their final testing, snapping
them against the bags with satisfaction, knowing that Kitty
would hear, knowing that, for once, she would welcome
this signal that he was all set.

He turned away from the car, half expecting to see Kitty
and the children already on the porch. But they were still
upstairs, of course; and breakfast had to be eaten yet. Even

Dad Parker seemed to have disappeared from the porch. But, no, there he was, hiding behind the banisters. What was he up to? Usually the old gentleman kept his dignity, no matter what. It didn't matter, though. Dwight would pretend not to notice. He dropped his eyes to the ground. . . . As he advanced toward the house, he resolved that this one time he was not going to be impatient with Kitty about setting out. He would keep quiet at the breakfast table. One impatient word from anybody, at this point, might set off fireworks between Kitty and her mother, between Kitty and her father. (He glanced up, and, lo, Dad Parker had popped up in a normal position again.) Between Kitty and her ineffectual old bachelor brother, even. (He wished Henry would either get away from that door or come on outside where he could be seen.) And if she got into it with them, Dwight knew he could not resist joining her. It would be too bad, here at last, but their impositions upon Kitty this summer had been quite beyond the pale— not to mention their general lack of appreciation of all she and he had undertaken to do for them, which, of course, he didn't mind for *himself,* and not to mention their show of resentment against *him,* toward the last, merely because he was taking Kitty away from them ten days earlier than the plans had originally called for. The truth was that they had no respect for his profession; they resented the fact that his department chairman could summon him back two weeks before classes would begin. . . . For a moment, he forgot that, in fact, the chairman had not summoned him back.

As Dwight approached the porch, in his slow, lumbering gait, Judge Parker suddenly rocked forward in his chair. Stretching his long torso still farther forward, he rested the

elbows of his white shirtsleeves on the banister railing.
Dwight, out there in the morning sun, seemed actually to
be walking with his eyes closed. Perhaps he was only looking down, but, anyway, he came shambling across the lawn
as though he didn't know where he was going. Judge
Parker had noticed, before this, that when his son-in-law
was let loose in a big open space, or even in a big room, he
seemed to wander without any direction. The fellow was
incapable of moving in a straight line from one point to
another. He was the same way in an argument. Right now,
no doubt, he had a theory about where the porch steps
were, and he would blunder along till he arrived at the
foot of them. But what a way of doing things, especially
for a man who was always talking about the scientific approach. It had been, this summer, like having a great
clumsy farm animal as a house guest. It had been hardest,
the Judge reflected, on his wife, Jane. Poor old girl. Why,
between the fellow's typewriter and record-player, she had
hardly had one good afternoon nap out. And, oh, the ash-
trays and the glasses that had been broken, and even furniture. For a son-in-law they had the kind of man who
couldn't sit in a straight chair without trying to balance
himself on its back legs. . . . Out-of-doors he was worse, if
anything. He had rented a power mower and cut the grass
himself, instead of letting them hire some mountain white
to do it, as they had in recent years. He had insisted, too,
on helping the Judge weed and work his flower beds. As
a result, Judge Parker's flowers had been trampled until
he could hardly bear to look at some of the beds. A stray
horse or cow couldn't have done more damage. All at once,
he realized that there was an immediate danger of Dwight's
stumbling into his rock garden, beside the porch steps, and

crushing one of his ferns—his *Dryopteris spinulosa.* Somehow, he must wake the boy up. He must *say* something to him. He cleared his throat and began to speak. As he spoke, he allowed his big, well-manicured hands to drape themselves elegantly over the porch banisters.

"Professor Clark," he began, not knowing what he was going to say, but using his most affectionate form of address for Dwight. "Is it," he said, casting about for something amiable, "is it thirty-eight miles to the gallon you get?"

Dwight stopped, and looked up with a startled expression. He might really have been a man waked from sleepwalking. But gradually a suspicious, crooked smile appeared, twisting his chin still farther out of any normal alignment. *"Twenty*-eight to the gallon, Dad Parker," he said.

"Oh, yes, that's what I meant to say!"

What could have made him say *thirty,* he wondered. Not that he knew or cared anything about car mileage. It always annoyed him that people found it such an absorbing topic. Even Jane knew more about his Buick than he did, and whenever anyone asked him, he had to ask her what mileage they got.

But he couldn't let the exchange stop there. Dwight would think his slip was intentional. Worse still, his son Henry, behind the screen door, would be making *his* mental notes on how ill the summer had gone. The Judge had to make his interest seem genuine. "That does make it cheap to operate," he ventured. "And it has a four-cylinder motor. Think of that!"

"Six cylinders," said Dwight, no longer smiling.

The Judge made one more try. "Of course, of course. Yours is an Ambassador. It's the Consul that has four."

"Mine is called a Zephyr," Dwight said.

There was nothing left for Judge Parker to do but throw back his head and try to laugh it off. At any rate, he had saved his fern.

At the steps to the porch, a porch that encompassed the cottage on three sides and that was set very high, with dark green latticework underneath, and with the one steep flight of steps under the cupola, at the southwest corner—at the foot of the steps Dwight stopped and turned to look along the west side of the house. Dad Parker's lilac bushes grew there. Wood ashes were heaped about their roots. Beyond the lilacs was the rock pump house, and just beyond that Dwight had a view of Dad Parker's bed of forget-me-nots mixed with delphiniums. Or was it bachelor's-buttons mixed with ageratum? He was trying to get hold of himself after the Judge's sarcasm about the car. In effect, he was counting to a hundred, as Kitty had told him he must do this morning.

For the peace must be kept this morning, at any price— for Kitty's sake. For her and the children's sake he had to control himself through one more meal. And the only way he could was to convince himself that Dad Parker's mistakes about the car were real ones. With anybody but Judge Nathan Parker it would have been impossible. But in the case of the Judge it *was* possible. The man knew less than any Zulu about the workings of cars, to say nothing of models of foreign makes. This father-in-law of his most assuredly had some deep neurosis about anything vaguely mechanical. Even the innocent little Italian typewriter had

offended him. And instead of coming right out and saying
that Dwight's typing got on his nerves, he had had to ask
his rhetorical questions, before the whole family, about
whether Dwight thought good prose could be composed on
"a machine." "I always found it necessary to write my
briefs and decisions in longhand," he said, "if they were to
sound like much." And the record-player, too. The Judge
despised canned music; he preferred the music he made
himself, on his violoncello, which instrument he frequently
brought out of the closet after dinner at night, strumming
it along with whatever popular stuff came over the radio.
. . . There was not even a telephone in the cottage. That
seemed to Dwight the *purest* affectation. Dad and Mother
Parker were forever penning little notes to people over in
the resort grounds, or at the Hotel. They carried on a vo-
luminous correspondence with their friends back in Nashville. During the week, they wrote notes to brother Henry,
who had to keep at his job at the courthouse in Nashville
all summer long, and only came up to the Mountain for
weekend's. In fact, three weeks ago, when the generator on
Dwight's car went dead, Dad Parker had insisted upon
writing brother Henry about it. The garage in the mountain village could not furnish brushes and armatures for
an English Ford, of course, but from the telephone office
Dwight might have called some garage in Nashville, or
even in Chattanooga, which was nearer. Instead, he had
had to tell Dad Parker what was needed and let Henry attend to it. Henry did attend to it, and very promptly. The
parts arrived in the mail just two days later. When the
Judge returned from the village post office that morning,
he handed Dwight the two little packages, saying, "Well,
Herr Professor, here are your 'foreign parts.' " Every-

body had laughed—even Kitty, for a moment. But Dwight hadn't laughed. He had only stood examining the two little brown packages, which were neatly and securely wrapped, as only an old bachelor could have wrapped them, and addressed to him in Henry's old-fashioned, clerkish-looking longhand.

At the foot of the porch steps, Dwight was listening hopefully for the sound of Kitty's footsteps on the stairs inside. He remained there for perhaps two or three minutes, with his eyes fixed in a trancelike gaze upon the mass of broad-leaved forget-me-nots. (They *were* forget-me-nots, he had decided.) Presently he saw out of the corner of his eye, without really looking, that Dad Parker had produced the morning paper from somewhere and was offering him half of it, holding it out toward him without saying a word. At the same moment, out in the rock pump house, the pump's electric motor came on with a wheeze and a whine. Someone had flushed the toilet upstairs. It was the first flush since Dwight came downstairs, and so he knew that Kitty and the children would not be along for some minutes yet. There would have to be one more flush.

As he went up to the porch to receive a section of the paper, the pump continued to run, making a noise like a muffled siren. That was its *good* sound. It *wasn't* thumping, which was its bad sound and meant trouble. Probably the low ebb in understanding between Kitty and her mother this summer had been during the second dry spell in July. Kitty had come to the Mountain with the intention of relieving her mother of the laundry, as well as of all cooking and dishwashing. Those were the things that Mother Parker had hated about the Mountain when Kitty was growing up. She had missed her good colored servants in

Nashville and couldn't stand the mountain "help" that was available. But it seemed that Kitty didn't understand how to operate her mother's new washing machine economically —with reference to water, that is. During that dry spell, Mother Parker took to hiding the table linen and bed-sheets, and the old lady would rise in the morning before Kitty did, and run them through the washer herself. No real water crisis ever developed, but, realizing that Dad Parker would be helpless to deal with it if it did, Dwight got hold of the old manual that had come with the pump, when it was installed a dozen years before, and believed that he understood how to prime it, or even to "pull the pipe" in an emergency. Having learned from the manual that every flush of the toilet used five gallons of water, he estimated that during a dry spell it wasn't safe to flush it more than three times in one day. And as a result of this knowledge it became necessary for him to put a padlock on the bath-room door so as to prevent Dwight, Jr., aged four, from sneaking upstairs and flushing the toilet just for kicks.

It seemed that the pump, like everybody else, was try-ing to make only its polite noises this morning. But just as Dwight was accepting his half of the newspaper, the pump gave one ominous, threatening thump. Dwight went tense all over. There had been no rain for nearly three weeks. There might yet be a crisis with the pump. In such case, brother Henry would be no more help than Dad Parker. It could, conceivably, delay Dwight's departure a whole day. If that happened, it might entail his pretending to get off a telegram to the chairman of his department. More-over, he would have to do this before the eyes of brother Henry, in whom Kitty, in a weak moment, had confided the desperate measure they had taken to bring the summer visit to an end. It was Henry, lurking there in the shadows, that really depressed him. It seemed to him that Henry had come up for weekends this summer just to lurk in the shadows. Had he joined in one single game of croquet? He had not. And each time Dwight produced his miniature chess set, Henry had made excuses and put him off.

Dwight looked into Dad Parker's eyes to see if the thump had registered with him. But of course it *hadn't* registered. And when the motor went off peacefully, and when everything was all right again, that of course didn't register, either. To Dwight's searching look Dad Parker responded merely by knitting his shaggy brows and putting one hand up to his polka-dot bow tie to make out if anything was wrong there. Everything was fine with the Judge's tie, as it always was. He gave Dwight a baffled, pitying glance and then disappeared behind his half of the morning paper.

II. THE GARDEN HOUSE

Dwight sat down on a little cane-bottomed chair and tilted it on its back legs. He opened his half of the paper. His was the second section, with the sports and the funnies. He had learned early in the summer to pretend he preferred to read that section first. Dad Parker had been delighted with this, naturally, but even so he hadn't been able to conceal his astonishment—to put it mildly—that a grown man could have such a preference. To the Judge it seemed the duty of all educated, responsible gentlemen to read the national and international news before breakfast every morning. He liked to have something important—and controversial, if possible—for the talk at the breakfast table.

Dwight, tilting back in his chair and hiding behind his paper, was listening for the pump to come on again. He felt positively panicky at the prospect of staying another day, or half day. One more flush of the toilet and he would be free. To think that five gallons of water *might* stand between him and his return to his own way of life! He found that he could not concentrate on the baseball scores, and he didn't even try to read "Pogo." Then, at last, the pump did come on, and it was all right. And again it went off with a single thump, which, as a matter of fact, it nearly always went off with.

Dwight sat wondering at his own keyed-up foolishness, but still he found it irksome that Dad Parker could sit over there calmly reading the paper, unaware even that there was such a thing as an electric pump on the place. It seemed that once the pump had been installed, the Judge had deafened his ears to it and put it forever out of his mind. This was just the way he had behaved during the worst dry spell. But Dwight understood fully why no water shortage could ever be a problem for Dad Parker. To begin with, he watered his flowers only with rain water that he brought in a bucket from the old cistern—water that was no longer considered safe for drinking. And Dad Parker, personally, still used the garden house.

The garden house! Dwight was alarmed again. The garden house? Was there any reason for the thought of it to disturb him? There must be. His subconscious mind had sent up a warning. The garden house was connected with some imminent threat to his well-being, possibly even to his departure this morning. Quickly, he began trying to trace it down, forming a mental image of the edifice itself, which was located a hundred yards to the east of the cottage, along the ridge of the Mountain. This structure was, without question, the sturdiest and most imposing on the Parkers' summer property. "Large, light and airy, it is most commodious"—that was how Dad Parker had described the building to Dwight when he and Kitty were first married and before Dwight had yet seen the family's summer place. And Dwight had never since heard him speak of the building except in similar lyrical terms. Like the pump house, it was built of native rock, quarried on the mountainside just three or four miles away; but it had been built a half century back, when masonry work done on the Mountain was of a good deal higher order than it was nowadays. Family tradition had it that one spring soon after Kitty's grandfather had had their cottage built, the men of a local mountain family had constructed the garden house for the grandfather free of charge and entirely on their own initiative. It was standing there to surprise "the Old Judge," as the grandfather was still remembered and spoken of locally, when he and the family came up to the Mountain that July. The Old Judge had not actually been a judge at all, but an unusually influential and a tolerably rich lawyer, at Nashville, and he had befriended this mountain family sometime previously by representing them in a court action brought against one of their number for disturbing the peace. They had repaid him by constructing a garden house that was unique in the whole region. Its spacious interior was lighted by rows of transom windows, set high in three of the four walls. Below these windows, at comfortable intervals, were accommodations for eight persons, and underneath was a seemingly bottomless pit. Best of all, the building was so situated that when the door was not closed, its open doorway commanded a view of the valley that was unmatched anywhere on the Mountain. . . . It was there that Dad Parker usually went to read the first section of the paper, before breakfast every morning. And frequently he read the second section there, after breakfast. Suddenly a bell rang in Dwight's conscious mind, and the message came through. Dad Parker had, this morning, already read the first section of the paper once! From the east dormer window, half an hour before, Dwight had seen him returning from the garden house, paper in hand. It was extremely odd, to say the least, for him to sit there poring over the news a second time. Usually, when he had read the paper once, he knew it by heart and never needed to glance at it again—not even to prove a point in an argument. What was he up to? First he had hidden behind the banisters, now behind the paper.

Involuntarily, almost, Dwight tilted his chair still farther back, to get a look at Dad Parker's face. The chair creaked under his weight. Remembering he had already broken one of these chairs this summer, he quickly brought it back to all fours. Another broken chair might somehow delay their getting off! The chair wasn't damaged this time, but the glimpse Dwight had had of Dad Parker left him stunned. The old gentleman's face was as red as a beet, and he was reading something in the paper, something that made his eyes, normally set deep in their sockets, seem about to pop out of his head.

By the time the front legs of Dwight's chair hit the floor, the Judge had already closed the paper and begun folding it. As he tucked it safely under his arm, he looked at Dwight and gave him a grin that was clearly sheepish— guilty, even.

But deep in the old man's eyes was a look of firm resolve. A resolve, Dwight felt certain, that *he,* Dwight, should not under any circumstances see the front section of the paper before setting off this morning. Dwight couldn't imagine what the article might be. He had but one clue. He had observed, without thinking about it, that the Judge had had the paper open to the inside of the last page. That was where society news was printed, and it was one page that the Judge seldom read. Dwight realized now that Dad Parker had given him the second section as a kind of peace offering. And while going through the first section again he had stumbled on something awful.

From inside the cottage there came the sound of Kitty's and the children's footsteps on the stairs.

III. AN OLD BACHELOR BROTHER

Henry Parker, just inside the screen door, heard Kitty and her children start downstairs. He pushed the door open and went out on the porch. Through the screen he had been watching his father and his brother-in-law, hiding from each other behind their papers. He believed he knew precisely what thoughts were troubling the two men. He had refrained from joining them because ever since he arrived from Nashville last night he had sensed that his own presence only aggravated their present suffering. Each of them was suffering from an acute awareness that he was practicing a stupid deception upon the other, as well as from a fear that he might be discovered. His brother-in-law was leaving the Mountain under the pretense that he had been called back to his university. The Judge was concealing the fact that there was a party of house guests expected to arrive from Nashville this very day—almost as soon as the Clarks were out of the house—and that an elaborate garden party was planned for Monday, which would be Labor Day. Each man knew that Henry knew about his deception, and each wished, with Henry, that Henry could have stayed on in Nashville this one week-end. Henry couldn't stay in Nashville, however—for good and sufficient reasons—and just now he couldn't remain inside the screen door any longer. Kitty was on the stairs, and his mother was coming up the hall from the kitchen. His lingering there would be interpreted by them as peculiar.

Just as Henry made his appearance on the porch, Dwight and the Judge came to their feet. They, too, had heard the footsteps of the women and children. It was time for breakfast. Henry walked over to his father and said casually, "Wonder if I could have a glance at the paper?" The Judge glared at him as though his simple request were a personal insult.

"The paper," Henry repeated, reaching out a hand toward the newspaper, which the Judge now clutched under his upper arm. The Judge continued to glare, and Henry continued to hold out his hand. Henry's hands were of the same graceful and manly proportions as his father's, but, unlike the Judge, he didn't "use" his hands and make them "speak." He also had his father's same deep-set eyes, and the same high forehead—even higher, since his hair, unlike his father's, was beginning to recede. He glared back at his father, half in fun, supposing the refusal to be some kind of joke. Finally, he took hold of the paper and tried to pull it free. But the Judge held on.

"May I just glance at the headlines?" Henry said sharply, dropping his hand.

"No, you may not," said the Judge. "We are all going in to breakfast now."

Dwight stepped forward, smiling, and silently offered his section of the paper to Henry. Henry accepted it, but his heart sank when he looked into Dwight's face. Dwight's face, this morning, was the face of an appeaser. Only now did Henry realize that both men imagined he might, out of malice or stupidity, spill their beans at the breakfast table. The Judge, it seemed, meant to bluff and badger him into silence; Dwight intended to appease him.

Henry took the paper over to the edge of the porch, leaned against the banister, and lit a cigarette. His mother and sister were standing together in the doorway now, and his father had set out in their direction.

"Breakfast, everybody," said his mother. By "everybody," he knew, she meant him, because he was the only one who had ignored her appearance there. He glanced up from the paper, smiled at her and nodded, then returned his eyes to the paper, which he held carelessly on his knee.

"Henry has taken a notion to read the newspaper at this point," he heard his father say just before he marched inside the cottage.

His brother-in-law lingered a moment. There seemed to be something Dwight wanted to say to Henry. But Henry didn't look up; he couldn't bear to. Dwight moved off toward the doorway without speaking.

"Don't be difficult, Henry," his sister Kitty said cheerfully. Then she and her mother went inside, with Dwight following them.

Henry heard them go back through the cottage to the screened porch in the rear. He knew he would have to join them there presently. He supposed that, whether they knew it or not, they needed him. They were so weary of their own differences that any addition to their company would be welcome, even someone who knew too much.

And how much too much *he* knew!—about them, about himself, about everybody. That was the trouble with him, of course. *He* could have told them beforehand how this summer would turn out. But they had known, really, how it would turn out, and had gone ahead with it anyway; and that was the difference between him and them, and that was the story of his bachelorhood, the story of his life. He flicked his cigarette out onto the lawn and folded the paper neatly over the banister. No, it wasn't quite so simple as that, he thought—the real difference, the real story wasn't. But he had learned to think of himself sometimes as others thought of him, and to play the role he was assigned. It was an easy way to avoid thinking of how things really were with him. Here he was, so it appeared, an old-fashioned old bachelor son, without any other life of his own, pouting because his father had been rude to him on the veranda of their summer cottage on a bright September morning. Henry Parker was a man capable even of thinking inside this role assigned him, and not, for the time being, as a man whose other life was so much more real and so much more complicated that there were certain moments in his summer weekends at this familiar cottage when he had to remind himself who these people about him were. For thirteen years, "life" to him had

meant his life with Nora McLarnen, his love affair with a
woman tied to another man through her children, tied to a
husband who, like her, was a Roman Catholic and who,
though they had been separated all those years, would not
give her a divorce except on the most humiliating terms.
Henry had learned how to think, on certain occasions with
the family, as the fond old bachelor son. And he knew that
presently he, the old bachelor, must get over his peeve and
begin to have generous thoughts again about his father,
and about the others, too.

It *had* been a wretched summer for all four of them,
and they had got into the mess merely because they
wanted to keep up the family ties. His mother was to be
pitied most. His mother had finally arranged her summers
at the cottage so that they were not all drudgery for her,
the way they used to be when she had two small children,
or even two big children, in the days when their cottage
was not even wired for electricity and when, of course, she
had no electric stove or refrigerator or washing machine
and dryer. But in making their plans for this visit Dwight
and Kitty had completely failed to understand this. Kitty
had moved in and taken over where no taking over was
needed. Not only that. Because Dwight had to do his writing—for ten years now they had been hearing about that
book of his—and because Dwight and Kitty so disdained
the social life that Mother and Dad had with the other
summer residents, she had forgone almost all summer social life. Henry had it from his mother that the party on
Monday was supposed to make it up to Dad's and her
friends for their peculiar behavior this summer, and was
not really intended as a celebration of their daughter's
departure. To have concealed their plans was silly of

them, but Mother had been afraid of how it might sound to Dwight and Kitty.

Kitty had to be a sympathetic figure, too, in the old bachelor's eyes. Kitty had written her mother beforehand that they would come to the Mountain only if she could be allowed to take over the housekeeping. Yet her mother had "frustrated" her at every turn. She wouldn't keep out of the kitchen, she wouldn't let Kitty do the washing. Further, Henry agreed with his sister that the cottage had suffered at their mother's hands, that it had none of the charm it had had when they were growing up. It was no longer a summer place, properly speaking. It was Nashville moved to the Mountain. There was no longer the lighting of kerosene lamps at twilight, no more chopping of wood for the stove, no more fetching of water from the cistern. The interior of the house had been utterly transformed. Rugs covered the floors everywhere—the splintery pine floors that Mother so deplored. The iron bedsteads had disappeared from the bedrooms; the living-room rockers were now used on the porch. Nowadays, cherry and maple antiques set the tone of the house. The dining room even ran to mahogany. And, for the living room, an oil portrait of the Old Judge had been brought up from the house in Nashville to hang above the new mantelpiece, with its broken ogee and fluted side columns. With such furnishings, Kitty complained, children had to be watched every minute, and could not have the run of the house the way they did when she and Henry and their visiting cousins were growing up. It was all changed.

As for the lot of the two men this summer—well, he should worry about them. When thinking of *them,* he couldn't quite keep it up as the sympathetic old bachelor who took other people's problems to heart. What was one summer, more or less, of not having things just as you wanted them? Next summer, or even tomorrow, or an hour from now, each of them would have it all his way again. And by any reasonable view of things that was what a man must do. A man couldn't afford to get lost in a laby-rinth of self-doubts. And a man must be the head of his house. They were the heads of their houses, certainly, and they knew what they wanted, and they had their "values." Both of them knew, for instance, that they hated lying about small domestic matters, and tomorrow, or the next hour, would likely find them both berating their wives for having involved them in something that was "against their principles." Henry sighed audibly, took out another cigarette, then put it back in the package. If they but knew how practiced *he* was—without a wife—at lying about small domestic matters! If they knew his skill in that art, they wouldn't be worrying lest he make some faux pas at the breakfast table.

Finally, Henry bestirred himself. He crossed the porch and opened the screen door. Passing from the light of out-of-doors into the long, dark hall, which ran straight through the cottage to the back porch, he was reminded of something that had caught his attention when he was leaving Nashville, yesterday afternoon. As he was enter-ing a railroad underpass, he glanced up and saw that there was something scrawled in large black letters high above the entrance. He had driven through his same tun-nel countless times in the past, but the writing had never caught his attention before. It was the simple question *Have you had yours*—with the question mark left off.

Perhaps it had been put there recently, or it might have been there for years. Some sort of black paint, or perhaps tar, had been used. And it was placed so high on the cement casement and was so crudely lettered that the author must have leaned over from above to do his work. Somehow, as he drove on through the tunnel, Henry had felt tempted to turn around at the other end and go back and read the inscription again, to make sure he had read it correctly. He hadn't turned around, of course, but during the eighty-mile drive to the Mountain the words had kept coming back to him. He thought of the trouble and time the author had taken to place his question there. He supposed the author's intention was obscene, that the question referred to fornication. And he had the vague feeling now that the question had turned up in his dreams last night; but he was seldom able to remember his dreams very distinctly. At any rate, the meaning of the question for him seemed very clear when it came back to him now, and it did not refer to fornication. The answer seemed clear, too: *He* had not had *his*. He had not had his what? Why, he had not had his Certainty. That was what the two men had. Neither of the two seemed ideally suited to the variety of it he had got; each of them, early in life, had merely begun acquiring whatever brand of Certainty was most available; and, apparently, if you didn't take that, you took none at all. Professor Dwight Clark was forever depending upon manuals and instruction books. (He even had an instruction book for his little Ford, and with the aid of it could install a new generator.) And Professor Clark had to keep going back to Europe, had literally to see every inch of it in order to believe in it enough to teach his history classes and do his writing.

And the Judge's garden, while it contained only flowers
and combinations of flowers that might have been found
in any ante-bellum garden, was so symmetrically, so regularly laid out and so precisely and meticulously cared for
that you felt the gardener must surely be some sweet-
natured Frankenstein monster. And the decisions that the
Judge handed down from the Bench were famous for their
regard for the letter of the law. Lawyers seldom referred
to him as "Judge Parker." By his friends he was spoken of
as "Mr. Law." Amongst his enemies he was known as
"Solomon's Baby." . . . But what was Henry Parker
known as? Well, he wasn't much known. He was assistant
to the registrar of deeds. He was Judge Parker's son; he
was a Democrat, more or less. At the courthouse he was
thought awfully well informed—about county govern-
ment, for one thing. People came to him for information,
and took it away with them, thinking it was something
Henry Parker would never find any use for. He had passed
a variety of civil-service examinations with the highest
rating on record, but he had taken the examinations only
to see what they were like and what was in them. He did
his quiet, pleasant work in his comfortable office on the
second floor of the courthouse. The building was well
heated in the winter and cool in the summer. Two doors
down the corridor from him, Nora McLarnen was usually
at her typewriter in the license bureau. Their summers,
his and Nora's, were all that made life tolerable. With *his*
parents at the Mountain, and *her* two sons away at camp,
they could go around together with no worry about embarrassing anyone that mattered to them. Their future
was a question, a problem they had always vaguely hoped
would somehow solve itself. That is, until this summer.

During past summers, Henry had come to the Mountain on weekends for the sake of his parents, or for the
sake of making sure his mother had no reason to come
down to Nashville on an errand or to see about him. But
this summer he had come mostly for Nora's sake. Her
older boy was now sixteen and had not wanted to go to
camp. He had been at home, with a job as lifeguard at one
of the public swimming pools. Nora had wanted to devote
her weekends to Jimmy. And by now, of course, the
younger boy had returned from camp. For Labor Day,
Nora had agreed to attend a picnic with the boys and their
father—a picnic given by the insurance company for
which John McLarnen was a salesman. All summer it had
been on Nora's mind that the boys' growing up was going
to change things. In the years just ahead they would need
her perhaps more than before, and they would become
sensitive to her relationship with Henry. She was thinking
of quitting her job, she was thinking of letting her husband support her again, she was wondering if she mightn't
yet manage to forgive John McLarnen's unfaithfulness to
her when she was the mother of two small children, if she
hadn't as a younger woman been too intolerant of his
coarse nature. She would not, of course, go back to her
husband without Henry's consent. But with his consent
Henry felt now pretty certain that she would go back to
him. They had discussed the possibility several times, very
rationally and objectively. They had not quarreled about
it, but they seemed to have quarreled about almost
everything else this summer. He thought he saw what
was ahead.

He was so absorbed in his thoughts as he went down the
hall that when he passed the open door to his parents'

bedroom he at first gave no thought to the glimpse he had of his father in there. It was only when he was well past the door that he stopped dead still, realizing that his father was on his knees beside the bed. He was not praying, either. He was stuffing something under the mattress. And Henry did not have to look again to know that it was the newspaper he was hiding. He hurried on back to the screened porch, and, somehow, the sight of Dwight, bent over his grapefruit, wearing his traveling clothes—his dacron suit, his nylon tie, his wash-and-wear shirt—told Henry what it was the Judge had to conceal. There would be an article on the society page—something chatty in a column, probably—about those two couples who were driving up to visit the Nathan Parkers, and even a mention of the garden party on Monday.

IV. THE APPLES OF ACCORD

Kitty was determined that the two children should eat a good breakfast this morning, and she saw to it that they did. Mrs. Parker, who had insisted upon preparing and serving breakfast unassisted, was "up and down" all through the meal. The two women were kept so busy—or kept themselves so busy—that they seemed for the most part unmindful of the men. They took no notice of how long the Judge delayed coming to the table, or even that Henry actually appeared before his father did. When everybody had finished his grapefruit, and the men began making conversation amongst themselves, the two wives seemed even not to notice the extraordinarily amiable tone of their husbands' voices or the agreeable nature of their every remark. The only sign Kitty gave of following the conversation was to give a bemused smile or to nod her dark head sometimes when Dwight expressed agreement with her father. And sometimes when the Judge responded favorably to an opinion of Dwight's, Mrs. Parker would lift her eyebrows and tilt her head gracefully, as though listening to distant music.

Henry's first impression was that there had not, after all, been a crying need for his presence. His father and his brother-in-law, who a few minutes before had been hiding behind their papers to avoid talking to each other, were now bent upon keeping up a lively and friendly exchange. The Judge was seated at his end of the table, with Henry at his left and with Dwight on the other side of Henry at Mrs. Parker's right. Across the table from Henry and Dwight, Kitty sat between the two children.

The first topic, introduced by Dwight, was that of the routing to be followed on his trip. Dwight thought it best to go over to Nashville and then up through Louisville.

"You're absolutely right, Professor," the Judge agreed. "When heading for the Midwest, there is no avoiding Kentucky. But keep *off* Kentucky's back roads!"

Henry joined in, suggesting that the Knoxville-Middleboro-Lexington route was "not too bad" nowadays.

"I find the mountain driving more tiring," Dwight said politely, thus disposing of Henry's suggestion.

"And, incidentally, it is exactly a hundred and fifty miles out of your way to go by Knoxville and Middleboro," the Judge added, addressing Dwight.

Then, rather quickly, Dwight launched into a description of a rainstorm he had been caught in near Middleboro once. When he had finished, the Judge said he supposed there was nothing like being caught in a downpour in the mountains.

But the mention of Knoxville reminded the Judge of something he had come across in the morning paper, and his amnesia with regard to his hogging and hiding the first section was so thoroughgoing that he didn't hesitate to speak of what he had read. "There's an editorial today on that agitator up in East Tennessee," he said. "Looks as though they've finally settled his hash, thank God."

"I'm certainly glad," said Dwight. It was the case of the Yankee segregationist who had stirred up so much trouble. Dwight and the Judge by no means saw eye to eye on segregation, but here was one development in that controversy that they could agree on. "That judge at Knoxville has shown considerable courage," Dwight said.

"I suppose so. Yes, it's taken courage," said Judge Parker, grudgingly, yet pleased, as always, to hear any favorable comment on the judiciary. "But it is the law of the land. I don't see he had any alternative."

Henry opened his mouth, intending to say that the judge in question was known to be a man of principle, and if it had gone against his principle, Henry was sure that he would have . . . But he wasn't allowed to finish his thought, even, much less put it into words and speak it.

"Still and all, still and all," his father began again, in the way he had of beginning a sentence before he knew what he was going to say. "Still and all, he's a good man and knows the law. He was a Democrat, you know." His use of "was" indicated only that it was a federal judge they were referring to, and that he was therefore as good as dead—politically, of course.

"No, I didn't know he was a Democrat," Dwight said, hugely gratified.

Here was another topic, indeed. Dwight and the Judge were both Democrats, and it didn't matter at the moment that they belonged to different wings of the party. But Dwight postponed for a little the felicity they would enjoy in that area. He had thought of something else that mustn't be passed up. "I understand," he said, pushing the last of his bacon into his mouth and chewing on it rather playfully, "I understand, Judge, that the Catholics have gotten the jump on everybody in Nashville."

The Judge closed his eyes, then opened them wide, suppressing a smile—or pretending to. "They've integrated, you mean?"

The machinations of the Catholic Church was a subject they never failed to agree on. "Not only in Nashville," Dwight said. "Everywhere."

"Very altruistic," said the Judge.

"Ah, yes. Very."

"If the *other* political parties were as much on their toes as that one, politics in this country would still be interesting."

Henry felt annoyed by this line they always took about the Catholic Church. Perhaps *he* should become a Catholic. That would give him his Certainty, all right. He grimaced inwardly, thinking of the suffering Nora's being a Catholic had brought the two of them. He realized that he resented the slur on the Church merely because the Church was something he associated with Nora. Silly as it seemed, Nora still came in the category of "Nashville Catholics." She was still a communicant, he supposed, and yet this proved that you could be a Catholic without developing the Certainty he had in mind. . . . But he didn't try to contribute anything on this subject. He had already seen that contributions from him were not necessary. Perhaps his father and his brother-in-law were no longer consciously trying to keep him silent, but they were in such high spirits over their forthcoming release from each other's company that each now had ears only for the other's voice. And, without knowing it, they seemed to be competing to see who could introduce the most felicitous subject.

From the subject of Nashville Catholics it was such an easy and natural step to Senator Kennedy, and so to national politics, that Henry was hardly aware when the shift came. Everybody had finished eating now. The men had pushed their chairs back a little way from the table. Dwight, in his exuberance, was happily tilting his, though presently Kitty gave him a sign and he stopped. Neither the Judge nor Dwight was sure of how good a candidate Kennedy would make. They both really wished that Truman—good old Truman—could head the ticket again. They both admired that man—not for the same reasons, but no matter.

Meanwhile, Kitty and her mother, having finished their own breakfasts and feeling quite comfortable about the way things were going with the men, began a private conversation at their corner of the table. It was about the basket of fruit, which Mrs. Parker still hoped they would find room for in the car. In order to make themselves heard above the men's talk and above the children, who were picking at each other across their mother's plate, it was necessary for them to raise their voices somewhat. Presently, this mere female chatter interfered with the conversation of the men. Judge Parker had just embarked on an account of the Democratic convention of 1928, which he had attended. He meant to draw a parallel between it and the 1960 convention-to-be. But the women's voices distracted him. He stopped his story, leaned forward and took a last sip of his coffee, and said very quietly, "Mother, Dwight and I are having some difficulty understanding each other."

Mrs. Parker blushed. She had thought things were going so well between the two men! How could *she* help them understand each other?

"Is the question of the basket of fruit really so important?" the Judge clarified.

Mrs. Parker tried to laugh. Kitty rallied to her support. "It's pretty important," she said good-naturedly.

Henry hated seeing his mother embarrassed. "I imagine it's as important as any other subject," he said.

The Judge's eyes blazed. He let his mouth fall open. "Can you please tell me in what sense it is as important as any *other* subject?"

Dwight Clark laughed aloud. Then he looked at Henry and said, unsmiling, "Politics is mere child's play, eh, Henry?" And, tossing his rumpled napkin beside his plate, he said, "Oh, well, we must get going."

"No," said the Judge. "Wait. I want to hear Henry's answer to my question."

"I do, too," said Dwight, and he snatched his napkin from the table again as if to prove it.

"We're waiting," said the Judge.

"At least theirs is a question that *can* be settled," Henry said, lamely.

"Oh," Dwight rejoined in his most ringing professorial

voice, "since we can't, as individuals, settle the problems
of the world, we'd best turn ostrich and bury our heads in
the sand."

"That won't do, Henry," said Judge Parker. "We're
still waiting."

So they *had* needed him, after all, Henry reflected. A
common enemy was better than a peacemaker. He understood now that his own meek and mild behavior on the
front porch had assured both men that he was not going
to spill their beans. And in their eyes, now, he saw that
they somehow hated him for it. But, he wondered, why
had they thought he might do it, to begin with? Why in
the world *should* he? Because he was an old bachelor with
no life of his own? He knew that both the men, and the
women, too, were bound to have known for years about
his love affair with Nora McLarnen. But to themselves, of
course, they lied willingly about such a large and unpleasant domestic matter. . . . He was an old bachelor
without any life of his own! Oh, God, he thought, the
realization sweeping over him suddenly that that's how it
really would be soon, when he told Nora that she had his
consent to go back to John McLarnen. He thought of his
office in the courthouse and how it would seem when
Nora was no longer behind her typewriter down the corridor. And he realized that the rest of his life with her,
the part that had been supposed to mean the most, didn't
matter to him at all. He couldn't remember that it *once*
had mattered, that *once* the summer nights, when his
parents and her children didn't have to be considered, had
been all that mattered to him. He couldn't, because the
time had come when he couldn't afford to remember it.
All along, then, they had been right about him. All his

hesitations and discriminations about what one could and could not do with one's life had been mere weakness. What else could it be? He was a bloodless old bachelor. It seemed that all his adult life the blood had been slowly draining out of him, and now the last drop was drained. John McLarnen, who could sell a quarter of a million dollars' worth of life insurance in one year, and whose wife could damned well take him or leave him as he was, was the better man.

While Dwight and the Judge waited for him to speak up, Henry sat with a vague smile on his lips, staring at the basket of fruit, which was placed on a little cherry washstand at the far end of the porch. He saw the two children, Susie and her little brother, slip out of their chairs and go over to the washstand. He heard his sister tell them not to finger the fruit. Suddenly he imagined he was seeing the fruit, the peaches and apples and pears, through little Dwight's eyes. How very real it looked.

"The basket of fruit," he said at last, "is a petty, ignoble, womanish consideration. And we men must not waste our minds on such." Intuitively, he had chosen the thing to say that would give them their golden opportunity. But before either of the men could speak, he heard his mother say, "Now, Henry," in an exasperated tone, and under her breath.

V. THE JUGGLER

Judge Parker rested his two great white hands limply, incredulously on the table. "Henry," he said, "are you attempting to instruct your brother-in-law and me in our domestic relations?" He gazed a moment through the wire screening out into his flower garden. He was thinking that Henry always left himself wide open in an argument. Even Dwight could handle him.

"If that isn't an old bachelor for you," Dwight said, rising from his chair. He wished Henry would wipe the foolish grin off his face. He supposed it was there to hide his disappointment. He had observed Henry, all during the meal, trying to work up some antagonism between his father-in-law and himself—about the roads, about religion, about politics.

The Judge was getting up from the table now, too, but he had more to say. "While we discussed all manner of things that you might be expected to know something about, you maintained a profound silence. And then you felt compelled to speak on a subject of which you are profoundly ignorant."

"'Our universities are riddled with them,'" Dwight said, savoring his joke, feeling that nobody else but Kitty would get it. "Old bachelors who will tell you how you can live on university pay and how to raise your children. I know one, even, who teaches a marriage course."

"*You* might try that, Henry," said the Judge. And then he said, "We're only joking, you know. No hard feelings?" He had thought, suddenly, of the extra liquor that Henry was supposed to have brought up from Nashville for the party. Then he remembered that Jane had already asked Henry. It was locked in the trunk of his old coupé.

"Henry knows we're kidding," Dwight said.

Kitty was helping her mother clear the table. Mrs. Parker was protesting, saying that she had nothing else to do all day. Presently, she said to Henry, "Henry, would you take the famous basket of fruit out front? I haven't given up." She *hadn't* given up. How really wonderful it was, Henry thought. And Kitty, too. She could so easily have agreed to take the whole basketful along, could so easily have thrown the whole thing out once they got down the Mountain. But it wouldn't have occurred to her.

"Will you gentlemen excuse me?" he said to the two men, smiling at them. And the two men smiled back at him. They felt very good.

When they were all gathered out on the lawn, beside Dwight's car, Kitty looked at her mother and father and said, "It's been a grand summer for us. Just what we needed."

"It's been grand for *us*," Mother Parker said, "though I'm afraid its spoilt us a good deal. We shouldn't have let you do so much."

"But we hope you'll do it again," Dad Parker said, "whenever you feel up to it."

"I never dreamed I'd get so much done on my book in one summer," said Dwight, really meaning it, but thinking that nobody believed him. He saw that brother Henry was pulling various little trinkets out of his pockets for the children. He had bought them in Nashville, no doubt, and they would be godsends on the trip. Henry knew so well how to please people when he would. He was squatting down between the two children, and he looked up at Dwight to say, "You're lucky to have work you can take all over the world with you."

"Well, I'm sure it requires great powers of concentration," Mother Parker said. She went on to say that she marveled at the way Dwight kept at it and that they were all proud of how high he stood in his field. As she spoke, she held herself very straight, and she seemed almost as tall as her husband. She had had Henry set the basket of fruit on an ivy-covered stump nearby. It was there to plead its own cause. She would not mention it again.

At breakfast, the children had been so excited about setting out for home that Kitty had had to force them to eat. In fact, even the night before, their eagerness to be on the way had been so apparent that Dwight had had to take them aside and warn them against hurting their grandparents' feelings. Yet now, at the last minute, they seemed genuinely reluctant to go. They clung to their uncle, saying they didn't see why they couldn't stay on a few days longer and let him enjoy the tiny tractor, the bag of marbles, and the sewing kit with them. It seemed to Dwight that their Uncle Henry had done his best to ignore the children during all his weekends at the Mountain, but now at the last minute he had filled their hands with treasure. And now it was Uncle Henry who was to have their last hugs and to lift little Dwight bodily into the car. When he turned away from the car, with the two children inside it, Henry took Dwight's hand and said, "I'm sorry we never had that chess game. I guess I was afraid you would beat me." It was as if he had seized Dwight and given him the same kind of hug he had given the children. Probably Henry had really wanted to play chess this summer, and probably he had wanted to be affectionate and attentive with the children. But the old bachelor in him had made him hold back. He could not give himself to people, or to anything—not for a whole season.

When finally they had all made their farewell speeches,

had kissed and shaken hands and said again what a fine summer it had been, Dwight and Kitty hopped into the little car, and they drove away as quickly as if they had been running into the village on an errand. As they followed the winding driveway down to the public road, Dwight kept glancing at Kitty. He said, "Let's stop in the village and buy a copy of the morning paper."

"Let's not," she said, keeping her eyes straight ahead.

"All right," he said, "let's not." He thought she looked very sad, and he felt almost as though he were taking her away from home for the first time. But the next time he glanced at her, she smiled at him in a way that it seemed she hadn't smiled at him in more than two months. He realized that this summer he had come to think of her again as "having" her father's forehead, as "having" her mother's handsome head of hair and high cheekbones, and as "sharing" her brother's almost perfect teeth, which they were said to have inherited from their maternal grandmother's people. But now suddenly her features seemed entirely her own, borrowed from no one, the features of Dwight Clark's wife. He found himself pressing down on the accelerator, though he knew he would have to stop at the entrance to the road.

In the mirror he saw his two children, in the back seat, still waving to their grandparents through the rear window. Presently, Susie said, "Mama, look at Uncle Henry! Do you see what he's *doing*." They had reached the entrance to the road now, and Dwight brought the car to a complete halt. Both he and Kitty looked back. Mother and Dad Parker had already started back into the cottage, but they had stopped on the porch steps and were still waving. Henry was still standing beside the ivy-covered stump where the basket of fruit rested. He had picked up two of the apples and was listlessly juggling them in the air. Dwight asked the children to get out of the way for a moment, and both of them ducked their heads. He wanted to have a good look, to see if Henry was doing it for the children's benefit. . . . Clearly he wasn't. He was staring off into space, in the opposite direction, lost in whatever thoughts such a man lost himself in.

Dwight put the car into motion again and turned out of the gravel driveway onto the macadam road, with Kitty and the children still looking back until they reached the point where the thick growth of sumac at the roadside cut off all view of the cottage, and the sweep of green lawn, and the three relatives they had just said goodbye to for a while.

ABOUT THE AUTHOR

Born in Trenton, Tennessee, in 1917, Peter Taylor has spent most of his life in the South and in the Middle West. During his childhood he lived for a time in Nashville, in St. Louis, and in Memphis. With his wife and two children he now lives in Columbus, Ohio, where he is on the staff of the English Department of the Ohio State University. He divides his time about equally between his teaching and his writing. In 1955 Mr. Taylor was a lecturer at the Seminar in American Studies, University College, Oxford. He spent a year in France on a Fulbright Grant, and has received numerous other fellowships and awards in recognition of his literary achievements. Mr. Taylor's short story "Venus, Cupid, Folly and Time" received first prize in *The 1959 O. Henry Memorial Awards*. He has previously printed two collections of short stories: *A Long Fourth and Other Stories* and *The Widows of Thornton*. He has also published a novel, *A Woman of Means,* and a play, *Tennessee Day in St. Louis.*